WASTED LUST

321

A 321 SPINOFF

WASTED LUST

321

A 321 SPINOFF

JA HUSS

Edited by RJ Locksley

ISBN-978-1-936413-90-4

Cover Photo: Daemon Donigan
Cover Model: JD
Formatted by Tianne Samson with E.M. Tippetts Book Designs

E.M.
TIPPETTS
BOOK DESIGNS

emtippettsbookdesigns.com

Other Books By
J.A. HUSS

Standalone Books

Three, Two, One (321): A Dark Suspense
Meet Me In The Dark: A Dark Suspense
Wasted Lust (321 Spinoff)
Sexy (Coming September 9, 2015)

Rook and Ronin Books

TRAGIC
MANIC
PANIC
TRAGIC, MANIC, PANIC BOX SET

Rook and Ronin Spinoffs

SLACK: A Day in the Life of Ford Aston
TAUT: The Ford Book
FORD: Slack/Taut Bundle
BOMB: A Day in the Life of Spencer Shrike
GUNS The Spencer Book

Dirty, Dark, and Deadly

Come

Come Back

Coming for You

James and Harper: Come/Come Back Bundle

Social Media

Follow

Like

Block

Status

Profile

Home

Young Adult

Losing Francesca

Science Fiction Series

Clutch

Fledge

Flight

Range

The Magpie Bridge

Return

ABOUT THIS BOOK

A standalone spinoff of the New York Times bestselling novel, Three, Two, One (321): A Dark Suspense.

A GIRL WITH REGRETS...

Sasha Cherlin died the night she let Nick Tate walk out on her for a life of crime. Her very essence was destroyed when they broke their promise to one another.

A MAN WITH REMORSE...

Nick Tate made his choice with her future in mind. He loved Sasha enough to know that leaving her behind was the only way to keep her safe.

A PATH TO REVENGE...

Special Agent Jax Barlow understands the bond of love and he plans to use it to get justice. Nick and Sasha will do anything to rewrite their past. He's counting on that to bring them down.

CHAPTER ONE

"Miss Aston?" The man is the kind of tall that makes you look up. He's wearing a dark suit with a skinny black tie, and even though we're indoors, he's got sunglasses on.

Anyone over the age of six can spot him for what he is. I stop walking so ten years of manners and settling can fall away and the girl I am underneath can take over. "Who's asking?"

"I'm Special Agent Jax, Miss Aston. And I have a few questions for you. Please come with me."

"Am I under arrest for something?" Holy fuck. He leads me through a set of double doors, and then another door, and then another door, until I'm three layers deep inside the fucking Denver International Airport. We finally come to a small office, where he waves me in and says, "Please, take a seat."

WASTED LUST

I take my seat as my mind races with all the possible reasons the FBI could be interested in me.

Just be cooperative, Sasha, Ford tells me in my head. We've covered my tracks well since he adopted me ten years ago. But we've always planned for the day when people discover my history is a lie.

"Am I under arrest?" I ask again, trying not to take deep breaths. Trying not to sit on my hands and fidget in my seat. Trying not to wonder if this is the end of the line for me.

"No, ma'am," he says. "I just need to ask you some questions, if that's OK."

"What if it's not OK? What if I want to call my dad?"

He sits down at the table opposite me and opens up a folder. His hands are large and his fingers are long and slender. I concentrate on those two characteristics as he shuffles some papers around. Who uses papers anymore? You'd think they'd have this shit on a tablet. It's a ploy. To unsettle me. Make me think they've got dirt on me. Make me fuck up and talk. Make me—

Hush, I tell the killer locked away deep inside me. *Be cool, Sasha.*

"You are Sasha Aston, correct?" He waits as I process things. Not smiling, not frowning—impassive. Typical.

I can be impassive as well. I learned from the best. "You know I am. I just got off that plane. So I was checked in."

"You came from…"

"Peru." I fill in the blank for him.

"What was your business in Peru, might I ask?"

"I was at an archeological dig. They found bones."

"Bones?" He cocks an eyebrow at me.

"Dinosaur bones. I'm a paleontologist. Well, a grad student. It was a summer internship. Why?"

He looks at me for a moment. I have been questioned by enough dangerous men to recognize the pause as reevaluation. I tend to have that effect on people. "Impressive. And your father is Rutherford Aston IV?"

"Yes." I swallow hard. Jesus Christ, we are totally busted for something. "I need to know what's going on. You're scaring me. Did something happen to my dad?"

"No, ma'am."

"Stop calling me ma'am. I'm twenty-four and you look like you're about thirty."

He eyes me down the bridge of his nose. "Thirty? I don't look thirty. I'm twenty-seven."

"What?" I have to shake my head at that. "What do you want, Special Agent Jax? If I'm not under arrest, then I'm leaving."

He flips the page in the folder just as I begin to stand up, and produces a photograph that steals all my breath away.

"Do you know this man, Miss Aston? Can you identify him for us?"

I shake my head as I study Nick's face. His perfect face. The blond hair, the brown eyes. The steely gaze. I can picture him smiling at me in that hotel room in Rock Springs back when I was only thirteen years old.

Thirteen and already a killer several times over. Thirteen and I had lost everything. There was absolutely nothing left of me that day. Thirteen and wanting to die so bad because this boy here left me. *Live your life*, he told me. *Grow up, move on. You will love again.*

I never had a choice, did I? Because just a few days later I was on a boat heading out to sea and he was standing on a beach. Didn't even wave goodbye.

"Never seen him before," I say, lying right to Special Agent Jax's face. "Why?"

"Take another look, Miss Aston. How about this one?"

This time, Nick is shirtless. His whole body is covered in tattoos. His chest, his arms, his neck. And when I look closely, even his hands have tattoos on them. It pains me—emotionally and physically—not to reach out for that photo.

I shake my head again. "No, sir. Sorry."

"Hmmm," Jax says. "Well, that's interesting, Miss Aston. Or should I call you Miss Cherlin?"

I stare him in the eyes and do not flinch. I don't deny or confirm. From this point on, I do not talk. I say nothing until I'm given a phone and then I call my dad and tell him I need Ronin. Ronin, the liar. Ronin, the one who talks for all the Team members if we get in trouble. Ronin. That's the only name on my mind right now.

"They call him Santino down in Central America. But here in the US, they call him Holy Boy. He's white with blond hair—but somehow, he's the second highest-ranking member of the *Mara Perro*, Gang of the Dogs."

"Very interesting. But what's this have to do with me?" Shit, I just broke the no-talking rule.

"That's what I'm trying to figure out, Miss Cherlin. If that's who you are, it makes a lot more sense."

"How so?"

"I think you know how so." He grins at me and flashes a dimple. His eyes are blue and his hair is light. Not quite blond, but not quite brown, either. He's handsome. That's probably why they sent him to me. Thinking I'm easily distracted by a pretty face.

"I don't have time for this. I don't know that man—"

"He knows you, Miss Aston. He knows you very well. Because he's sent more than two dozen people here to find you while you've been digging down in Peru this summer."

"What?" My heart thumps.

"Did you two have some unfinished business? Before you took on this new identity?"

I can't breathe.

"Or some prearranged agreement to meet up in the future?"

I shake my head no as I close my eyes to picture the prearranged meeting that never happened. "We didn't."

"But you do know him?"

I just gave myself away. I lean on the desk with my palms down and bow my head to try to think clearly. Agent Jax places his hand on mine.

"Miss Aston, I'm not here to arrest you or pry into your past. I understand your fear right now, I do. Better than most. But if you know him, and if he's looking for you, you should understand… he's probably planning on kidnapping you."

"*What?*" I pull my hands away from the desk to take my mind off the fact that Agent Jax is touching me.

"We've intercepted several of these men he's sent to look for you. Three of them confessed to this plot. Now I don't expect you to tell me much. Just yes or no. Is this man, the one they call

Santino, Nicholas Tate?"

I nod. "That's him. I'd recognize him anywhere. But I haven't seen him in ten years. I don't know anything about this stuff. I was in Peru, not Central America—"

"You're not under suspicion, Miss Aston."

"Then why did you ask me here?"

"We don't want to arrest you, Sasha. We want to recruit you."

My childhood flashes through my head. Stalking, hunting, shooting, killing. Being blown up, being tracked, being hated and wanted dead. The anger I had, the love I lost, the life that was ripped away.

Ford Aston did his best with me. It was better than anyone else on this planet could've done, that's for sure. I respect him. I love him. I love my brother, Five, my sister, Kate, and my mom, Ashleigh. I had dogs, and cats, and a nice house, and trips around the world. I had my own room. I was sent to private school where I made friends and got good grades.

James, Harper, Merc and I made a lot of money off that final job we pulled. Nick never got his cut. Nick never got the chance because he took off with a Central American drug lord in order to save the rest of us.

And no, none of it was perfect. We ran into troubles here and there over who I am. Who we all are. But it got handled. I graduated college and I'm on the verge of completing my oral examinations and being fully invested in my career in anthropology as a PhD candidate.

I. Am. A success.

"I moved on," I tell Agent Jax. But I know it's a lie. And he knows it's a lie. Because even though I'm the toughest girl you will ever meet—I am the killer of killers, for fuck's sake—just one picture of just one man can take me back to the moment I realized… I lost.

I lost everything.

And no amount of money—not new mothers and fathers, not new friends and schools, or college degrees, or even the simple satisfaction that comes from my grad school research—can make up for it. None of that can fix the fact that I lost.

My father is dead. Mother dead. Grandparents dead. Home gone. And Nick—the one thing I held onto after the Company took my childhood away and turned me into a murderer—left me behind. Left me all alone. Because only a Company kid can understand what I am. We don't walk the edge, we live on the other side of it.

Harper has James. Merc wasn't a Company kid, but he was a Company assassin. And Sydney has him to keep the crazy at bay. So good for them. I'm glad they have each other.

But I've been alone on the other side of things for ten years because my partner *left* me. And yeah, I'm tired of it. I want my past back. And just a glimmer of the future I was promised and denied, just one more conversation with Nick, would be worth it for me.

But if this agent thinks I will sell my soul to the government to see Nick Tate again, he's wrong. I'm not a snitch. So if he wants to play a game of cat-and-mouse with me, fine. I'm in.

"I'd like to leave now." I fold my arms over my chest and zone him out. I don't even hear him as he uses the next thirty minutes trying to persuade me.

He threatens me with a forty-eight-hour hold, felonies that

list into the dozens, and a visit to my grad school mentor at University of Kansas.

That last part is the only thing that gives me pause. My mentor is cool. I chose her for a reason when I decided to take KU's grad school offer. She thinks the world of me and I'd hate for her to find out I'm such a lowlife piece of shit.

But it can't be helped. I am stone, that's how firm I am in this. There is no way in hell I will work with the corrupt FBI to take down the only person I ever called a partner.

If Nick Tate is looking for me, then I can make myself available without any help from this asshole.

CHAPTER TWO

"**S**asha," Agent Jax says calmly. He's switching tactics. "Please."

I shake my head and laugh.

"I don't know your whole story—"

"You don't know shit." My calm is fading just as his is building. I stare up at him, the rage finally getting to me. "You don't know shit. And whatever it is you think you do know is not even a fraction of what's happening."

"I know about the Company, Sasha."

"Do you want a medal?" Snide and sarcastic Sasha is threatening to come out right now, and I've spent all ten of the years between then and now trying to rein her in. This Jax guy is bad news. Bad in every way.

I don't want that girl to come back. I don't want to feel these feelings. I don't want that anger and hate to build inside me to the point of overflowing. So I take a deep breath. I don't care about the things I've gained since Nick left. I love my family and I enjoy my work, but the only gift I got out of all that loss is this girl I became. I am strong, and rational, and *normal*.

I exhale that breath and say, "I can't help you. I don't know that man anymore and I have no intention of seeing him again. And that's the end of it." I tip my chin up and set my jaw, making sure he knows this is final. "Arrest me. I will bail myself out. Follow me, bug my apartment, threaten me with twenty-four-hour surveillance. I don't care. I have nothing to hide. I'm not going to get dragged into some government sting operation just to satisfy your curiosity or give you some upper hand in whatever political war you think you're fighting."

He sighs, looking at me from across the table. I see a lot of things in his gaze. Frustration, mostly. "I'm going to do all that, you know. Aside from the arrest."

"It's your game, Agent. Not mine. Do whatever you have to do. If you're not going to arrest me, then I'd like to leave now so I can pick up my luggage before someone at baggage claim steals it."

"Do you have a ride home?"

"I don't need a ride."

"You have a taxi taking you to Fort Collins?" He smiles when I look at him.

"I don't live in Fort Collins," I sneer back.

"Taking a bus to Kansas, then? I know you have no connecting flight back to school. And I know you don't have an apartment."

I just smile.

"You do have one." He frowns. "So it's not in your name? Or your father's name? And you haven't been there in a very long time. Because I know a lot more about you than you think."

"If you follow me, then I guess you'll find out where I'm going, won't you?"

He shrugs with defeat. "You're free to go. But I'll walk you to baggage to make sure your luggage wasn't stolen."

Whatever. I get up and walk to the door. It's locked from the inside, I know that much, so I stop and wait for him to press in the code that releases the lock. He waves me forward and we head down the corridor the way we came.

Agent Jax clears his throat when we finally get back out to the concourse, and then we get on the moving sidewalk. He stands behind me as I walk, making the gates fly by, and he is quiet all the way to the train.

We are alone there, which is strange, but I don't doubt they have security manipulating every step of our journey out to baggage, so I just wait.

When the train finally appears—and it takes several minutes, so I know for sure they are manipulating my exit—it's empty. I step in thinking about how many travelers they had to piss off to make sure we had this time alone.

When we get to the main terminal, I exit the train and take the escalator up to the bustling airport. I walk across the mall-like building, looking up at the atrium ceiling briefly as I find my way to baggage. I stop for a moment when I get there. I don't know what carousel my flight came out of, and none of the electronic boards have the number on them anymore.

Asshole had to make this difficult for me.

"Miss Aston," Agent Jax says, tapping me on my shoulder. "Your luggage."

He points to a porter standing with, yes, my luggage. There are stickers plastered on the hard plastic explaining TSA has rifled through them due to a 'random inspection'.

"I hope you found what you were looking for," I say, snapping up the handle of my roll-away and slipping the oversized backpack over my shoulder. My purse makes that three bags I have to maneuver as I make my way over to the rental cars.

And what do you know. Every counter is closed. Every one of them has a sign that says, *Out of cars.*

I turn to look back at Jax. He frowns, like this is unfortunate. But we both know he did this.

No matter. I walk down the long corridor until I find the doors that will take me out to the taxi waiting area of the garage.

Empty.

I'm not the only one dismayed, either. There are crowds of people looking around for taxis. And I know, the longer I stay here pretending I am not going to be riding home with Agent Jax, the longer they will wait for a taxi.

I turn to him. "Why are you doing this?"

"I'm sure your father can come pick you up." He offers me his phone. "Give him a try."

I stare at the phone.

"He doesn't know you came home early, does he?"

"What?" Asshole. "So you were pretending ignorance about where I was all summer? You knew I was in Peru. You knew I had no car here. You knew my dad wasn't picking me up."

"I know school doesn't start for two more weeks, Sasha Cherlin." He smiles when he says my old name. "I know you've got plans. But what those plans are, I'm still not sure. Which is why you're being followed. I think you lied to me about Nick. I think you're a very good little actress and that Nick Tate contacted you while you were in Peru. I also know he's not in Honduras. Not in Central America at all, in fact."

My heart skips a little. He's here.

"And I think you have a secret meeting with him right now."

I turn and consider my options. I do not have a secret meeting with Nick. I really haven't talked to him. He's not why I came back to Denver. But I can't go where I was going to go either. I can't call my dad. He thinks I'm in Peru for another eight days. And as far as he knows, I'm not flying into Denver at all. I was supposed to fly right back to Kansas.

So now what?

"Where are you going, Sasha?"

I laugh and turn back to him. "You mean, where am I *not* going, now that you're here?" God, I hate this guy. He just fucked up something important to me.

"Where are you going?" His tone is harsher now. "If you tell me, maybe I can help you get there."

I calculate how many plans just got ruined over this asshole's quest to find Nick and it pisses me off so bad, I just start walking. There is nowhere to walk to, but I walk anyway. I cross the empty street on the fifth level of the parking garage and start weaving through cars. I drag that stupid suitcase up and over curbs, trying to make Agent Jax give me some space so he can't see my disappointment, but he's on my heels the entire time. And when

I finally make my way to the very edge of the garage and there is nowhere else to go I stop and lean on the concrete wall, my head in my hands.

"Sasha," Jax says, putting a hand on my shoulder. I turn and swat it off in a single move. My eyes are blazing with the killer I used to be and not the normal person I'd like to believe I am. "What are you doing?" He's confused now, but the look on my face must tell him my mood has changed. "You were meeting him, weren't you?"

I shake my head. "I'm not lying about Nick. And to be perfectly honest, I'd like to see him again. But I'm not home early for him. Or anything that requires your attention. And I just want to go."

"Who were you meeting? Just tell me, we'll check it out, and then you can go."

"I can't tell you that. I will *never* tell you that. So whatever. You want to take me somewhere? Or get me a car so I can drive back to school? Because my plans have changed."

CHAPTER THREE

"I have a private plane waiting," I tell her. And then I take the backpack off her drooping shoulder and grab the handle of her roll-away suitcase and turn away.

I walk by myself for a few moments, but then I hear her reluctant footsteps and smile to myself. Sasha Cherlin has a secret. I will get that out of her before we get to Kansas, that's for sure.

She's good. I've read all about her upbringing in the Company. That insane massacre she helped orchestrate out in Santa Barbara ten years ago. I admit, I had trouble imagining that until I met her today.

When you imagine a thirteen-year-old girl you picture them thinking about boys, parties, school, and friends. You do not picture Sasha Cherlin with a gun, a mastermind plan to take down a network of people who make grown men tremble, and the skills to actually carry it out.

Granted, her partners—all other Company-trained assassins—helped. But without this one girl they wouldn't have gotten very far.

No. The demise and fall of the Company was a product of Sasha Cherlin's loss, anger, and heartbreak.

Note to self. Do not cross this girl.

That makes me smile, even though I'm serious. I chance a glance over my shoulder and find her walking, not close, but not far back, either. Five steps. Her back is straight and her chin is up.

That look says, *You cannot touch me.* Whether she knows it to be true or just knows she can kill me should the need arise, I'm not quite sure.

We weave our way through the level five parking garage until we get to the arrivals lane. The taxis are back. And shuttles. Travelers have already forgotten that things seemed unnatural when they came outside to an empty pick-up lane.

I have a car waiting with my driver, Madrid, who is the same age as Miss Cherlin. Chosen for a reason. Discretion.

Madrid opens the trunk of the government-issue sedan. I plop the luggage in without fanfare, then open the passenger's side door and wave Cherlin in.

"No, thank you," she says politely. I guess her composure is back. "I'll take the back."

I close the door and walk around to the other side of the car. There's no way I'm letting that girl sit *behind* me.

She pulls a pair of sunglasses out of her purse—round ones

that cover a good portion of her face—like she's a movie star trying to escape the paparazzi.

Madrid pulls out into the lane of traffic and exits level five, heading towards the exit. When we get back on the only highway that services the airport, I direct her. "Fort Collins airport, Special Agent Madrid."

I expected a small snort from Sasha over our destination, but she holds in any reaction she might have.

I'm not quite sure what to make of her, still adjusting to the assignment. Still trying to put all the pieces together. I'm on edge, in fact, because Sasha Cherlin legally died nine years ago. A body was recovered in a small Mexican village in the Gulf of California. Mostly eaten by fish. And somehow, some back-village Mexican official managed to not only identify Miss Cherlin's remains, but also alert the US Embassy, feign ignorance when the body disappeared—misplaced, they said—and then declare her legally—and finally—dead.

It turns out she has dual citizenship. I'm not sure how Ford Aston managed that one, since every bit of evidence I've been given points to her being home-birthed on a ranch up near Sheridan, Wyoming.

That could be her real story, or it could be her manufactured one, put in place by her adopted fathers, Ford and Merc—both on internal CIA blackhat lists, one associated with the Company, one not. This girl covers her bases, doesn't she?

Regardless, on paper, Sasha Cherlin no longer exists.

I look over at her as she pulls out a tube of balm and slides it across her lips. She sneers at me, so I look away quickly, so as not to appear watching. But she's damn cute.

For a murderer.

"You know," she says, breaking her silence once we settle into a comfortable eighty-five miles per hour on the I-25 north, "there are a lot of airports between here and Fort Collins you could've used."

"Sure," I say with a smile. "But why miss an opportunity?"

"What opportunity?" She slides her sunglasses down her nose. Not with apprehension though. With annoyance.

"How could I pass up a chance to meet the infamous Ford Aston?"

Her flat expression does not break.

"He's your father, right?"

"You know he is," she returns. "But he's out of the country, unfortunately. Left for New Zealand last week."

"Lies," I say. "I can check that shit, you know."

"So check that *shit*." She slides her glasses up her nose again. "At any rate, we are not going to the Aston house today. And if you try I will make sure this conversation is over. For good."

"Already playing cards, Cherlin?"

"If you call me Cherlin again, we're done. And yes," she says smugly, "when one has the upper hand, they write the rules. These two are just the beginning if you want information from me."

"Let's start that talk now. Where were you going today?"

"None of your business. And it has nothing to do with this"— she waves her hand at me with disdain—"business."

"Then tell me what it was."

"No."

She crosses her legs. Her shorts are not exactly sexy. Loose tan cargo shorts with lots of pockets. If she hadn't just come out of an airport, I'd be wondering what was in those pockets. One of the reasons I wanted to catch her getting off the plane. But her legs are long and bronze from spending a summer in Peru. She has on a pair of cream-colored wedge sandals and sleeveless blouse trimmed in lace that gives her a sophisticated look. Her style says she has taste. And money. The purse is white leather, some designer I've never heard of, but definitely expensive.

She certainly doesn't look like a killer. But I guess that's the point, right? You never see those Company kids coming. Little girls are not supposed to be your number-one suspect. High-society women either, for that matter.

I'm still looking at her legs as I think all this and when I finally glance up at her face, she's got a crooked smile. "See something you like, Agent?"

"I was admiring your style, Miss Aston."

Sasha returns her attention to the back of Madrid's head, and Madrid gives me a quick glance in the rear-view, rolling her dark brown eyes.

It's not my fault Sasha Aston makes me look twice.

Sasha shakes her head a little, like she's reading my thoughts.

We ride in silence the rest of the way up to Fort Collins Airport, and then Madrid parks the car at the entrance, where some local agent is waiting to take possession of it.

"This way, Miss Aston," I say, placing my hand at the small of her back—barely touching her at all—to guide her around the front entrance and towards the tarmac, where a stairway has already been extended up to the Agency jet.

Sasha moves ahead of my hand, maybe to avoid any contact.

I take a moment to wonder if she likes the touch or not. I'll get information on that soon enough, so I put that thought aside and wave her forward when we reach the stairs.

I let her get a few steps ahead so I can look at her ass on the way up, but just as I'm about to climb behind her, Madrid shuffles past and blocks my view.

"Don't be a pig," she whispers as she passes. "She's not that kind of girl."

"Madrid," I sigh, wanting to tell her to shut up. But Madrid is not under my direction. She is along to make sure nothing inappropriate happens. Not sexually, of course. Legally. I am not to make offers. I am not to make promises. I am not, my DC superiors stressed, to become friendly with her, anger her, or push her into a corner which might make her flee or react with force.

Why don't we just kill her? It would make all this fuss go away immediately. I guess they're afraid of what her friends might do in retaliation. Or perhaps the gold mine of information is worth all these precautions and risk?

The only other idea I can come up with is that they really do want her to join the Agency.

We take our seats, Sasha on one end of a long leather couch, and myself on a chair that faces her. I'm not going to miss an opportunity to look at her. She immediately puts her seatbelt on and doesn't gape around the interior cabin, which is nice, but nothing more. This jet can seat between twenty and twenty-two people comfortably. It has a small dining area, an office section, and a nice lavatory. There's a staff of five, two in the cockpit and three back here.

Sasha closes her eyes and crosses her legs again. I stare openly this time. Madrid is asking for orange juice and isn't paying attention. Sasha opens her eyes, busts me, and then turns her attention to the closest attendant. "Did I hear you have orange juice?"

"Yes, ma'am," the attendant replies. "Would you like some?"

"Yes," Sasha says, with a sigh. "With vodka, please."

I smile at that. "Are you a rebel, Miss Aston?"

"I'm a paleontologist, Agent Jax. I spend my time digging in dirt for ancient bones, hoping to find some small scrap to give my day meaning. I live alone in a great big house, and all my friends are other diggers. So do *you* think I'm a rebel?"

I wink at her with a smile. She pulls her chin back, as if offended. Perhaps Madrid is right. She's not that kind of girl. But what she lacks in social rebellion, she makes up for professionally. Not the digging. How boring that is. But she's failing to mention her ties to hackers and killers. "I think you have potential, Miss Aston."

She looks over at Madrid, and when I look at Madrid she's mouthing something derogatory about me. "Agent," I say, stopping her mid-word.

But when I look back at Sasha, she's smiling at Madrid like they are sharing a secret.

Girls.

"Would you like to see a recent picture of Nick Tate, Miss Aston?" I ask, flipping the authority and control back to me. "I have one. Madrid, bring me my case."

Madrid huffs a breath as she unbuckles her belt, walks over to a cabinet, gets the case, hands it to me, and then sits back down just in time to buckle up before the drinks are served and the captain begins to taxi the plane towards the runway.

Sasha stares at the case in my hands, then recaptures her composure. "How old is the photo?"

"Three months," I say, and then add, "We think. This was the last thing this particular insider sent before she disappeared."

"She?" Aston has a very hard time hiding her contempt for the gender of my insider.

"It could be because she's dead or it could be because she's turned on us. We're not sure."

"The picture?"

A few moments pass as I try to work out if she's jealous, or if she thinks she might know who our infiltrator is.

"Yes," I say, setting the case down on a small table as the plane accelerates for takeoff. I wait until we're climbing before opening it and then shuffle around inside until I find the most recent picture and hand it out for her to take.

She does not touch it, but uncrosses her legs and leans forward with her hands in her lap.

So composed for someone so young. So disciplined. So careful. So passive.

"Take it," I say, still offering.

"I see him," she says. And then, like that picture is the last thing on her mind, she crosses her legs again and shoots me a smile. "I'm going to have to decline your offer, Agent Jax. I'm just too busy at school." Her snob has been turned on, I realize. That thirteen-year-old assassin has been transformed over the years into a very classy lady. She lost it momentarily back at the airport. But she's collected herself since then.

My interest is piqued. I allow a smile as I withdraw the photo and tuck it back into the briefcase. I'm going to enjoy playing high society with her. Not many women these days are interested in manners and polite conversation. "Would you change your mind if I told you what he's been up to all these years?"

"No, Agent. I think if I knew…" She pauses here, I'm sure picturing the life he might've carved out for himself down in crime-ridden Honduras. "If I knew, I'd be very much inclined to run the other way as fast as possible."

Hmmm. "I disagree. I think Nick Tate is the only thing you've thought about for ten years. The fact that he left you behind while he went out to meet his future wasn't in the plan, was it? And what happened to you, Miss Aston? Did it break your heart? That he left you? That he chose that life over the one you imagined you'd live out with him?"

She swallows, but her expression remains solid. Stoic. Utterly unemotional. "Very few people know the details of that night. And you are not one of them."

"Ah," I say, and a small laugh that I can't tuck down comes forth. "I know some of them. I know you didn't want him to leave. I know you traveled around the west that summer with James Fenici—AKA Assassin Number Six—and Nick's twin, Harper Tate. I know they dropped you off at Aston's soon after. I know *everything*, Sasha Cherlin."

She stiffens at that name. Her mouth becomes an angry line.

"Your next question isn't *how*, Miss Aston. But *who*. Who told me these things?"

"No one told you anything," she says, her calm back. She swings her sandaled foot a little and I can't stop a quick glance at her tanned leg as it moves. When I look up she's smiling. She knows she's pretty and she's using it against me now. "Because what you just said is like the icing on the cake. But the only thing that really matters is what's inside. And you have no details about what's inside, Agent. You have no idea what it tastes like."

"Maybe," I say back, using her metaphor as an excuse to picture eating her like cake. "But I'm close. And I'm gonna be tasting those details about you before you know it."

She picks up her orange juice, takes a sip, and then rifles through her purse until she comes up with some earbuds. She plugs them into her phone and switches me off.

Madrid gives me a knowing smile behind some trashy magazine she's reading and I have to wonder if she knows more about what's going on than I do. She certainly doesn't like me much. But she seems willing to befriend Sasha. For what purpose? Has she been sent here to acquire Miss Aston? Disrupt my plans, possibly? Or is she just trying to play good cop to my bad?

I'm not sure about Madrid. I've only known her ten days. The exact number of days I've been on this assignment. She came from DC, like me. And she's well-connected. She has to be in order to work on anything that involves the Company. But beyond her sparkling service record—most certainly scrubbed for my eyes—I know nothing about her.

It unsettles me.

And then there's the little issue of where Sasha was headed today. Nick? Or not Nick? Is he here already? The border is so porous these days, he could walk over on his own. Or is he biding his time because our infiltrator has been discovered?

There are a lot of unknowns here. A lot of possibilities, too.

And the short plane trip to the local airport near her school isn't enough time to get anything more out of Miss Aston.

When we land in Kansas, she follows me to a car. She doesn't bother telling me her address, which I already know. She lives off-campus, but very close to the Museum of Natural History. Only a few blocks down. And when we stop in front of her three-story historic craftsman-style-home on Ohio Street and 14th, Madrid pops the trunk and gets out, giving us about thirty seconds of privacy.

Sasha already has her fingertips on her door handle, ready to escape me. But I put a hand on her shoulder like I did back at the airport. "Look, I get it. You have secrets. And I'm not interested in most of them. You can keep those to yourself. But I have things you need to know. And I'll warn you now, you will have twenty-four-hour surveillance until you decide to work with us."

"*Until?*" she asks, stressing the word. "You're pretty presumptuous, Agent Jax. I'm a grad student. I work fifteen-hour days on research that is the epitome of boring to ninety-eight percent of the population of this whole planet. So you will be far more inconvenienced than I will, if that threat of twenty-four-seven surveillance is true." And then she hikes her purse up on her shoulder and exits the car.

I get out as well, but Sasha is already dragging her luggage up to her house before I can think of anything else to say.

CHAPTER FOUR

My house is a couple blocks off campus, less than a five-minute walk to the Museum of Natural History where I have an office on the top floor, and big enough to house a family of six. I get a small stipend from the program, but I've had my own money since I was thirteen years old.

We stole that. It's enough to last... well, hell. Longer than I have in this life, I'm sure.

So when I announced that I was gonna take this offer here at KU, my whole family came out here to find me a suitable place. I went to undergrad at The School of Mines in Golden, Colorado. It's a great school if you're a nerd—and I am. Plus I wanted to stay close to home.

Just in case.

WASTED LUST

I shove my key in the locked box that sits eye-level to the right of the front door and then open the flap that hides the security keypad so I can punch in the code. A high-pitched alarm sounds. Someone yells, "Sasha!" from a few porches down and I look over and wave at Mr. Banjengi. "You're home!"

"I'm home," I yell back, nodding at him since my hands are full right now.

All the overprotective men in my life thought this house was perfect. There are more lifetime residents on this street than on any other street near school. They are all older, nosy, and not afraid to shake a fist at someone.

I smile as I pull open the screen door and hold it with my hip as I key in another code to gain access to the real door. Another alarm sounds and then I pull all my luggage in and close it behind me so I can make the fifteen-second delay on the real alarm. I key in the final code you must have to enter my home and not have phones ringing all across the world. And believe me, you do not want their attention. James is on a yacht in the middle of the ocean, Merc is at home in the Mojave Desert, and Ford is in New Zealand—but if those phones ring, the shit hits the fan.

It freaks me out, but this is what it takes to keep me safe, I guess. I've learned to live with it.

After all that stress is over, I look around my house.

I've been gone for months and it smells dusty and stale. But other than that, it looks unchanged. I press another code on the keypad and the metal security shutters begin to lift up from the windows, finally letting in the sunshine. They are mounted on the interior of the house instead of the outside, and my adopted uncle, Spencer, painted the outside-facing panels to look like they are white plantation shutters. You really cannot tell they are sheets of metal. He even painted fake cracks with a view inside, in case anyone got close enough to try to peek in the window.

I press another button and each window in the house slides open six inches. That's the default setting, just in case I lose power and can't get them down without attending to each one manually.

I'm used to this by now. They've been freakishly overprotective since I was thirteen. Add in a successful kidnapping two years ago, just before I bought this place, and yeah. It just got worse. I'm locked up tight in here, that's for sure.

My bedroom is on the first floor, even though I have two more floors above me where I keep all my stuff. It's easier to escape the house from the first floor. But there's a planned escape route from every room in the house. I have a basement too, a really old, creepy one that no one in their right mind would use. But it's fitted with access to a storm door that leads outside.

It's overkill. I know that. And I resented all the security insisted on all through my teen years, but that last incident really shook me up.

It still does.

I drag my suitcase to the laundry room and stuff all the clothes into the hamper, and then put the suitcase away on a top shelf. The rest of my baggage is all little things. Trinkets I collected from the village near the dig site while I was in Peru. Little souvenirs I kept.

Twenty minutes after I arrive home, I'm done. And after an entire summer of meticulous, backbreaking work, I've got nothing to do… except think about what just happened.

Nick.

WASTED LUST

My promise who left me behind. To give me a chance at a regular life, he said back then when I was thirteen. But I didn't believe that then and I don't believe it now. In fact, this visit today from that Jax guy is my long-awaited proof.

Because if Nick did leave to give me a new chance, then why is he back? Why come looking for me ten years later when my life is on track, when the stark reality of who I am has faded, when the sting of his rejection is finally dying away to nothing... why come back and open all that stuff up again?

There is only one reason to do that.

He lied. Nick Tate is a liar.

He lied back on that beach in Santa Barbara when he said was there was no *us*. He said we had no future, even though he and I were promised. In Company terms, that promise is law. I was destined to marry Nick Tate. We were friends—even though he was several years older than me. And we had even talked about it a few times when he first found me back when I was an innocent eleven-year-old with braces.

And I don't know if that was all a lie to get me to go along with his plan to end the Company and free himself and his sister, but I was a little girl and I took that shit seriously.

Maybe it was just as hard for him to walk away from me that night as it was for me to watch him do it?

Or he was telling the truth back then and now he needs me for something. Some job, probably. He wants me to watch his back as he does something dangerous.

Ford would flip his lid and insist I join him in New Zealand if he knew this was happening.

James would probably just kill Agent Jax, no questions asked.

Merc would kill Nick. And everyone else who stood in front of him. He was never happy about how that ended.

But they see this through the eyes of men. And while I'm quite capable of seeing things that way too, when it comes to Nick, I see what my heart feels.

My phone starts buzzing in my purse, reminding me where I should be right now instead of home.

But she would not call me. She knows better than most that this secret we have cannot leak. We're on our own.

I grab my purse and fish the phone out, tabbing the lock off with a swipe. It's a text message from that asshole, Agent Jax.

Wanna get some dinner? We can talk.

I text back, *Fuck you.*

He does not reply. Wise man. And I don't need to leave the house for food, anyway. It's called a freezer. I don't have anything fresh, but hell, I drank plenty of powdered milk in my day.

I laugh at that as I plop down on the couch. *Gross.* Some things you just never go back to. And powdered milk is one of them. But I've eaten all kinds of shit.

Growing up with my dad—my real dad, not Ford—was an experience like no other. We spent a lot of time just rolling around the West in an RV selling guns at gun shows and supplying weapons to Company men. I learned to camp, shoot, and survive. Once we settled down from the nomadic life, my dad opened up a surplus supply store in an old antiques mall in Cheyenne. I ran a booth there across from his. My booth didn't have secret weapons for Company assassins though. I sold used books, figurines, jewelry, and various other small things that kids think are valuable.

WASTED LUST

I didn't make much money, but it kept me out of trouble and gave me a routine. I liked it there. It's a time filled with good memories. Reading *Little House* books and playing dress-up with the lady who sold vintage clothing in the booth near mine. Those antiques people were almost like family. Of course, everything that came out of my mouth was a lie. But I liked those lies. Liked that pretend life I was living. It was fun before Nick showed up and everything started to change.

I never went to school. Not until Ford got a hold of me and put me in Saint Joseph's in Fort Collins for eighth grade. But I'm not stupid, obviously. My real dad did OK with me. I'm not wild anymore. I've been living a very civilized life for ten years now. And maybe it took me a while to get the hang of things like boys, and hair, and clothes, but I came around.

I graduated from a private Jesuit high school down in Denver—the same one Ford went to—and studied geological engineering at The School of Mines for my undergrad. So those things aren't exactly typical. But eventually I fit in. In a grad school kind of way. I mean, people who go into research aren't normal anyway. They live in the lab or on the dig site. They get excited over data and results. They have little time for socializing.

I spend my time teaching undergrads, studying fossils, and running experiments. So maybe I planned it this way? Maybe I chose this field not because I was a dinosaur freak when I was growing up with my real dad, but to isolate myself from the rest of the world?

It works, that's for sure. Because while I know all my fellow research freaks here at KU, and I know plenty of undergrads from the classes I teach, I have no real friends.

I had Jimmy up until last summer. I look at the only photograph I have on display in my home and smile. I miss that stupid dog. He was just too old to stay here at home by himself while I worked. And even though he has a service vest that will get him into any place in the US, my department here at school made it clear they did not want one of my dad's face-eaters trailing me around everywhere. So I took him home to Fort Collins.

And now I live in this secure house alone.

That's exactly how I feel right now. Alone.

I had that side project planned before school started and now that's all fucked up too. And even though no one in their right mind would consider that a social activity, I was looking forward to it.

Fucking Jax ruined it by showing up at the airport.

And Nick. I do want to see him. I'd like to know why he left. I'd like to know if he ever loved me or if he was just using me to take people down in the Company.

I want to punch him in the face and fall into his arms at the same time. I feel like he is the last piece of the puzzle that is me. The one thing in my past that is unresolved.

I lie down on the couch holding my phone. Maybe he will call? Maybe he's watching me right now?

I don't close the windows or the shutters. I'm hoping that he will slip into my house and wake me up with some declaration of his undying love. Apologize for leaving behind the only girl he ever loved. Insist that he did it all for me. To give me a chance, and make my life good, and get me away from the death and destruction that we grew up with as Company kids.

But I don't even get that in a dream. I wake up the next morning cold, and just as alone as I was the night before.

FOUR MONTHS
LATER...

CHAPTER FIVE

"Yeah," I croak into my cell phone.

"You awake?"

Adam. I take the phone away from my ear and check the time. Two AM. "Do I sound awake?"

"Max called me. Said you're taking too long. Something's going down a couple days from now and he wants you to put things in motion."

I sit up in bed. "What? Since when?"

"I dunno. I'm just the messenger."

I sit there thinking about this for a moment.

"You got any ideas?"

"About?"

"Sasha Cherlin, who else."

WASTED LUST

I have a lot of ideas about that girl, I chuckle to myself. But none of them have to do with this job. "Maybe one or two."

"Then do it. Call me if you need anything."

I get the hang-up beeps from Adam and fall back into my pillows. Sasha Cherlin. What an enigma. I've thought of nothing else but this girl since the moment I laid eyes on her. I'm glad Max is getting restless. I've been restless for months. I'm tired of waiting around for something to happen. And I might have a way to get her to move.

I set my alarm and close my eyes so I can picture it in my head. And then I fall back asleep wondering what it would be like to kiss her.

Sasha Aston—AKA Sasha Cherlin
Place of birth—unknown. No official birth certificate for Sasha Cherlin exists. Sasha Aston, however, was born in Denver, CO to parents unknown.
Age—twenty-four
Blonde hair, blue eyes, five-six
Attended and graduated from Regis Jesuit High School, Aurora, Colorado
BS in Geological Engineering from Colorado School of Mines, Golden, Colorado
Current position—PhD student at University of Kansas in anthropology, Lawrence, KS
Job history—none
Criminal history—none

That's it. After four months of digging, surveillance, and greasing palms with favors and promises to gain access to files I have no clearance for, this is the extent of my information about Sasha Cherlin. No parents, not even her real ones, are listed. But I know she was a Company kid.

I have my sources, and she admitted it in that one encounter we had at DIA when she acknowledged she knew Nicholas Tate. She never went to an elementary or middle school before she moved in with Ford Aston from what I can tell. I've checked every school in the west and found nothing.

But I've known one other kid with this very same background. The pattern fits—with one exception. Sasha is still alive.

I'd like to know how she managed that, to be honest. I'd like to know who raised her, what secrets she's keeping, how she got inducted into a makeshift family of con men and killers. I'd like to get inside her house. Turn over every mattress, pry up every floorboard, and peek into every crevice. But that place is locked up tight unless she's entering or exiting.

What kind of grad student has security like that? What kind of person, period?

I've looked into her adopted father's personal history, and it almost reads as true. He has parents, at least. Very rich family with a long history in Denver and the surrounding areas. He has children, a home, and a job. Two, actually. A semi-famous television producer of reality shows and one long-running science-fiction series on a major cable network. And he's on a CIA watchlist for criminal hackers. That guy's history is a case all its own.

But I don't care about her adopted father's indiscretions. I want more info on Sasha and the only way to get that info is *through* Sasha.

Max is right. We need to move this case forward and I need to do whatever it takes to make that happen. We can't afford to wait until Nick makes a move. If we let this opportunity slip by we'll lose any ground we've gained over the past four years.

But Sasha does not seem to be on the same timeline as us. I've followed her relentlessly. I've bugged her office phone. I've even gotten two students to spy on her. One asked her out on a date, which she declined. She does not party, she does not have friends, she does not do anything even remotely suspicious.

But I know who she is. So I'm not falling for any of it.

Sasha Cherlin might be the most dangerous woman in this entire country. She has no weapons registered to her, but if my sources are right—and I believe they are—she has guns. She possibly has explosives. And she knows how to use them. Furthermore, just the fact that she admitted to being Sasha Cherlin is enough to put her on every watchlist in the country. Probably every watchlist in the world.

But the fact that she is not on any of these lists—even though her adopted father *is*—tells me something I can't ignore.

The Company is still taking care of her.

It all adds up to something and even though I can think of a few scenarios that might involve the Company reasserting their claim on this girl, none of them are good for her.

They want her skills for a job. They want information. Or they want to kill her. These are the only three possible reasons for Nick's renewed interest in Sasha Cherlin.

I want her for all those things too. I don't want to kill her, but if she's working for them again—if that meeting I interrupted when I approached her at DIA has something to do with the Company—then I will.

They have a serious blood debt with me and I've waited a long time to get even. I've lost a lot trying to get to this moment in time. I've put things on the line. *People* on the line. And Sasha Cherlin will not yank the only opportunity I have for payback away from me because she's careful.

She has to fuck up sometime. And I need that fuckup to happen soon or years of waiting and work will all go down the drain. Hell, I might lose my position at the FBI over this if anyone finds out. And that's not all. I could be charged with treason just for looking at the information Max gave me.

And Madrid. She's been professional and she was sent by Max. He's one of the only people I can trust, so I accept her as a partner. But who is she? Why is she here? Why is she on this case that isn't even a case? How did she manage to get assigned to a top-secret mission like this?

There's only one answer for that.

She's involved.

Like me. Like my brother. Like Sasha.

Madrid and I don't work the same shift. She takes days, trailing Sasha discreetly at school using campus cameras from a remote location. And I take nights watching her house. No one comes. No one goes. At school, she's an exemplary student, teacher, and citizen. No parties, no drugs, no drinking, no friends, no men, no nothing.

Sasha is a living, walking ghost.

I check my watch from the front room of the apartment

across the street from her. She leaves every day at seven-fifty and walks to school. That's in three minutes. So I grab my keys and walk out the door. Today, she will have company.

I paid the student who rented this place four months' rent to get him to move out and let me have it, still under his name. And my four months are just about over. We need to change the course of things and I plan on doing that today.

When I get out onto the street it's seven forty-nine. I wait in the front-door vestibule until she exits and pushes through into the rain, locks up that fortress she lives in, and crosses the street.

I take her in as I exit the building. She has a look to her. A style specifically for school. When she came home from Peru she was casual class. But she's changed since last summer. At least on the outside. She started school wearing slacks and blouses. Kinda nerdy, if you ask me. But as the weeks went on her style morphed into jeans and grungy t-shirts. She wears a coat that one might find on a cowboy—those short jackets made out of tan canvas. Her hair started the semester in a tidy up-do, but now it hangs, covering her face. When she turns and sees me, I catch a moment of surprise. But it only lasts a moment, and her expression never changes. I'm just very good at reading people.

She walks down her front steps and turns left, towards the main street that leads to campus. I join her on the sidewalk as she opens her umbrella. "Miss Aston. May I walk with you?"

She smiles without turning her head. "I doubt I can stop you." She gives me a one-second onceover. "I've been wondering when you'd show up again."

"Oh, I never left."

"I know." She snorts. "I see you."

Hmm. "How's school going? Anything going on I should know about?"

"Well, if you like hearing about lab results, student teaching woes, and plans for winter break, I'm happy to tell you all about it. These are the only thing I'm enjoying these days."

"I'm not surprised."

She sighs, like I'm boring her. And I probably am.

"I mean, lab results, I don't know what you're doing as far as that goes. I can see you enjoy your field of study, so the joy you get from teaching seems in line, and the fact that you have no plans for your break pretty much sums up the rest of your social life here on campus."

I get a scowl from this and that makes me smile because I know she has no plans.

"Do you have something you'd like to discuss with me, Agent?" She stops walking. The rain is dripping down the sides of her black umbrella, and I'm well on my way to soaked. "Because I already told you what I know and I've got nothing to add."

"Well," I say, lowering my voice to something just above a whisper, "I've got some news." I clear my throat to give her time to react, but she is passive and still. "There's been some buzz in the Agency that Nick Tate might be planning a trip to the US."

She shifts from one foot to the next, like she's anxious to get away from me. "I'm not sure what that has to do with me."

"I think he's coming to see you. And quite honestly, I'm worried about it." I frown to illustrate my concern. "You're locked up tight in that house of yours, but you walk to school. Maybe you can let me drive you from now on?"

She shakes her head and starts walking again. "No, thank

you."

I walk alongside her until we get to the corner and have to cross the street. We let a car pass and then step off the curb together. "I'd make it worth your while."

"What's that supposed to mean?" She walks faster now. School is only two blocks away, and we're not very far from the museum where she has her tiny grad school office. I glance over my shoulder and see one of the students Madrid has placed on Sasha, and give him a nod. He drops back into a crowd of girls and lets them pass.

I only have a few minutes to make my move. "I've just noticed you're not very social. No boyfriend, no dates, not even a girls' night out. Nothing on your calendar the entire semester. And I get it. You're not one of those pretty, popular girls—"

"Excuse me?" She huffs out a laugh.

"—so I thought you could use a date."

Now she lets off a guffaw. "Wow, that was a pretty pathetic way to ask a girl on a date. And even though I might appear hard up and undesirable, I'm going to have to pass on that."

I take her arm, gently, not wanting to startle her. Something tells me a startled Sasha is a bad thing. I lean into her space. She smells like shampoo and flowers. "Miss Aston, I'm not saying you're undesirable at all. I'm just saying you could use a night off."

She looks down at my hand on her arm and I remove it, but when her blue eyes meet mine, I feel a little wave of apprehension. "I said no, thank you."

She starts walking again. I let her get a few paces ahead, so she can wonder if I will pursue, and once she shoots that glance over her shoulder I jog a little to catch up. "OK," I say calmly. "But everyone needs to have some fun, Sasha. And I've been on this boring job for months. I'd like to have some fun."

"Agents don't have fun with suspects." She laughs.

I like the sound of that laugh. It was real and this girl is so serious. I had started wondering how deep her unhappiness runs. "I told you months ago, you're not a suspect. We just want to work with you."

"Agents don't have fun with prospective agents, either."

"Since when?" I chuckle.

"So date Madrid if you need to get laid. I'll let her spies know that you're interested. She's pretty, but I doubt she's getting much action the way she's all over me."

"Madrid isn't even in town." She is, but she's behind the scenes. Only watching from remote locations. "Besides, she's not my type."

"So what's your type?"

"Ah, I knew you were interested." I take her arm and wrap it in mine as we walk. She tries to pull away, but it's a half-hearted attempt at best. So I grab hold with my other hand. "Madrid is all sorts of tough, you know? Those women who have a chip on their shoulder. They work a man's job and—"

"Whoa, whoa, whoa! You did not just say that." She stops again, and by this time I'm good and wet. Rain is dripping down my face. But this is a reaction I can work with. "So she's a bitch, is that what you're saying?" A snort from Sasha at that. "She's serious and goal-oriented, so that makes her tough. Well, I have news for you, Agent Jax, I'm not a soft girl either, so I have no idea what you're talking about when you say I'm your type."

WASTED LUST

We're at the corner of the last street we need to cross before we get on campus and Sasha pushes the walk button repeatedly.

"You seem soft to me." I say it in a low voice again. This makes her stiffen a little. "And I'm not disparaging Madrid. I don't know her very well, actually. I just don't like career women."

"Oh my God," Sasha says, shaking her head. Another student standing at the light with us shoots me a disgusted look. "If you haven't noticed, *I'm* a career woman."

"Ah," I say, waving my hand at her just as the walk light illuminates. We head across the street with her once again struggling to free herself from my arm, but I hold onto her tightly. "You're not, Sasha. you're playing at it. Dabbling. You're filthy rich, you have a thing for dinosaurs, I guess. So you figured you'd waste some time at school because you don't know what else to do with yourself. Nick left you behind. You never got over it. And so you spend your days immersed in science labs and boring lectures. You stay away from men and friends because you can't relate. And maybe Nick isn't coming back. You think about it all the time, don't you? Are you saving yourself for him?"

"I'd slap the shit out of him," the girl in front says over her shoulder. "Punch him in the face."

"Hey," I bark at the feminist. "This is private."

"Then maybe you shouldn't be saying that shit in public," she retorts before veering away from us.

Sasha finally tugs her arm from my grasp and starts walking fast towards the museum. We are steps away and I'm not sure my approach is working yet. I did get her to talk, but it's not enough. I need movement on this case and I need it today. So I jog to catch up and then get ahead of her so I can open the door.

She rolls her eyes at me, but she steps through, folding up her umbrella. I follow her in as she makes her way to the stairs. "What are you doing?" she asks in a hushed, but angry, whisper. There's no one in here. The museum isn't normally busy this early in the morning and there's no classrooms in here. Just the grad school offices on the third floor. "Go away. I'm at work. I'm pretty sure agents are not allowed to harass upstanding citizens at work for no reason."

The stairs are not enclosed. The building is old and elaborate with dark hardwood banisters and marble steps. But it is a little dark in this area since there are no windows. She takes the steps two at a time but when she gets to the landing between the first and second floors, I grab her hand and pull her close for a moment. "I think that girl was right. We need some privacy."

"Agent Jax," Sasha growls. "I'm not interested in your offer, your work, or your interest in me. And if you touch me again"— she pulls her arm away a final time—"I will break all your fingers."

I put my hands up in surrender. "OK, look. I heard some news, I said. And I think he's about to make his move. I don't think you're safe."

"I'm quite capable of taking care of myself, Agent." She says it with determination as she unbuttons her raincoat, but I catch a moment of doubt in her eyes. It throws me for a second. Because I know she's quite capable. If I had to bet which of us was more capable, I'd put my money on her. So this is interesting. "I don't need you to protect me, I have not heard from Nick Tate in ten years, and I have no interest in a—"

I cup my wet hands around her face and kiss her.

She drops her umbrella and struggles for a moment, but

when my tongue slips between her lips, she stops. Not quite giving in—her hands are gripping my biceps as I play with her mouth—but she doesn't pull away. I push her backwards until she bumps up against the wall, pressing my wet clothes into her open coat. And I slide one hand behind her neck to draw her closer while the other one fists her hair.

Her tongue responds, twisting together with mine. Her chest begins to rise and fall more rapidly, and then she is panting in my mouth. Fuck.

I pull back and release her hair so I can palm her cheek. I slip my thumb up to her lips and she actually moans. And when I try to slip my thumb into her mouth, she opens for me.

Good God.

I stare down at her as she looks up at me. My hair is dripping water down her face, but she stays absolutely still. "I want to take you out tonight, Miss Cherlin." She swallows when I call her by her real name. "I'm not taking no for an answer. So I'll pick you up at eight."

And then I kiss her again—this time no tongue—and turn away to jump down the stairs.

When I get to the bottom I turn around. "Hey," I call up to her. She's still backed up against the wall, her mouth open from the kiss. It makes me grin to see her so caught off guard.

"What?" she whispers, her hand reaching towards her heart.

I hold up both hands, palms out, and laugh. "I've still got all ten fingers, killer. Looks like you've lost your game." And then I drop the smile and give her a stern look that makes her face scrunch up. "If we hire you to help us, you're gonna wanna get that game back, understand?"

I don't wait for an answer, just turn and walk away. Out of her line of sight from the stairs, and then out of the building. It's still raining outside, but the only wet thing on my mind right now is that girl's mouth.

CHAPTER SIX

"Who the..."

That asshole. He walks away before I can finish my sentence.

Pick me up at eight. Work for them. Asshole.

"Hey, Sasha," Mike, my office-mate, says as he walks up the stairs. He stops on the landing in front of me. "What are you doing?"

I let out a breath and mutter, "Nothing."

"You OK? You sound stressed. And your face is all wet. Didn't you use your umbrella?" He looks down at it on the floor. "You never get stressed. So the world must be upside down right now."

I paint on my trademark smile. "I'm fine, just thinking about my orals today. How about you? Are you ready for them?"

"I took mine yesterday."

"What?"

"Yeah, I'm skipping town for winter break, going to see some family in Europe, so they let me take them early."

I pick up my umbrella and we start walking up the stairs towards our office on the top floor. "How'd you do?"

"Passed." He grins. Mike is average-looking in all ways but one—that smile. He's got a nice smile and I've been lucky to be sharing an office with someone so upbeat for two years. "So I get to spend all next semester interning for Professor Ling in Montana."

"That's wonderful!" I say it enthusiastically, but I'm ready to explode with jealousy. I wanted that internship. I figured I had it in the bag.

"You're not mad, are you? That I got it?"

"Oh, no," I say, patting him on the shoulder like friends do. "Congrats, really. You deserve it."

"Thanks. I know you'll get a good one too. Probably that dig site in Utah everyone's been scrambling for."

We get to the office door and I throw my bag down on my desk and start pulling out my computer. I have some last-minute work to get my class grades in on time, and then the rest of the day is going over notes for the oral examination later this afternoon. "Yeah, one can hope." I smile at him, and then his phone rings and his face lights up. Must be his girlfriend. He walks out of the office, chatting happily about his promising future.

I drop into my crappy desk chair and despair over mine.

And then I remember Agent Jax and my anger is back. Kissed me! Said we're going on a date tonight! Said I lost my game!

I have game, dammit. I've got more game than anyone. I'm like a game master. I just stopped playing a long time ago. That game ended and this one began. I'm in a new game.

The only problem with this new game is that I'm really not a VIP player. And it sucks to admit it, but grad school is not as easy as my mom made it sound. She got a master's in psychology. In a foreign country, for fuck's sake. Speaking a whole other language.

But I'm here in the US, speaking English, and everything I do seems to be average.

I sigh. This has been my life for two years. I like teaching. I like the dig sites I get to go to in the summer and over breaks. But I don't have an internship lined up for this break. In fact, this is the first year in a very long time that I won't be off doing something over Christmas. Usually I go with my parents to New Zealand and we stay for a few weeks if I don't have academic plans.

And now I've got nothing, because they aren't going to New Zealand this year. The show my dad was producing ended last spring. They're not even staying home, so I can't go visit. They're taking my little genius of a brother, Five, to look at colleges. He's ten. Ten, for fuck's sake. And he's probably gonna have that PhD before I do.

"Ugh." I pull up my faculty account and start checking messages before I get started. Professor Brown wants to see me in her office at three. Probably to give me encouragement before my orals. Other than that, I've got nothing. Finals for undergrads ended last week, so the campus is nearly dead. Only us lowly grad students and work-study people are left.

I get busy on finalizing the grades for my classes. Mike

comes back and does the same, interrupted by many, many, many annoying calls from fellow students and faculty members congratulating him on his success.

I'm happy for him. He's a total anthropology nerd. He deserves all this, he really does.

But I'm jealous. I can't help it. I'm a nerd. I like anthropology. I love dinosaurs more. But you can't major in dinosaurs. That was a real bummer when I figured that out. Which is why I got a practical undergraduate degree in geological engineering. I figured that would look really good on a resume. Especially coming from The School of Mines.

But I was wrong about that. Mike has a BS in human evolution. That's the ticket to anthropology success. Because no one cares about dinosaurs. No one over the age of twelve, anyway. They all go fangirl over human shit.

I could spend my whole life with ancient reptile bones and be happy. But those internships are few and far between. That one I had last summer in Peru was the only thing scheduled for years.

I sigh. Which is why I will be spending this Christmas alone. Shut up in my fortress. Trying to forget about my past and be hopeful about my future.

But I don't feel very hopeful right now. And I know it's just nerves before my orals. I can't wait for those to be over. Once I finish those, I will officially start my research.

Only a few more years, Sasha, I tell myself. *Then you can go forth and conquer your passion for dinosaurs with academic support.*

It seems so far away though.

"Ugh." Back to work. I finish up the final grades for my class, send them to the registrar's office, and then pack my stuff up to go see Professor Brown.

The temperature has dropped since I came in this morning, and the rain is just starting to turn to sleet when I open my umbrella and head out the door. Professor Brown's office is a few buildings over, so I jog there, trying not to slip in the slush that has accumulated over the day. When I finally pull open the door of the administrative offices, my stomach does all kinds of tumbling. Orals are a big deal. It's normal to be nervous. Once this is over I will feel so much better. I can start planning my research and really begin moving towards this goal I've had since I was a kid.

Professor Brown's door is open when I get there. I knock politely, just to let her know I'm coming in. "Hey!" I say, cheerfully.

"Sasha." She smiles. She's only in her mid-forties, so she is beautiful in a way that says sophisticated and smart. Her blonde hair is styled into a fashionable bob, her makeup is perfect but not overdone, and her eyes are always bright with wonder about the world around her. She's brilliant and I'm very lucky she agreed to mentor me. "Come in and close the door behind you."

"Ut-oh," I laugh, closing the door as she asked. "I feel like I'm in trouble." I say it jokingly, but when I turn to take a seat in front of her large mahogany desk, she has a frown on her face. "What?" My anxiety starts creeping out.

She takes off her glasses and that's when I realize I really am in trouble. "Sasha, we've cancelled your orals for today. I'm sorry I didn't tell you earlier, but I thought this was a conversation that deserved a face-to-face meeting."

"What?" Oh my God. What's happening?

"We don't think you're ready to commit to your candidacy. You are a smart girl…"

It goes on like that for twenty minutes. I feel the sting of tears. She comforts me. Tells me I'm brilliant. But if I was brilliant, then why are they insisting I take a semester off?

I walk out of her office stunned.

I've been ordered to think about my future. What do I really want out of this degree? *Why* do I want this degree?

What the hell?

Why the fuck does she think I want this degree? I want to study bones! It's not rocket science! You need a PhD to get grants, and dig sites, and authorization from local governments. You need academic backing and to get backing you have to have a degree!

Of course, I didn't say that. I told her what she wanted me to say. That I have a passion for anthropology. And it's a not a lie. I like it. But it's just a stepping stone to dinosaurs.

I stopped mentioning dinosaurs years ago once I figured out no one would take me seriously. So yeah, this program is not about dinosaurs. This program is about all kinds of old stuff. Fossils and human evolution and all that shit. What I'm doing is not so out of the ordinary. People use degrees to get other places all the time.

But this university, and specifically this program, does not want to be used as a stepping stone. And even though I never used those words in our conversation, she's on to me.

I push through the doors of the museum so I can go upstairs and collect my things.

Collect my things! I've been ousted. I don't even get to prove myself!

I am so glad Mike left for the day once I get upstairs. How humiliating it would be to have to pack up and walk out knowing he just got the dream assignment.

When I get to my desk I realize I have very few things to collect. Some office supplies in my desk drawer. Some notebooks with my lab results. And my dinosaur Chia Pet.

All my samples can stay in the freezers until I come back, Professor Brown said. If I choose to come back. She actually said that.

I slump down into my chair and struggle with this very unexpected ending to a day that was supposed to plant my feet firmly on the ground. I feel… defeated. And small. Insignificant.

But beyond that, I feel… cheated.

And, if I'm being perfectly honest with myself, outed.

I'm a fraud. And she knows it.

I put my head on my desk and close my eyes. How many years have I painted this fake smile on my face, just trying to fit into this world? Ten years, that's how long. Ten long years of pretending that I am normal. And what good has it done me? I'm on the cusp of success. I have the golden ticket in my sights, and it's all pulled away in an instant because they know.

I'm not normal.

I'm a liar.

I'm a killer.

And even though she didn't say any of that, that's how I took it. Because it's all true. I've been deceiving these people. Pretending that I'm one of them when I'm not. I'm damaged.

WASTED LUST

And no amount of studying, no college education or PhD degree or fake smiles painted on my face, can change that.

I was never Sasha Aston. She doesn't exist.

I was born, and have always been, Sasha Cherlin. Company kid. Daughter to a traitor. Child assassin.

CHAPTER SEVEN

After Sasha returns to the museum—looking down at the ground her entire way, so she never even notices me—I wait under the eaves of the building for her to come back out. But after a while I get cold and antsy, so I slip inside and take a seat on a bench near the stairs so I can catch her coming down.

Two hours later, I've done all the crap I can think of on social media, watched a few YouTube videos, and I'm just about sick of looking for new music to buy when she finally makes an appearance. I stand, smiling, waiting for her to notice me. But she's got her hands full with a box and her head is still down.

She walks right by, tipping her hip into the door to make it open, and then disappears into the dark evening with a swoosh.

Hmmm.

WASTED LUST

I follow her out, surprised to find she is already at the stoplight. I jog over to her and reach for the box in her hands. She drops it, whirls around, and delivers a chop to my neck that almost has me choking.

"It's me," I say, half laughing, half gasping for air. "Whoa, calm down, killer."

"Dammit! Don't sneak up on me." And then she looks down at her overturned box and lets out a groan. "Now look," she says, picking up some broken piece of pottery. "The only real thing I had up there is broken." She takes a deep breath and leans down to pick her things back up, but I beat her to it.

"Sorry about your"—I squint at the pottery—"damaged Chia Pet."

She laughs a little, but only a little. "I'm not going to dinner with you, OK? That kiss was out of bounds and I'm an in-bounds kind of girl. So you screwed up." The light has changed so she grabs the box out of my hand and starts walking across the street. I follow her, grabbing her umbrella out of the box, and since she doesn't have an extra hand to hold it up herself, I push it open and hold it over her head.

"What the hell are you doing? I said go away."

"Hey, no man would leave a lady to carry a box in the freezing rain. So you can let me carry the box and you can hold the umbrella, or you can carry the box and let me hold the umbrella. Choose, Sasha Cherlin."

"It's Aston, OK? And I just want to be left alone. So fuck off."

I smile, still walking with the umbrella over her head, and then I laugh at her outburst. "OK. We're making progress, Miss Aston. You are letting me in on your feelings. Which means you're softening to my wily techniques."

She rolls her eyes but I catch a slight grin.

I put a hand on her shoulder, asking her to stop. She does. But she looks at the ground. "Please, Agent Jax. Just leave me alone." And then she looks up and I realize she's on the verge of tears. "I've had enough and I just want to go home."

"OK." I nod, my face somber like hers. "OK. But I'm still gonna walk you there. So one more choice today, killer, and then you can put this day to bed. Box? Or umbrella?"

She stares down into her box and doesn't answer. So I do the only thing I can. I take the box in one arm, the umbrella in another, and slip that arm around her shoulder so it can keep her covered while we walk.

Her body tenses up when we make contact, but she lets out a sigh and accepts my offer to walk her home in the rain, leaning into me a little as we start on our way.

"Bad day?"

She says nothing, so I take the hint. We stay like this all the way to her house a few blocks away. It only takes a few minutes—much too fast for my liking—and then we are climbing the steps to her front porch.

I set the box on a small table off to the side of the door, and then fold the umbrella away as she unlocks her fortress. I even have a moment of hope that she will invite me inside. But instead she opens her door with a shove of her hip and then reaches for the box without looking at me. "Thank you," she says in a small voice that tells me this is no ordinary bad day. "I appreciate the help."

I nod as she sets the box down inside and makes to close the door. But I stop her with the folded umbrella. "Hey," I say. She looks up at me with blurry blue eyes. "I'm happy to listen if you need to talk."

But all I get is a shake of her head, and then she grabs the umbrella and closes the door before I can say anything else.

I wait there for a second, maybe hoping she's peeking through the peephole, still thinking about the man on her porch. But I hear the beeping of her alarm and then footsteps as she walks away.

There's a lot on her mind tonight. But it isn't me.

So I jog down her steps and walk back to my car. Madrid is in there. We're a team again, it seems. She knows this can be a career-making case, she's in for the teamwork.

I open the driver's side door and slip into the rental car.

"Damn, boy. You're wet!" She scoots away from my dripping coat and presses herself against the passenger door. "Anything?"

"Nope," I sigh. "You wanna eat?"

"Eat?" she says, scrunching up her face in a way that makes her upturned nose crinkle. "We are on a deadline. We ain't eatin'. We're gonna work." Her thick Southern accent comes out when she's annoyed. And it clashes with her fake, trashy persona. She comes off as half streetwalker and half gang member, but over the past few months I've gotten to know her a little better. Madrid Marano usually talks like she came straight out of Brooklyn, but she is from Savannah, Georgia. A real Southern belle from a family that has been in the Agency for three generations.

Which is funny if you compare us. I'm actually from Brooklyn, but lost the accent when I took my first assignment down south in Miami.

"She's having a bad day, Madrid. It's not a good time to move this forward."

"We don't have time for good times," Madrid says, her voice rising a little. "You're a man. A somewhat attractive man. If you like blue eyes and blond hair. Which I don't," she says, her hand on her chest like she needs to clear this up right now. "I like them dark, understand. So don't be all accusing me of inappropriate conduct when I have to turn you down 'cause you're hot for me."

I just shake my head. She's always on this kick about how desirable she is and how I secretly lust after her.

"So get your move on, boy. You need a plan to seduce this girl into helping us. We have no time for pansy-ass, pouting girls and pussyfooting, 'fraidy-cat men who don't know how to get a job done. Get your game on, Jax." She opens her door, steps out, and then leans back in, dripping water everywhere. "I'm going back to the apartment to check footage. You wrap this shit up tonight and we'll reconvene in the AM. Madrid out."

And then she slams the door and walks away.

Fucking women. I sigh as I start up my car.

Moves. I have moves, but Sasha Cherlin doesn't look like she takes kindly to moves. Plus she had a bad day. I need to make sure I don't add to it, or it will set us back further.

"Well," I huff, pulling away from the curb. "Just take a play out of yesteryear, Jax. Treat her nice and let the chips fall where they may."

CHAPTER EIGHT

After I shut the alarm off I press myself against the door, a feeling of defeat trying its best to wash over me, but I square my shoulders and walk off, dropping my bag on a chair as I make my way to the stairs. My feet find the places on the old wooden steps where no boards will creak out of habit and I silently ascend to the upper bedrooms. There are three. I don't need three, since I am alone, and this makes the place feel empty and cold. A shudder erupts in my body as I walk into the elegantly decorated master bedroom—which I don't normally sleep in since I'm a paranoid freak—and throw myself face-first on the bed.

Am I stupid?

Yes. I am the dumbest girl alive. I am the biggest fool to ever live. I am naive and gullible in ways I can't even describe right now. Because I believed that if I worked hard, got good grades, took the path most traveled, every step away from the broken-hearted thirteen-year-old who sat and cried over a broken promise would lead to something else.

Something better. A new life. A new family. A new opportunity.

And where do I find myself now? Not digging up dinosaurs—which is also the foolish dream of a child. Kicked out of the world of the legitimate. *Take time off to think about things*, that's what Professor Brown told me. But I can read between the lines just fine, thank you. What she was really saying is, *We don't think this program suits you.*

And since digging in the earth to find ancient bones so I could put the puzzle pieces of the past together was the only thing that ever made me feel a part of society at large—well, the words 'complete devastation' run through my mind.

Growing up the child of a man who trains shadow government assassins was not a choice I ever got to make. It was my fate. I did not come into this world declaring myself to be a killer. I didn't teach myself to hold and shoot a gun. To throw knives and shoot arrows. I didn't drag myself across this country in an RV knowing secrets that certain people might kill for.

My father did that to me.

And while I don't blame him—he did his best and all that training saved my life over and over again—I fucking hate that this is who I am.

And I have regrets. I have big-time regrets. And I have questions. Like why is this my destiny? Why do I have to live on the outside, forever looking in at all the things I want but can't have?

This career was obtainable. I felt it. I still feel it. I'm qualified, I'm smart, I'm inquisitive, I'm a hard worker, and I get good grades. I didn't fuck up anything too big doing my lab work. I made mistakes, like anyone new to the process of discovery. But I had no major missteps.

And a lot of good it did me.

There is something about me. I feel it burning inside me. Something attached to my soul that declares me *different*.

I don't want to be different. I want to be *same*.

I roll over on my back and stare at the ceiling. Ford and Ashleigh did a good job as my parents after my father was killed and my fellow assassins and I fought our way into a tenuous illusion of peace. I traveled and made friends. Obtained a first-class education. Had a few boyfriends even. Nothing serious. And not because of Nick.

I was making progress in the love department. Steady progress. I had dates to dances in high school. One serious boyfriend freshman year of undergrad. Three one-night stands the rest of college.

All that came to an abrupt end in my senior year when I was abducted by a sick man looking for revenge over an old debt that wasn't even mine. He did not rape me. It could've been so much worse than it was. I know that. But it affected me. It shut me down. Not right away. I put on that fake face I had practiced over and over again while I was adjusting to living the life of a normal girl. I went back to school after I was saved by my assassin friend, Merc. I finished up school in Colorado and moved here to this very house.

WASTED LUST

Merc and I never told Ford and Ashleigh anything about the abduction. Ford is a security freak and it was his idea to take most of the precautions. But once they left to go home—Ford holding me tighter that day than any other time in my life—I called James and everything just spilled out. He flew in specialists to fortify the house. He brought me guns and ammo. He even brought me some Kevlar clothing made special by a friend in Central America.

I insisted I wasn't scared. The man who wanted to hurt me was dead. And I really wasn't scared. I was terrified.

That realization was enough to rock my whole world, because I was always the fearless one. I was the one with all the answers. I was the one who would do the job no matter the consequences. And even though this thought I had today walking home with the FBI agent has been in the back of my head since that abduction— right now is the first time I will admit to it.

I am weak. I am small. I am a girl. Worse than a girl. I am a Company *girl*. And I have pushed all my fucked-up moments away into a place that hides the truth in order to protect this fragile part of me that lingers. The part of me that knows I will never be OK. I will never get over the things I have seen, the acts I have committed, and the violence I am part of.

I am damaged.

Terrified and damaged.

I swallow hard as I turn over on my back and stare up at the ceiling. The only thing holding my illusion together was school. My objective. Get that PhD and slip into a world of isolated academia. A world of digging in the earth searching for clues to the past. A world where only the joy of discovery matters. A world where I was no longer Sasha Cherlin, the child who can kill. I was Sasha Aston, the woman who clung hard to the only innocent thing about her upbringing.

A love of dinosaurs.

My father fostered that love like my life depended on it. He took me to museums and places here in the West where bones were found, tracks were still visible, and all the unanswered questions were about what these ancient creatures ate, how they raised their young, and lived out their days until the final blow that wiped them off the face of the earth.

And maybe he knew? Maybe he knew all those years ago that I needed this innocent hobby to get me past the person I truly was? To blind me to the facts and make me forget that I was born a Company girl.

I will not cry about the end of this life. I will not.

I have ended my life before. I can pick up and move on. I can even find another, more suitable, program to join and continue the illusion that I am normal.

I could.

But I know I won't.

Because Nick Tate still holds me captive. His broken promise still hurts. The way he pushed me aside that last night I saw him still stings my heart. The scream that came out of my mouth as I was led down the dock to a waiting boat by James and delivered into the hands of Merc.

I watched Nick fade that night. But he never disappeared for me. As much as I tried to say he did, even after Agent Jax told me Nick was looking for me, it's just not possible to forget the person you were meant to marry and spend the rest of your life with.

And I wonder, and have wondered all this time, if being a Company girl would've been so bad if I'd been with Nick.

It's a frightening thought. Especially after seeing first-hand what they did to the girls who were not raised by my father. The ones not raised and loved by the Admiral, like Harper was. His little princess was spared the brunt of the consequences, just like me.

But the child assassin fate was tempered by the fact that my destiny was Nicholas Tate.

And yet it wasn't.

It's so wrong to wish for the life I never had. It's wrong. Because so many people put their lives on the line to give me this second chance. They made sacrifices for me.

I am filled with shame because if Nick had offered his hand that night when I was thirteen and kept his promise to make me his, I would've said yes. I would've walked away from all the friends and family who love me so much, and they would be the ones left behind instead of me.

I would take Nick's hand. I would gladly take his hand and disappear into a life of crime and uncertainty. Death and lies.

Shame on you, Sasha.

Yes. Shame on me for wanting my only chance at true love.

"Yeah," I say to the ceiling. "I should feel so much shame because my future was stolen from me." It's ridiculous and it maddens me that every one of my old friends from the Company days got their happy ending. It infuriates me. It makes my whole body rage with heat that I must suppress my dreams to make things right.

Why? That's my only lingering question. "Why did you leave

me, Nick Tate? Why was everyone allowed to determine what was best for me back then except me? Why am I stuck here, on the edge of fulfillment, while you live the life you chose? Why am I not allowed to make my own choices?"

And most importantly, why are you looking for me again?

I don't think it's because I'm in danger. Nick would not contact me, of all people, if that was the case. He'd call James or Merc. They'd leave me out of everything, like they always do. They'd gather their guns and ammo. Call up old favors. Turn back into the dangerous and insane men they used to be.

They'd take care of things and I'd probably never know about it.

So why is Nick looking for me?

I've tried to put it out of my mind since Agent Jax corralled me into that interrogation room at the airport last summer. I came home and went back to my studies. Went through the motions of work and pretended that this was the life I chose for myself.

But it was all a lie.

Nick. Nick. Nick. The name reverberates in my head every moment of every day. Hidden. Secret. But still there, no matter how many times I try to deny it.

"You're mad, Sasha."

I am mad. In every sense of the word. I'm furious and insane. "Call home."

My words startle me for a moment. Enough that I reach into my pocket and pull out my phone and dial the number.

"Aston residence," Five says on the second ring.

"It's me, Five." I can almost feel him smile. "Is Mom there?"

"Sasha," he breathes in that all-knowing way, unnatural for a ten-year-old. "Did you know that we are leaving for New Zealand tomorrow?"

"What? Since when? I thought you were all going to look at colleges?"

"Since Ford—"

"You mean Dad." Ford hates it when Five calls him by his name.

"Whatever. He got a call to shoot a new pilot show."

"Oh, well, that's great, I guess."

"Great? Great? No, it's not great. Sparrow Flynn's birthday is tomorrow and Princess Shrike tells me they are having a party. I was not invited to this party, Sasha. And now my plans to crash it are ruined."

"Why the hell would you want to go to an eight-year-old girl's birthday party?"

"The Princess will be dressed up like a biker, Sasha. It's a biker theme and I have purchased her a leather jacket for the occasion. I wanted to be there to see the joy on her face when…"

I tune him out as I think about what the fuck is going on at home. Princess Shrike's father—her real name is Rory, only Five calls her Princess—is world-famous custom bike builder Spencer Shrike. So this only makes sense in that context. And I don't even bother asking how he got his hands on a leather jacket fit for a nine-year-old. This is Five we're talking about. "I got nothing for that, Five. Can you get Mom?"

"How would you like to hear my proposal for my newest invention? I'm seeking early investors for my new technology app. I project that if a prototype can be developed in the next twelve months, we can go public in two years."

"Five," I say patiently. He's had a dozen of these ventures over the past few years. "You're ten years old. I'm not investing in your gaming apps."

"It's not a game this time, Sasha. It's an app that will change death as we know it."

"Morbid," I reply. "Get Mom."

"Morbidity has nothing to do with it. People will pay for years to have what I'm developing right now. A subscription that will last until infinity."

"Five, I need to talk to Mom *now*." I sigh into the phone and he stops his protest.

"You're upset," he says in that unaffected way he has. A tone he's perfected to make people believe he's never emotional, only objective. My little brother is a freak of a genius, just like Ford. He speaks six languages and he's well on his way to a seventh— Icelandic, of all things—and could probably have passed my orals today without a glance at the topic beforehand. They've been trying to get him into summer college programs for two years, but he's afflicted with the most overpowering of emotions, and has been since he was four.

Love.

I almost snort into the phone thinking about it.

He loves Princess Rory Shrike. The name alone makes me smile, makes me happy that I called home to talk to my mom about this new development in my long career of developments.

"I can tell you are crinkling your nose at this very moment."

"I'm gonna hang up and call Dad and tell him you're looking for investors again if you don't call for Mom right now."

"Fine." he huffs. "Mom!" he screams. "Your eldest is on the phone with disappointing news."

Neither him, nor Kate, my little sister, are my real siblings, obviously. But Kate was one and Five was newborn when I came to live with Ford and Ashleigh. So it was just easier to become one of the kids. Of course, they know who I really am. We are not a family of liars. But I like calling Ash Mom and Ford Dad. Even if the kids aren't around.

The phone makes some muffled noises and then Ashleigh is there, a little out of breath.

"Hey," she says. "How did the orals go?"

I can hear excitement in her voice and all the questions I had a few moments ago are replaced with regret. She's smart too. Not a genius like Ford, but she's got her master's degree in psychology and has a private practice that specializes in treating children with autism-related disorders. She's always encouraged me to follow my dream of digging up old bones and she's been my biggest cheerleader from the moment I walked into their house and she became the mother of a teenager at the young age of twenty-four.

I can't bear to tell her the truth, so even though we are not a family of liars, I lie. "Awesome," I say through my fake smile. "I passed easily."

"And the internship?" She's still breathless, like she's got all her fingers and toes crossed that I get the one that went to Mike. The one I've been talking about for months. "Did you get the one you wanted?"

I can't lie that much. Maybe I can still go back to the program. Give it a few weeks of soul-searching and figure out where I went wrong in my lack of enthusiasm for anthropology. I could still get back in. But that internship is gone. "No," I say with genuine disappointment. "I didn't. Mike did. Mine is still up in the air, but I'm OK with it. He really deserved it."

"Aww, I'm sorry, Sasha. But you'll get something great, I just know it." Her brightness comes back when I agree, and then we talk for several more minutes about Ford's new show and their Christmas plans. I tell another little lie and say I'm going home with friends.

She accepts that easily. I used to have friends. She has no clue I've gotten so antisocial since I moved here. Of course, that's because she has no idea about the abduction that spurred my melancholy in the first place.

I hang up with a false laugh and promises to come home and see them in the spring when things settle down.

I throw my phone on the bed feeling dirty for lying, as well as ashamed for being ungrateful for the full life I have. The sadness threatens to overtake me, so I get up and go run the water for a bath.

The tears are coming. Today was just too much, and I only allow myself to cry in the tub. I have done this for years. I lock myself away from the world, dip my whole body under the water, and let the tears flow undetected. It feeds my illusion that not a single tear has touched my face since I walked out of that hotel room for the last time. The hotel room where Nick left me but promised to come back. The hotel room where James explained the facts of life.

Not sex.

Loss.

WASTED LUST

Loss is a fact of life. And he pounded that home good and hard.

But I remember when the dream was fresh. The day Nick walked into my life and promised me the world. Promised me a future filled with his smiling face. Promised me a life with him by my side.

I take off my clothes and step into the tub, waiting for the hot water to pour out of the tap in a waterfall that drowns out the reality outside my house.

My tears are falling for his broken promises the moment I slip under.

CHAPTER NINE

There are no lights on in the house even though it's not even eight PM. But there are never lights on in her house. At least from the outside. She has security shutters that keep the world at bay. I climb the steps a little more nervous than I should be for the circumstances.

I'm not usually a second-guesser. I rewrite the rules all the time. I make demands and expect them to be met. I ask, people give. But being turned down by Sasha Cherlin has affected me in a way that's new.

For one, she refuses to engage. Most of the time when a woman puts up a wall, I can force her to engage with flirting. It gets the banter going, loosens things up a little, breaks down a few bricks in the wall. So far, Sasha has not done that.

This tells me two things—she is a deliberate person. Not one who reacts out of emotion, but one who calculates and plots her actions. And the reason she has not fucked up and made contact with anyone is because she's on a course I haven't yet recognized.

What is that course she's on? Where is she headed? What was she doing that day I confronted her at the airport?

It occurs to me that I would've found out if I had not approached her. But how was I to know Nick wasn't making contact with her? Everything pointed to it. It felt so... imminent.

I stop in front of her door and hesitate, shifting the bags in my hand to free up a finger to push the doorbell. There's something else that's been nagging me since I walked her home earlier as well. Why choose this path of academia? It's always seemed like a copout to me. A way to prolong an entrance into the real world. A reason to push life away.

What is she hiding from?

She has plenty of reasons to hide from her past. Growing up the way she did would make anyone want to prolong an entrance into society. But I don't think that's it. I don't think it's Nick, either. I have an idea of what they were to each other, but why join this small world of ambitious nerds, a world she so clearly does not belong in, only to push it all away and cloister herself in this tower of her own making?

It doesn't add up.

I sigh as I push the doorbell. I can't hear it, so I'm not even sure it works. But after a few seconds I hear a whirring noise of some well-hidden camera trying to focus. "Sasha?" I ask out loud, knowing full well she is watching me. "Open the door."

"I'm not interested in your date, Agent Jax. In fact, I'm very busy tonight. You have five seconds to remove yourself from my porch before I call the police."

I bow my head so she can't see me smirk, and then look up. "I am the police, Miss Aston."

"No," she says calmly from the safety of her intercom. "You're some kind of rogue agent. I'm not sure. I really haven't thought about you much over the past few months. But if I wanted to figure you out, if I were interested enough, I would have you all figured out. And you are here under someone's orders, but I'll bet they are not legitimate. In fact, you've been here far too long. So I'm betting that you had to make contact today for some specific reason. Perhaps you've been called back. Perhaps your rogue superior has had enough. Or perhaps there is another lead that you must follow. Either way, I have a feeling that if I just hold out a little bit longer you will disappear as quickly as you came."

Jesus Christ. She's a fucking mind-reader too. I straighten my tie to buy me a moment to gather myself, and then say, "Astute observation, Miss Aston. But you're wrong. I have carte blanche in this case. All the time in the world, in fact."

"Whatever—"

"But listen," I say, lowering my voice. I imagine her leaning in to the speaker on the other side of her fortress to hear me better. "We had a date. It's eight o'clock and I'm here to make good on my promise this morning."

"Not interested, Agent—"

"You can't possibly know that, Miss Cherlin, until you hear my offer. So please open the door and let me explain your options face to face."

"This conversation is over. Goodnight, Agent."

WASTED LUST

I drape the one bag over a nearby porch chair, set the other bag down on a small table next to it, and then remove the photograph from my breast pocket and hold it up. Her cameras are not visible, so I pan it across the front entrance. "We made contact with Nick Tate, Miss Cherlin. We don't have him in custody and we don't know where he is. But we know he's about to make contact with you. We think he's going to kill a lot of people, Sasha. And we need your insight to stop that."

Silence.

And then the whirring of the camera lens. I hold the image still. It's a much better photo than the ones I showed her months ago.

"I know you two have a history. If you open the door and talk to me face to face right now, I'll let you have this photograph."

Silence.

And then the unmistakable sound of disengaging locks on the other side of the door. Her face appears in a small crack. "You have ten seconds."

I tuck the photograph back into my breast pocket and her eyes track that movement.

She wants that photograph pretty bad.

I pick up the bag draped across the chair and the other one on the table and hold them up in the air for her to examine. "You have two choices if you want the photograph, Miss Cherlin." I shake the garment bag. "Put this dress on and go out to dinner with me." I shake the paper bag, wet with grease stains. "Or we dine in tonight."

She looks me in the eye. "My third choice, Agent Jax, is to tell you to fuck off."

Ah! Finally, I have her engaged. "Alu gobi," I deadpan back at her, still holding up the bag from the restaurant. "Or the dress."

She crinkles her nose when I say the name of the dish I brought. She hates Indian food. Our spy invited her out a few months ago and this was one of the only tidbits of information we got from that conversation.

"The dress is beautiful. When was the last time you went out on a date? Years ago?" I smile, tucking down a chuckle. "It's sad, really. A woman like you all buttoned up in here like a spinster."

Sasha opens the door a few more inches. She's in a robe, her hair is wet, and now that some light from the street lamps can get past her walls, I realize her eyes are red.

"You've been crying."

"I don't cry," she says defensively. "I'm tired. I had a very bad day, and I'm not hungry or feeling up to going out." I wait for her to close the door in my face. But she looks at my breast pocket again.

She really wants that photograph.

I set the bag of food back down on the table and push the dress towards her. "Let's go out, Sasha. I promise not to ask you a single question about this case. All I want is an opportunity to unwind."

"With me?" She sneers, far from convinced. "Surely there are slutty co-eds you can pass the time with."

"I didn't say I wanted to simply pass the time with you, Sasha. I said unwind. I think we're a lot alike."

"I think we are complete opposites."

"We could laugh."

"We'd probably fight."

"I could buy you a drink and a nice dinner."

"I can buy my own drinks and dinner."

"I'd like to hold your hand and take a walk afterward. Do you like to look at the stars?"

She hesitates. I know she does. There is a small observatory on the roof of her house. It took me weeks to figure out what that little dome-shaped structure was up there. I thought it was hiding an air conditioner. Like a camouflaged utility room. But one night a while back, the dome slid open and I took pictures and sent them to a friend to see if he had any ideas what she might be doing.

A small observatory, he replied. To house a telescope.

Anyone who builds that on the roof of their house has a love for stars.

"No," she lies. "I'm sorry, you can keep your photo—"

But she stops mid-sentence when I reach inside my pocket and pull it back out. "How about a show of good faith then," I say, holding it out to her. "You take it now. And the dress." I shake the garment bag again. "And I'll come back and pick you up in thirty minutes when you're ready."

She stares at the photograph as I hold it up.

"I have years and years of pictures of him, Sasha." Her eyes dart up to mine. "An entire history, actually. We've had people on him for more than a decade." I see the disbelief in her eyes. More than a decade is longer than he's been missing, so I play the last card I can right now, and give her the truth. "I knew him, Sasha. I knew him growing up. We were almost friends once."

"You're lying." But it's a whisper. And her words are the lie, not mine. She knows this.

"I'm not," I tell her. "I have pictures of us together to prove it. But I want this night." I gently grasp her hand and push the photograph towards it. "Take it inside. Come out with me tonight and forget about him. Let your mind open up to me. Leave everything behind for a few hours and I'll show you what life in the real world can be like. You're hiding, Sasha. You've locked yourself away in this prison of your own making, and it's killing you. I can see it in your eyes. You live in the past when the present is all around you. Let me take it away for one night and I promise, I will fill in all those blank years for you in the morning. And when that's over, I'll ask you again if you'd like to help me. If you say no, I'll pack up and leave."

She takes the photograph and I give her the time she needs to look it over. I let her yearn for him. I let her imagine all the answers to all her questions. I let her soak it up and wish for more.

And then she nods. "OK. One night out with you and in the morning I want answers. But I'm telling you right now, Jax"—hearing her say my name without the formal Agent in front makes me smile immediately—"I'm not interested in you." She nods down at the picture. "I'm not interested in him that way either. I just—" She stops and lets out a long sigh. It's filled with emotion. Sadness and loneliness and maybe even regret. "I just need to know more."

"I understand." And I do. I need to know more as well. I have followed the lives of Company kids since I was a kid myself. I'm obsessed with them. With her, specifically. Everything I've done for the past four months is proof of how bad I have it. "But Sasha," I say with an edge to my voice, forcing her to focus her attention on me, "leave that photograph at home when you step outside."

She swallows hard and nods. And then she takes the dress from my hand, disappears inside, and closes the door with a soft click.

I grab the bag of food and walk across the street and up the path that leads to the apartments where I've been living for the past few months. Madrid is just pulling up in the parking lot with the car we hired. I walk towards her and hand her the bag of Indian food just as she steps out of the car.

"We've got it wired," she says, taking the food and inhaling the aroma of her favorite Indian dish. She walks off to her own car, sighing a little as she peeks into the bag and says, "Yum."

I go upstairs and change into my black Armani wool suit paired with a crisp white shirt and a dark-gray striped tie. I comb my dark-blond hair back and then put on a pair of cufflinks that will catch Sasha's eye.

It's been a long while since I've been interested in a girl. And even though I know I'm not supposed to be interested in Sasha Cherlin... I am.

I'm interested. And that kiss on the stairs at her school was just a tease.

I need more from her. It kills me to have to dangle Nick Tate in front of her face to get it. But I'm a man who gets what I want, no matter what it takes.

CHAPTER TEN

I walk over to the couch and take a seat near the lamp. My eyes never leave the image of Nick in my hand. He looks like my Nick from years gone by, except he has a tattoo on his upper arm. He's wearing a white t-shirt that hugs the well-defined muscles of his chest in a way that leaves little to the imagination. My heart is suddenly heavy with sadness.

I stare into his brown eyes. I can't see them well—the picture is mostly of his upper body, with the frayed edge of some faded jeans giving me a hint of his waist. But I don't need to see them in this picture to imagine them.

But dear God, I want more.

My eyes wander to the front door, beyond which is an evening with Jax. Going out with him tonight is not a big deal. Not when I can get more images of Nick and answers to my questions about what he's been doing. I've imagined all kinds of scenarios after he went off with Matias, the drug lord from Honduras who traded the lives of me, James, and Harper for Nick.

He traded himself so we could get away and start a new life far removed from the people who raised us into killers.

So he said, anyway.

I think he did it to get away from me. I've always felt that way. He never wanted me to be his promise. He never *wanted* me. He only wanted to *use* me.

I don't want that to be true. I want to see him again. I want him to see the woman I became and fall to his knees with regrets. Profess his love. Apologize and beg me to forgive him.

Such a stupid childhood dream.

I set the photograph down on the end table and stand up to get the dress and take it upstairs. I hang the garment bag on the hook in my bathroom and unzip it.

Inside is a red cocktail gown with a low-cut front and two slits that ride so high up on my thighs, my underwear might show if I take long steps.

Jesus Christ. This is what I've been reduced to? Playing dress-up fantasy girl to an FBI agent just to satisfy my twisted curiosity for a man who rejected me a decade ago?

I plop down into the hard wooden chair in front of my makeup vanity. When I moved in here I furnished this upstairs bedroom the way I had always imagined as a child. A four-poster bed made out of dark hardwood. A gauzy white netting draped over each post to create an intimate experience. The linens are top quality—Egyptian cotton sheets and a white cotton duvet filled with a plush down comforter. More pillows than one person has a right to own propped up against the headboard. The vanity table is also dark wood, with a matching chair. And the mirror is lit from a dramatic chandelier from above and small side lamps on either side.

Too bad I've had zero occasions to use it. I have not been out on any dates since I moved in and I can't fall asleep up here without tossing and turning all night worried about the escape route.

But that dream—the one where I fit in, where I was normal and had lots of chatty girlfriends and more men interested in me than I had days in the week… yeah. That never happened.

My closets are filled with dresses and shoes so high I would fall and break my ankle if I ever wore them. The en suite bathroom is like a spa. Completely remodeled, like the kitchen downstairs. I imagined dinner parties with dozens of guests and stimulating conversation about my interests.

How delusional was I?

I look at myself in the mirror and take it all in. I am not ugly. I've always been on the cute side, even as a gangly kid with braces. My eyes are a pretty blue and my hair is still dark blonde. I don't even have to dye it to keep that color. It has strands of light blonde that mimic an expensive trip to the salon.

But the hanging strands along the side of my face are the perfect frame for what I see in the mirror. Sadness.

"God, you are so dramatic, Sasha."

My hair is still slightly wet and has a bit of a wave that will certainly frizz if I don't dry it right now. I open a drawer in the vanity and take out the hairdryer and turn it on. The heat feels good now that it's night and a chill has taken over my house.

How did my reality get so far away from the fantasy I had imagined? Maybe a night out with a handsome man would do me good? Even if I'm not gonna fall for his charm, he could be fun. I mean, I realize he only wants to use me to get at Nick. But if I want to use him to get a chance at Nick too, then where's the harm of enjoying myself tonight?

I could do worse than Jax. Have done worse, in fact. I've dated mostly studious men. Men who mimic my ambitions. Men who like to talk instead of act. Men who are boring.

And I guess I'm boring too. I haven't put on makeup in months. Not since a small dinner party my mentor put on to welcome a new student to her lab last August. And I haven't made any attempts to find new friends. I had friends at my undergrad school. Not close friends. Not friends I'd ever tell the Story of Sasha to. But they were fun—in a serious sort of way. The School of Mines is for serious people. But I'm a serious person too. Right?

I sigh and turn off the blow dryer. Hair that was flying in all directions settles next to my face and falls flat again.

I need a change. I need more out of this life than what I've been settling for and the only way to get more is to put myself out there.

So Jax.

Maybe he's the first step?

I don't have to like him to use him for practice. Won't, in fact, like him. Ever. He's not my type at all. Because behind that badge that screams up-and-up there's a rule-breaker. I just know it. I've gone out of my way to avoid men like him. I'm a by-the-book kind of girl and he looks like a throw-the-book-away kind of guy.

Not my kind of guy.

Not after what happened two years ago.

But I don't want to think about that right now. I can't go back to that night when I was taken and held hostage. That experience changed me. Being held against my will was something I never want to repeat. Ever. And even though it could've been a whole lot worse than it was, even though I could've been raped instead of *almost* raped, and even though the only person who died in that event was the bad guy who deserved it—I still feel like Garrett is coming back. Like I'm waiting for him. Like he might be reanimated from the dead for the sole purpose of hurting me and the people I love.

I have issues, I admit, taking my makeup out of the drawer and laying it down on the table top before me, lining it up in order of use. I have trust issues. Love issues. Reality issues.

"Well, Sasha," I say out loud. "This *is* your reality. You have no present and no future because you live in the past. And if you ruin your life because you're stuck in the past, it's your own damn fault for giving up."

Those words startle me.

Have I given up? Is that why Professor Brown accused me of not being invested in the program?

Am I invested in the program?

I certainly don't want to be an anthropologist. I guess she can see that I lack the enthusiasm for her field of study. And why should she keep me on if I'm not invested? I'm her legacy. All her grad students are her legacy. If I won't go on to make a name for myself in her field, why should she invest in me now?

She was right to ask me to think about leaving. And maybe one day I'll figure all this out. Maybe one day I'll know what I want and how to get there without pretending to be someone I'm not. And maybe I will return to this university and finish what I started.

But I don't think so.

I think being asked to reflect on my future was a warning shot in the chest that life is about to change. Some sort of catalyst that will propel me towards my true purpose.

Or maybe this rejection will send me spiraling down into a black abyss of self-loathing and discontent?

But if it does, it will be a hell of my own making. Because I have the means right now, tonight—this moment, actually—to start a new life. To find the answers I crave and get them from the man who left me ten years ago.

I need Nick. And maybe we're not soulmates. Maybe that promise was empty and he always knew that. But if so, then why is he looking for me? Why seek me out after all these years?

I need Nick.

And my path to Nick—my path to my future—lies through Jax.

So I look at the line of cosmetics on my vanity and start my transformation. Concealer first. Then powder, eyeshadow, brows, liner, mascara, and finally lipstick. I put on the mask.

My reflection in the mirror is not me.

And that's OK.

I'm tired of being me.

I get up and walk to the dress. I could wear my own dress. I have so many nice things in my closet. But why? Why be me when I can be her? The woman I always dreamed I'd turn into? Why not let Jax help me make this change tonight?

I slip the dress on, tame my hair with a brush, and then slide my feet into the shoes that came in the bag.

I'm done being Sasha Aston. She's boring and sad. She's scared and confused.

But Sasha Cherlin was none of those things. Sasha Cherlin was strong, and brave, and filled with life.

I want to live again.

CHAPTER ELEVEN

When I'm ready I walk downstairs to the security room and unlock the door using the keypad attached to the wall. This is my safe room where I can check surveillance cameras placed in strategic locations on the property. I have most of the rooms wired with cameras too, just as a precaution.

I live by the Boy Scout motto.

I scan all the cameras, just like I do every morning and every evening, then check the computer attached to the cameras for any flagged moments. There are none—I would get a text message on my phone telling me if there were—but I'm overly paranoid these days. It's possible my messaging system could be offline. And I have several levels of suspicious programmed into the alerts. I don't get bothered with people who walk down the alley and don't linger, but I look at them anyway when I have time.

There aren't any to look at in the back. But Jax and I come up on a screen at the front door when he walked me home. I have a sensor on an anklet I wear at all times. It's a tracker and ID code and it sends my GPS location to this computer every thirty minutes and logs me in and out of my house automatically as I enter and exit.

Just in case.

I didn't tell Merc about this. Or my dad, for that matter. They don't need to know that I'm so worried about this stuff. It would only upset them. Especially Merc, since he feels responsible for what happened to me two years ago.

A feeling of dread washes over me as that moment flashes into my head and then my stomach churns, making me feel sick.

All my life I was the one in control. The girl who knew things. The girl with skills.

But that day I was abducted by a crazy man and held hostage for two days was an awakening that changed my life.

Never before had I felt so vulnerable. Never before had I felt so helpless. I was a child assassin. I killed several people over the course of my short career. Grown men and one teenage girl. I can still hear the gunfire as I took out those men when they came to kill me on my grandparents' ranch. I can still feel the cold knife handle in my palm when I threw it, striking that girl's throat and ending her life in a horrifying way. Choking on her own blood.

I don't regret any of that. Not one moment.

But my badass confidence did nothing for me the night that bastard Garrett drugged me and took me as his prisoner. He threatened me with rape. Had started taking off my clothes, even. Only some predetermined alert that beeped on his phone stopped him.

Luck. The fact that he never got his chance to take me like that, it was all luck.

I don't like luck. You can't depend on luck.

I like cameras, and guns placed all over the house. And martial arts training. I've had a trainer for years. Long before all that Garrett stuff happened. But it was only to keep my skills up.

It wasn't enough.

It will never be enough to just prepare. I have to embrace the coming confrontation as inevitable. Only that acceptance gets me through the panic and paranoia. Only that silences the nagging voice in my head that says, *This isn't over, Sasha. Not by a long shot.*

Will it ever be over? Will I ever put the Company behind me and have a normal life?

An alert beeps on the screen. A black car has pulled into my driveway. The door opens and Jax gets out wearing a long black pea coat that gives me a peek of the dark suit it's covering up. He checks his watch, then pushes the door closed before striding up the walkway to the porch like a man who owns the world.

I wish I had his confidence.

The doorbell rings, so I exit the security room and close the door behind me. I take a deep breath as I walk to the front of the house, and then pause for a moment before pulling the door open.

"Miss Cherlin," he says in that deep throaty growl. "You look lovely." He smiles at me, and God, what a smile. The dimple that reminds me a little bit of Ford. The confidence that reminds me of James. And the air of danger that reminds me of Merc. "You take my breath away."

God, what a player. "Please call me Miss Aston if you want to be formal. I left Sasha Cherlin behind a decade ago."

"May I come in?" he asks, ignoring my request and reaching for the security screen. It locks automatically through a mechanism on the anklet when I step into the house, so he doesn't get far. And his fruitless tug on the door makes me smile for some reason. But he recovers from that little surprise and shoots me a smile that is alarmingly disarming. "Or have you changed your mind?"

He backs away. Just a small step, but my heart flutters when I think he might take his invitation back. "No," I say calmly. His eyes brighten, as if he was the one who was worried we would not have our date tonight. But I'm dressed. And I answered the door. So he must know I'd come. "I didn't change my mind. I take a lot of precautions, that's all."

He nods. And it's not a nod that makes fun of me for being so careful, but one of understanding. "You don't have to worry about that stuff as long as I'm with you, Miss Aston. You're safe with me."

His use of my new name makes me blush for some reason. He didn't acknowledge my request, but he did honor it. And that eases my discomfort about what I'm doing just a little bit. Plus, he basically offered himself up as my protector with that statement.

I have never wanted or needed a protector. I've only ever had partners. James, Harper, and Merc. Ford became my *de facto* protector when he adopted me, I guess. But he's not a physical fighter. His brand of protection is more along the lines of highly trained attack dogs, military-grade security systems, and hacking skills.

Jax's offer comes off more threatening. Not like Merc, who can send grown men running with a glare. Or James, who you never see coming, because he doesn't make threats, he just makes good on them.

No, it comes off like a man with authority.

"Thank you," I say as I unlock the outer door, intending on walking out on the porch.

But Jax has the security door firmly in his grasp and he takes a step forward, like he wants to come inside. "You need a coat, Miss Aston. A cold front has moved in."

I panic for a moment, wondering if I want him in my house. But he takes away my choice when his imposing body blocks the doorway, and I have to step back to allow this move.

"Do you have one? Or should I find one for you?"

"A coat?" I laugh off the way he just intimidated me into letting him inside and turn away, heading towards the coat closet. "Of course I have coats." I open the door and take one off the hanger that will go with the formal dress. I don't think I have ever worn it, so I check the sleeve for a tag, and then let out a breath of relief that I don't have to rip it off in front of him and let him in on the fact that I never have an occasion to wear something so fancy.

Jax takes it from my hands, his body behind me, so very close to my own. So close I can feel his warm breath as he leans down and whispers, "Let me help you with that."

I swallow and slip my arms into the satin interior of a long black wool coat with silver fox lining the collar and cuffs, before turning round to face him.

"Are you nervous?" he asks.

"No," I lie. This makes him smile and I have to wonder what kind of training he's had. Merc was astute in reading me. He's trained to look at body language and expressions. He can tell a lot by the color of my face or the way I hold my shoulders. And Jax was trained by the FBI. He could have these skills, since Merc got them when he was in the Army.

"I like this," Jax says, eyeing my dress and coat appreciatively. His fingertips come up next to my cheek and plunge into the soft, thick fur. "It's real," he says, looking at the fur for a moment before dragging a heated stare up to my eyes. "I'm a little surprised such an educated girl would wear real fur."

I crinkle my nose at his insult. "If you think I'm some do-gooder college revolutionary who has time for stupid things like fur bans, then you don't know me at all. I eat meat, wear leather, and have killed at least a dozen foxes for threatening chickens on my grandparents' ranch. I skinned each one of them and turned them into useful articles. It's more of a sin to waste them by letting them rot than it is to wear them on a coat."

"I like it, Miss Aston," he says seductively as he leans into my ear. "I was joking."

"Oh," I say as my face heats up. That gives him yet another reason to smile at me. And now I know. He's watching my reactions very carefully and trying to make me react as he does it. "Well, I know the designer who made this coat. She's a native up in Alaska and only uses wild-caught foxes that she traps for her sustainability lifestyle."

He smiles even wider, and then a chuckle erupts. "I'd have

expected nothing less from you, Sasha. So thank you for clearing that up."

The way he says my name—or should I say, the way he makes me feel when he says my name—catches me off guard once again. It's not my face that heats up this time, but my whole body. I need to put a stop to this shameless flirting he's doing so I hold up a hand to his chest and push him backwards. He takes the hint and steps back. "Look, I need to clear something up before we go out tonight. That kiss on the stairs? That was not appropriate."

"No?" he asks, his eyes bright with mischief. He holds up both hands and wiggles his fingers again. "All ten fingers, Miss Aston. So I think you liked it more than you'd care to admit."

He takes two steps forward, forcing me to take two steps backwards. I'd take more steps back—because he's far too close to me—but I bump up against the closed closet door.

My heart starts to beat fast as he looks down at me. Races, actually. His hand presses up against my cheek as he leans down into my ear once again. "Sasha," he says, still in that gruff whisper. "The people in my department call you a lethal weapon. So if you hated the kiss you'd have made good on that threat. In fact"—he laughs a little and this sends yet another chill through my body—"I was very surprised you even bothered to threaten me. If you'd really hated the kiss, you'd have dropped me right there in the hallway and walked off as I lay writhing on the ground. So let's just stop with the pretenses, Miss Aston. And have a good time together tonight."

His palm slides up and presses against the side of my neck. I gulp air as I try to calm my beating heart. But it's too late. He's got his hand over my throbbing artery, assessing my reaction.

But just as quick as it appeared, it's withdrawn. I'm just about to breathe again when he replaces his palm alongside my cheek.

"What are you doing?" I whisper, the panic starting to set in. I'm fearful that my body will start shaking from all this touching.

"Pushing my luck, Sasha."

"Don't," I say, the panic finally coming through. I place both my hands on his chest and push him back. He sways a little from my demand, but only his upper body retreats. His feet stay firmly planted in the same space right in front of me.

"You don't do intimacy?" he asks. His palm is still on my cheek. My push had no effect on that. And now it slides down my cheek until his thumb is lightly gripping my chin. I'm so shocked, so mesmerized by his stare and his forward actions that I freeze as his thumb gently caresses my lower lip. "I get it," he says, his voice deep with desire, but controlled at the same time. "I'm taking you out of your comfort zone. But you've had yourself locked up here in this house all semester, Sasha. And I already told you. You're safe with me."

I suck in some air as his eyes shift from one side of my face to the other, trying to figure me out. "I don't need you to save me."

"Ah," he breathes. "I never said I'd save you, Sasha. You're in pretty deep, so I'm not even sure I *can* do that. It's"—he stops talking, but his thumb is still doing a sweeping tender arc under my lip—"it's a pretty complicated setup I have going right now."

"With me?" I ask, feeling a slight panic as my heart beats faster.

"Well, some of this has to do with you. Obviously. But there's a lot more going on here than you realize."

"Why can't you just leave me out of it? I don't understand

what you think I have that can help you. I admit I was filled with answers a long time ago, but most of what I know is outdated. Most of the people I had connections with are dead. And I swear to God, I have not seen or heard from Nick. I have not been involved in anything in a very long time."

"I don't need any of that, Sasha." But then Jax's lips are on mine. This time he's got my chin, and his grip on it tightens, like he's warning me not to pull away. His tongue sweeps between the seam of my lips and they part. I have a sinking feeling in my lower stomach, and I'm not sure if it's dread from giving in or just the fact that I haven't had sex in a very long time. Because there is no doubt in my mind right now—if he pushes, I will give in. One hand on the strap of my dress would have me begging him for more.

But he pulls back, ending the kiss. "You have the one thing I need, Sasha—Nick's heart."

CHAPTER TWELVE

Sasha's hands are flat on my chest, pushing hard, sending me back a step. A moment later, the sting of a slap cracks across my face.

"Get out," she growls. "I will not take part in this plot you have to capture Nick. I won't be used like some *thing*." Her blue eyes are burning bright with anger. But there's something else underneath. Something I can't quite place. "I said—"

"I heard you, Miss Aston," I interrupt her again.

"And don't think I will fall for those fake manners you have, either. Get the fuck out of my house or I will remove you myself." She glares at me, daring me to challenge her threat.

I can't stop the snicker that comes out. I mean, it's a bad move, considering her state of mind at the moment. But holy fuck, that was hot, cute, and even though I know it will piss her off, I want to accept that challenge.

My face is stinging with another slap, followed by a leg sweep that sends me falling over sideways. And any other tough guy might be embarrassed by her success, but my snicker has turned into a full-fledged guffaw. Instead of getting up, I stay on the ground as I throw my head back to enjoy the moment.

"Why are you laughing?" she growls, standing over me with a stern look on her face. Her legs are spread wide, allowing me to get a good long look. She notices my gaze and steps back. "What the fuck?"

"Oh, God." I laugh again. "I'm sorry," I say, still chuckling. "Really, I apologize. You're just so damn cute as the tough girl. And the dress, it's very revealing—"

"I know, asshole. You picked it out for this reason."

I laugh again and she puts her balled-up fists on her hips as she keeps her position of power. "I didn't imagine myself on the floor with you giving me a peek, no. But I'm not complaining. Can I get up now? Or will you kick me when I'm down?"

She turns on her heel and walks further back into the house. It's an invitation I can't refuse. I've been wanting to get a look inside here for months.

But as soon as I'm on my feet she's turned on her heel and headed back my way. I put a hand up to protect me from the possible slap, but she glides past and opens the front door. "Get out. I'm not going."

I grab her wrist and kick the door closed with a slam. Her pulse is throbbing beneath my fingertips and she draws back, ready to put the walls up again.

I tug her towards me, making her crash into my chest, and then I spin us around and push her against the coat closet door, pinning both wrists to the wall on either side of her hips.

"Every time I take a breath, Sasha Aston, you surprise me."

"Let go," she demands, wriggling against my hold.

"I expected a lot of things from you, but fear really wasn't one of them."

"I'm not afraid of you."

"I know," I tell her back, leaning my face into her long hair and drawing in her scent. No perfume. Just the clean, fresh smell of a recent shower. "You're not afraid of me," I say into the shell of her ear. My breath makes her shiver and I'm on the verge of being turned on. "You're afraid of life. And I just didn't expect it."

"I'm not afraid of anything. I can kill you right now if I wanted to. I could end your life. And if you push me, I won't hesitate."

"Mmmm," I say, leaning back so I can look her in the eye again. "We seem to find ourselves in this position a lot today." She stares up at me. I really didn't expect fear. But there it is. She's terrified. "I've had you backed up against the wall three times now. Is that how you like it? Forced?"

"Let go."

"I won't force you, so if that's how you want this relationship to start, you're out of luck."

"What the hell—"

"I'm just truly surprised that you're so scared of intimacy. I figured you were one of those academic nerds. Grad school and shit, right? But you've been floundering all semester. Even I could see it. And I know you had some big test today and you came out of your office carrying a box, all sad and depressed. So I'm guessing it didn't go well. But Sasha, you don't belong here."

"I do belong here. I came here to make my dream a reality and I can still do that."

"Can, sure. But you won't because you belong with me. You know it in your soul. You want what I'm offering." She opens her mouth to speak, but I let go of a wrist and place two fingertips over her lips. "Don't talk now. Just listen." Her eyes dart back and forth, anxious. Her other wrist, still in my grasp, allows me to continue monitoring her pulse. It races beneath my soft touch. "You don't belong with these people. You don't fit in with them. You and I really are a lot alike. We like adventure, justice, and a challenge. So I'm challenging you, Miss Aston. Get to know me tonight and think about what I can offer you."

"I know you well enough to understand we are not the same. Those things are not what I want. And I only accepted this to learn more about Nick Tate. And it's not because I have some girlhood fantasy of marrying him, either. It's because we were close and then he disappeared. Anyone who lost a good friend would want to know what happened to them."

I press myself closer to her body, my chest coming into contact with her breasts. She gulps in air and holds it when I slide my free hand behind her neck the way I did earlier. She almost came undone with that move and it has near the same effect this time around as well. "You might think you're safe enough on your own, and I might agree. But allow yourself the luxury of my protection for just one night. Let the guard down, Sasha. Let me bring you under my own armor and just try out what it means to simply exist without the stress and worry of who you were. Allow yourself to be who you are. And then at the end of the night I'll ask you one question before I change your life forever or walk away."

The breath she drew up finally comes back out in a rush. "What question?"

"Who do you want to be?"

She stares up at me like a child, filled with amazement. Like the thought she could make this decision and not have it made for her is a novelty that is almost too good to be true.

"I already know the answer to that question." Her sentence starts strong but finishes weak. She knows she's at a crossroads.

"Good," I say back. "Then you'll know just what to say when it comes up."

"Don't kiss me again."

"Done."

"And the next time you grab my wrists I will break a whole lot more than your fingers."

"Got it," I say, smiling. "Anything else?"

"I'm not afraid of you."

"I know." My surrender both surprises her and makes her suspicious at the same time. She's very good at reading me. "You have nothing to fear from me. But Sasha, there are still so very many, many things in this world to be afraid of. So"—I back up and give her all the space she needs as I open the front door and invite her through—"you're under my protection until you tell me you don't need it anymore."

"I don't need it anymore, Agent Jax. And I need to set the alarm from inside, so I'm sorry to interrupt your chivalrous moment, but you need to leave so I can do that."

I smile as I exit, and then wait for her on the porch as the sounds of a keypad alarm being armed leak through the door.

A long black car pulls up to the curb just as she reappears, back in control. Her head is high, the doubt is gone, and her back is straight.

"Our ride is here," I say, offering her my arm.

She accepts that gesture like a lady, lightly wrapping her fingertips around the crook of my elbow. "Your car is in the driveway, Agent Jax."

"No, Sasha," I say back as we descend the stairs of her porch. "That car belongs to the government. I, however, do not. And this night, as I promised, is not about them. It's about us."

I expect some questions, but she refrains and goes with the flow. Secrets are a part of her, just like they're a part of me. I played a card and she held one.

Game on.

CHAPTER THIRTEEN

What the fuck does that mean? I want to question him, but I'm not about to tip my hand and get lost in his secrets. I'm done with secrets. I had so many as a child, and it was so difficult to let them go that I refuse to go back to a time when everything that came out of my mouth was lies. I want to be fun, crazy Sasha Cherlin. But I've been Sasha Aston too long to just slide back into the secrets. They make me sick. They make my heart beat fast and my mind spin.

He can keep his secrets. And what do I care if he's on the up and up with the US government? It's not like I have any plans to join him in whatever little crusade he has going. I'm going on a date with him tonight so I can get answers tomorrow. That's it. And I refuse to feel dirty for wanting answers. I have a right to know certain things. Nick was my promise. We were supposed to get married and be partners for life. And yeah, that was dirty. Everything behind that was covered in the filth of the Company. But I have nothing to feel ashamed about. I was too young to understand the implications of what I wanted and what he refused to give me. But that doesn't mean I didn't have feelings for him. That doesn't mean I don't deserve to know what happened to him after he left me that night.

So screw Jax. He can keep his shit to himself.

"Let me get that for you," he says as we reach the black limo. I wait as he opens the door and waves me in.

I get in and scoot over, allowing him to get in beside me. By that time the driver is there to close us up and we have a moment of silence as he walks around the car and gets in the front seat. The divider is down and I wait for Jax to send the glass partition sliding upward to give us privacy, but he doesn't.

Instead he turns his body slightly, brushing his knee against mine in the process, and says, "This is Adam, Sasha. He's part of the security team."

I turn my head so he can't see me roll my eyes. "Nice to meet you, Adam," I say back, my manners taking over. And then I turn to Jax with my first question as Adam pulls away from the curb. "Where are we going?"

He smiles. No, not really a smile. A smirk that leads me to believe he thinks he's going to pull something over on me.

"Jesus Christ, Jax. Stop the bullshit. I'm not interested in you. I don't think you're cute or funny, and you're annoying me with all this secret stuff you have going."

"You don't think I'm cute?" he asks, smiling that smile again.

"Really?"

"Not my type, sorry," I deadpan back. Silence hangs in the air between us. I squirm in my seat a little. He is cute, but I'm not starting this game.

"Discretion, Miss Cherlin, is something I am always aware of. We need discretion tonight. I don't want too many eyes and ears on you until we have a deal."

"There's no deal in the works. We made a deal, yes. I go out to dinner with you and you give me answers about…" I trail off and glance at Adam, not sure if I should mention Nick's name.

"Oh, he's got clearance. He knows all about Nick Tate. More than me, probably."

Another worm dangled in front of me that I refuse to take as bait. And since I can say nothing that will put me in a position of power right now, I turn my body slightly away from Jax and stare out of the window.

"But I understand what you're trying to say. You're only here because I have something you need, and that's fine. Tomorrow I will give you everything you think you want to know about Nick. And maybe you'll be able to walk away. But maybe not. It's possible we will strike a new deal, and if that happens I will gladly bring you into the FBI family with me. All these… precautions can be over. But until then—"

"I'm a secret, right?" This makes me angry. So angry my face begins to heat up and I turn my body another fraction so he can't watch the way I react to his words.

He leans close to me, eliminating that small distance I was trying to create between us. "Not to me you're not."

I don't answer, just sit in silence as we drive towards the edge of town.

"What I do on the outside, Sasha, is not what I do on the inside."

"You don't say." I don't even know what that means.

"But let's drop that for now. And try to have a good time. By the way, I never did find out what you were up to that day."

"What day?" I say it with an attitude I didn't realize was brewing. *Control, Sasha*, I tell myself. *No emotions tonight.*

"When you came home from Peru early."

"I wasn't early," I say with even more edge. "The internship was over days before I left. I was late."

"Hmmm. OK. Regardless, you were up to something. And you knew I was on to you, so you curbed whatever it was and walked away from it. I admit, I was surprised you had so much self-control. At first I figured I was wrong about my suspicions. But then I realized you're very disciplined. So you walking away meant the opposite. It was something very important, wasn't it?"

"I have no idea what you're talking about now, Jax. And by the way, do you have a last name? I'd like to check your credentials with the FBI after I get what I want tomorrow."

"Barlow. Jackson Barlow. But everyone just calls me Jax. But back to my question. I have a feeling about what it might be. That secret you're carrying around. That's why I'm taking you out tonight."

"There's no secret. You're just some overeager agent who wants to play spies with me." His deep laugh comes out with a soft rush of air that hits the back of my neck. I pull away and look over my shoulder to find him very up close and personal. "Do you mind? I'm not—hey, where are we?"

"The airport, Miss Aston. I'm sure you recall it from when I brought you home."

"There better be a five-star restaurant at this crappy little airport, and we had better be dining there tonight. Because if you think I'm getting on a plane with you—"

"We're having dinner somewhere far better than a five-star restaurant. You don't go with the flow very well for a girl whose most valuable skill is adapting."

"I'm not getting on a plane with you." I cross my arms, signaling that this is final. But he puts an arm around my shoulders and gives the silver fox fur of my coat collar a rub between his fingers. "What the fuck are you doing?"

"Sorry." He smiles. "The fur is just... exquisite. But as I was saying, we are getting on that plane. Adam is a top-notch pilot, so you don't have to worry about crashing—"

"No," I say, reaching behind me to grab his hand and swing it back into his lap.

"—and you know how I know you're going to get on that plane, Miss Aston?"

"You don't know, Jax. Because I won't."

"Because I have someone you want to meet very badly waiting for us on the other end of the trip."

"Who?" I regret it as soon as it comes out, because I am picturing Ford, or Ash, or my little sister and brother on the other end. In the split second of silence I have to wait for his answer I am picturing everyone I love, tied up and near death from torture. My body trembles.

"Your aunt."

Relief rushes out in a long breath of air. "I never had an aunt,

Jax. So try again."

"I know you think that, Sasha. But your mother had a sister. A half-sister. And you and I both know what that means. She was a Company kid. Owned outright. But she was hidden from them by her father. Your grandfather. Don't you want to know more about the woman who gave up her life to save you? Your aunt is the only link you have to your mother, Sasha. And she's been wanting to meet you very badly. I said I'd bring you to her the first chance I had. I promised her that you'd hear her story before I let the FBI in on your decision to help us."

Why does it always come back to that? Mothers and daughters. This is how the Company keeps its ranks. Every mother who gives birth to a girl is given the same options. Pledge that child to the organization and let them turn her into a slave. Or give up your own life for hers, and she will be promised to a Company man when she turns eighteen.

It's a very effective policy. It's enslaved women for many generations.

The car pulls up to a waiting jet, about the size of the one we came on last summer, but it's all black with gold accents on it. I squint my eyes, wondering if I've ever seen a black jet before.

"I'm giving you far, far more than you asked for, Sasha. Two mysteries from your past revealed for the price of one. You can't say no. I understand enough about you to know that to be a fact. You are an empty girl today because of three events that changed your life in unimaginable ways. Your mother's death when you were born when she gave her life to give you a chance. Your father's death when you were twelve when he gave his life trying to set you free. And the promise Nick broke when you were thirteen. I know you got your answers about your father years ago. But the last two pieces of the puzzle that is Sasha Cherlin are within your reach. Right now. You can put aside all the questions and get answers. But you need to trust me."

I swallow down the feelings that are flooding through my body. Another living relative? Can it really be possible? The sting of tears rock my world. The overflowing pain of grief and loss floods my heart.

"Listen," Jax says, his hand on my shoulder again. "I said you're safe with me. I meant it."

I give him a sidelong look, trying to hide the sudden threat of tears.

"I'm not here to rip your world apart, Sasha. I'm here to put it back together. I can do that for you. I promise. I swear on my little brother's life. I swear on my honor as a man. My position in this fucked-up government as an agent. And the debt I owe to your aunt."

"What debt?" My words come out shaky and I suddenly feel like a child again. Not the thirteen-year-old assassin, but the twelve-year-old pigtailed girl who liked to read, and hunt dinosaurs, and who dreamed of a life filled with the love of a family she was denied since her first moment.

"She helped me once. She helped put me back together. I was broken too." Jax waves to Adam as he pulls open my door and steps aside, asking me to exit the car. "She helped Adam. And many, many more. She is a rock, Sasha. Like you. Only she is sure of her place in the world. She wants to give you that gift. And she gives it freely. My offer and her offer are not related. You can come with me tonight and say no to me tomorrow. But Sasha, don't refuse her because of me. She's too important to you."

WASTED LUST

I step out of the car, not because I want to take his offer and get in that plane, but because if I don't move quick the tears will fall. And if I cry in front of him, I might never stop. I might reach for his hand and find my cheek against his chest. And if that happens, I'm done. I'm gone. Because if I tell my story to someone, if I let out all the horrors that are hiding inside me... I might never stop crying. It might be a deluge of tears that refuse to end. I will spend the rest of my life wallowing in a pool of self-pity.

I cannot let him in. Not even for a moment. Because one moment leads to the next. They stack up on top of each other like a tower. And that tower will climb into eternity if I'm not careful. I will create an ever-growing tower of eternal sadness if I let one drop of what haunts me out.

So I walk to the plane in silence. My breathing hitches. One inhale with each foot forward, my mind swirling with fear, hate, and longing. One exhale with each emotion as I leave them all behind.

And by the time I'm being guided up the steps of the jet by Jax's hand on the small of my back, I have it all under control again.

The tears recede. The fear becomes courage. The hate turns to anger. And the longing—well, I keep the longing. I need the longing. I need the emptiness in my heart to remind me of what's possible.

A life.

Not a half-dead girl who lives in the past.

But a life. A real life filled with the promise of a future. All I need is Nick Tate to fill up the emptiness he left behind and I can be whole again.

CHAPTER FOURTEEN

The jet-black exterior of the plane is a stark contrast to the warm interior. The sand-colored floors gleam, and the reflection of my shoes makes me feel like I'm standing in a clear pool of water. I step forward into the cabin and take it all in.

The entrance leads to a sitting area complete with two sets of padded leather flight chairs on each side of a small meeting table. But off to my right, down the slim corridor, there is another room separated by pocket doors. All the walls are a warm ochre color, and the trim is a highly polished yellow-toned burl wood. My fingertips reach out to touch it as I take another step forward. So smooth.

Jax gives me slight encouragement at the small of my back again, turning me to the right, towards the partitioned part of the cabin. "We're going to skip the meeting room and have drinks in the lounge, Essie," he says to the nearest flight attendant. She's dressed like a waiter, with black wool pants, a crisp white shirt, and a black apron that falls below her waist.

"Of course, sir," she says as she helps me out of my coat and folds it across her arm. Jax takes his coat off and places it over mine. "Do you know what you want? Or would you like a drink menu?"

I tune out his response and start walking, eager to see what awaits me. I feel like I'm stepping into a new world. I've been on my share of private planes and I book first-class tickets when I need to fly commercial. But Ford never had access to a plane like *this*.

This is luxury, pure and simple.

"Here, Sasha," Jax says with a gentle prod that tells me to walk faster. "We're dining on board in the back."

The second room is much more informal, but still elegant. The butter-colored sofa stretches along one side of the fuselage, coming to a slight curve at the far end of the cabin, just enough to form a semi-circular dining area. There is a small table with enough room for two people to eat comfortably, set with china and silverware that sparkles under the subdued light.

I take a seat on the long side of the couch while Jax settles on to the curved portion. The leather is so smooth, I want to pet it.

"Pretty nice, huh?" Jax says, watching me take in the decor. There's art on the wall. I've never seen art on the wall of a private plane before.

"Wow. I feel like there's a world of hidden rich people and I've just been invited into the club."

"Like a secret, huh?"

I look at Jax and he gives me a wink. It unsettles me, even though it came with a smile. "Something like that," I reply back, looking down at my hands.

What the hell am I doing? *Getting involved with something better left alone*, is the reply in my head.

"Doesn't your father have a private jet?"

"We don't own one," I say with an edge to my voice, "if that's what you're asking. We use them. The studio he works for has them and they fly us places. But we don't get movie-star treatment."

"That surprises me," Jax says. And then Essie is there, placing drinks in front of us. "Thank you, Essie," he tells her, all charm and at ease. Like this is his world and he's comfortable in it. "I mean," he continues, his gaze redirected to me, "Ford Aston is very wealthy. Was born that way. He looks like the kind of man who likes the finer things in life."

"He does," I say back, the hair on the back of my neck rising. "Finer things being trained protection dogs worth as much as a well-bred racehorse, old comfortable houses in neighborhoods that have easy access to art museums and parks, private schools, and the finest food. But he's not pretentious. He doesn't flaunt his wealth. And he has never lived off his inheritance. He's a working man."

"Hmmm," Jax says, taking a sip of his whiskey.

I look at my drink, a pink concoction in a martini glass with a cherry on the bottom. It's pretentious. "I like beer."

"Oh, it's not a beer night, Sasha. Beer is for light conversation with friends while chatting at a local bar or in someone's living room. This is a celebration. And that's a Cosmo. Essie makes them a little on the weak side, so I'm not trying to get you drunk."

"Only I can get me drunk, Agent Jax. You have no hope of using such a simple trick to catch me off guard."

"You're right." His voice rumbles out of his chest, a hum that makes my stomach flip. "And besides, I'm not trying to catch you off guard. I'm trying to get you to lower it willingly."

"I'm not impressed by money, so you could give me the taxi cab version of this night and it would still turn out the same."

"I didn't imagine you would be," he says with a light-hearted chuckle. "You have so much of it yourself. Hidden away in all those secret accounts. You keep banks in the Caymans afloat with your checking account balance alone."

I'm not surprised that he knows I have money. But the fact that he knows where it's located makes my stomach churn. So I say nothing.

"We know what you did when you and your friends ended the Company a decade ago."

"Is that so?" I play along. "You're very good then. Because I'm not even sure what we did. Maybe you should enlighten me?"

He takes another sip of his Scotch and sets his glass down. The ice clinks as the door to the plane is closed and we are sealed up inside. For better or worse, I'm playing his game. I'm just not sure what the game is yet.

My family. My Nick. My past. He wants access to all of it. But he knows a lot already, so where is this going?

"Tell me, Sasha Cherlin—"

"Aston," I correct him, and then self-consciously pick up my martini and take a sip. He's right. It's not very strong. So I take a longer sip because I could use a little courage right now.

"Sorry, Miss Aston. Tell me something about you that's real."

"What do you mean? I'm real. Everything about me is real. I live in Kansas, I go to school, I love dinosaurs. You know more real things about me than most. So what more do you possibly want?"

He's shaking his head. "Mmmm, no. Those aren't the real parts I'm interested in. I'll be blunt then. We only have an hour on this trip. One hour to get a little insight into who you really are. Because once we get to the manor, I might not get a moment alone with you for a while. This might be the only date I get. So forget about Nick, and Ford, and your dinosaurs, and all the tragic things that happened to you as a child. And tell me something real about you *now*."

I fold my hands in my lap and lift up my chin. "I'm not a sharing kind of girl, Agent Jax. I'm a—"

"Very tightly buttoned-up kind of girl. I know. See, that's the part I hate about you."

"Excuse me?"

"The part I *hate*, Miss Aston, is the way you partition your life into neat little packages. Did Ford Aston teach you that? Did his personality overpower yours back when you were a teenager? Did he—"

"How fucking dare you?" The words blurt out before I can stop them. "Do not," I seethe, "talk about my father like you know him."

"Why not? I do know him."

"You do *not* know him. I have been his daughter for ten years and I have barely scratched the surface of what makes that man tick. We are very close, we have very close friends, and no one—"

"Ever gets inside that little team you grew up with. Is that it? They circled the wagons around you back when you were a teenager and pulled you into that life."

"You make it sound like that's a bad thing."

"Everyone needs friends, Sasha. But they are *his* friends. Where are *your* friends?"

"I have friends. James and Harper are my friends. Merc is my friend."

"Assassins?" Jax laughs heartily now. "Are you telling me your closest friends are all assassins? James Fenici and Harper Tate are your friends? That psycho Merc, he's your friend? I sincerely hope not. Because that means you chose them. And all this time I gave you the benefit of the doubt because I thought they were *family*. Family is family. You can't change that. But friends you choose. So tell me, what fantasy life do you live in where you choose murderers as friends?"

"I'm a murderer too," I growl. "And you better keep that in mind tonight."

"As am I, killer. As am I."

The plane accelerates on the runway and I brace myself for takeoff, grabbing my drink to prevent it from spilling as Jax does the same. The engine roar is too loud to talk, so I bow my head and try to check my anger. What is he playing at? Is he trying to make me react? Does he want to force me into a demonstration of how dangerous I am? Is he looking for a fight?

"I'll start then," Jax says once the plane evens out a few minutes later. He takes another sip of the Scotch in his glass and then sets it down. I mimic him, for lack of something better to occupy my time and hands. "I'll give you something real about me first. An example."

I roll my eyes and sigh, placing my hands back into my lap. I'm tired of him already. If I had a watch, I'd check it to let him know how much he's boring me right now.

"I grew up in Brooklyn. Well, not exactly." The initial half-truth grabs my attention even though I want to tune him out. "I bounced. You know that term, I think. Living here and there. Never having a real home. I was a foster kid. But one day, when I was twelve years old, I bounced into the home of Special Agent Max Barlow." Jax pauses for a moment. His eyes glaze over a little as he looks up towards the ceiling, like he's lost in a memory. "His house was big, but old. Not fancy," he says with a small smile. "The kind of house that says it's been lived in for a while. But not neglected. You know that kind of house, Sasha?"

I nod before I even realize I'm doing it.

"The furniture was nice, but worn. The leather couches all had butt indents in them. Like people had been sitting there comfortably for generations. He was the seventh generation to live in that house. Ever since his forefathers immigrated to America in the mid-eighteen hundreds. They built it over and over again, adding to it as the family grew and thrived in their new country. More generations were born, and with each one they grew a little more prosperous or a little less. But they always had that home. A place to gather and be with one another. But Max was the only child of his generation. And when his wife died after only two years of marriage and no children, he started to take in foster kids to fill the house back up."

I'm struck silent by this honest recollection of his history. I don't spend much time on the East Coast, but forming a picture of this house—standing and expanding as life comes and goes, a monument to the temporary nature of the human lifespan—I can see it in my head. I picture brown brick, a solid concrete front porch filled with children and neighbors. Holidays and dinners.

"Did you have a home like that, Sasha?"

I nod, once again before I realize I'm doing it. "My grandparents' ranch. My father's family raised cattle in northern Wyoming. They had a huge place. Thousands of acres. They ranched that land for over a hundred years."

"And the Company blew it up."

I look Jax in the eye and make a decision. I need this man to understand what it is I'm doing here with him. I need him to know who and what I am before he tries something he will regret. Something that will make me react on instinct.

And because he told me something real, I decide to reciprocate. "I had just turned thirteen. Lost my father less than a month before on Christmas Eve. I went from little girl to child assassin in the span of a few weeks. I killed four men the night they came. I was waiting for them." I let out a long sigh. "Looking back, I was always waiting for them."

"It must've been devastating."

"It wasn't, though. I mean…" I look down at my hands in my lap. The way I said it sounds so cold. "I mean, it was. Losing my father was the worst. I cried for weeks. But Ford came—" I have to stop and collect myself for a minute. I will not cry in front of this stranger. I refuse to let him break down the walls I've been building brick by brick for a decade. "I had met Ford the day before and he came to see me on Christmas Day. And he helped me." I look Jax in the eyes, in control again. "So when they came to kill me a second time, they got my grandparents. I didn't have enough training to save them. Just myself. I got out of the house by jumping out the second-story window into a snow drift and hid in the hills with a rifle. I got three of them from a distance. And the last one thought he'd get away, but I was in the back of his pickup as he drove off and I shot him in the head through the cab window."

He doesn't flinch. Even James flinched when I told him this story. "It must've rocked your world to kill at such a young age."

I shake my head. "No. It made me hard and calculating. The window shattered and bits of glass, and blood, and bone got stuck in my hair. And I refused to wash it for days as I waited for Merc to come find me. I wanted all that debris to remind me of the stakes. Of the harsh reality I was living in. It felt good, Jax. It made me feel powerful. And you can think I'm sick all you want for naming that psycho they call Merc as a true friend. But he is. And if that makes me sick, then I'm sick, I guess. My love for him took root when he picked me up on the hills outside my family ranch and took me in. Promised to make it right for me. And then I met James. And we went and found Harper. And the rest is history, isn't it? We crippled a global organization. Set them back years. They haven't yet fully recovered from that blow. But they will, Jax. They will recover. They are too big to take out all at once. So those assassins you look at with contempt are the people who would die for me when that happens. I'm sure you have a story to tell about your childhood, Jax. Everyone has one. But no one on this planet can understand my past except those three people. I won't help you get them, if that's what you're after.

I won't help you get Nick, either."

"Because he was your promise?"

I raise an eyebrow at that. "If you think you know what that term means, then you are a Company kid. And if you're a Company kid, you had better tell me now, or you will wake up with my knife slashing your throat."

He doesn't shoot me one of those disarming smiles or chuckle under his breath, like I'm so cute. He nods like a professional doing business. "I'm not a Company kid, Sasha. But I know a few. And that's why I'm taking you to see your aunt before I let the FBI know I have you."

"I'm going to make this very clear, Special Agent Jax Barlow. You have no idea what it means to be a Company kid. None. I don't care how many people you talk to, you can never, *ever* understand what it means unless you go through it. I barely know the horror of that title, and I grew up in that world. I've seen things, experienced things—things you can't even begin to imagine. So if you ever say it so casually again, I will end this association. And just so we're both on the same page, a Company assassin does that one way."

"You'll kill me?" he asks, as serious as I am. "For uttering words?"

"They aren't words. They're threats. You think you know me?" I stare hard at him as he tries to ease back by taking another sip of his drink. "You want Sasha Cherlin? You want that child killer back as a means to your end? Well, you've got her full attention. You have no idea how ruthless I can be, and if you cross me, I will not hesitate and I will not miss."

He sets his glass down with a clink of ice and leans back in his seat, trying to feign relaxation. "Well, Miss Aston, thank you for your honesty. Point taken. And now that we both agree who you *were*, maybe we can try to figure out who you actually *are*."

CHAPTER FIFTEEN

I take a deep breath as Sasha smiles thinly at Essie as her plate of lobster tail is set down before her. "Thanks, Essie," I say. "It looks fabulous, as usual."

She bows her head and retreats, pulling the burl wood pocket doors closed as she exits the main cabin.

Sasha is already poking her food with her fork. Trying to calm down, I suspect.

That was a moment I didn't expect. I mean, I was trying my hardest to get her to bare her soul to me, but I hadn't counted on the venom that came out with her threat.

She's wrong though. I do know what it means to be a Company kid. Maybe not as intimately as she does, but I know more than most. I've seen the way they deliver their misplaced justice. I've been on the receiving end of an attack. I've lived with the horror they leave in their wake.

I know a little.

Maybe not enough, though, my inner voice counters.

And I have to agree with that voice. I need to stay alert with Sasha until we are both working towards the same goal. Because I do not need another Company assassin as my enemy right now.

"Are you excited to see your aunt, Sasha?"

"No," she says, just before taking a bite of her lobster. She chews slowly for a few seconds, and then swallows and takes a sip of her martini. "If I have another living relative, then I'm angry." She looks me in the eyes and holds my gaze. "Pissed off, actually. Where the fuck has she been?"

"Well," I say, taking my own bite of food and chewing slowly. I wipe my mouth with my napkin and then take a sip of my drink. "I guess the formalities are gone now? You want to say fuck and threaten to kill me?"

"You have a problem with my language? Ha," she laughs. "That's funny. I'm sure you FBI guys are all about manners?"

"I'm just saying I enjoy treating you like a woman. I'd like to continue to treat you that way. But if you want to act like an assassin, I'll have to change my tactics."

I get nothing but silence.

"I get it," I say, trying to delete the edge from my voice. But she's dangerous. I knew this going in. I just forgot. She was so in control during most of our interactions. She lost a little of that control tonight, and even though that's my main goal for taking her out, I don't want to shoot myself in the back, so to speak, by drawing out the instincts the Company honed in her as a child.

She is lethal. They are all lethal. "I have a tendency to overstep. I didn't understand some things. The title, I guess. I'm sorry I upset you. I really do want you to like me and I really did plan all this to try to make that happen."

"By reminding me my family used me?"

"Is that what you think your aunt has been doing?"

"She left. Just like all the rest. She left me there to figure it out on my own. So when you insult my choice of friends and tell me you know what it means to be me, well, I get offended."

"I didn't mean it that way, Sasha. Truly. I thought your aunt would make you happy. I thought you could use a friend like me."

"What kind of friend are you, Agent Jax? The kind who comes to my house with an ultimatum and calls it a date?"

"OK," I say, putting my hands up like I surrender. "I admit, I was forward in that respect. But I'm on a deadline. You can understand that after watching you for several months and not getting the least bit of an answer to any of my questions that I might be a little bit desperate to move things forward."

"Tricking me isn't the way to do that. Twisting my arm to comply isn't the way either."

"So how can I make it better?"

"You can't."

She goes back to her meal and ignores my reaction. Which shouldn't be a surprise—I know how tough these Company people are—but it is. She's been so soft and careful these past few months. Almost timid. I've forgotten who she is.

"You said you wanted to figure out who I am now, like there is a distinction between this girl and the one from my past. But you're wrong, Jax. This is me. I am her. You will be very disappointed with Sasha Aston if you think she's different from Sasha Cherlin."

"OK," I say, giving in. If this is what she believes, I need to respect that. "But keep an open mind tonight when you meet your aunt. And if you want me to take you home tomorrow and let it all go, I will. Just keep an open mind. I have more to tell you, but I don't want to go there yet. When I asked for something real, what I should've said was something personal."

"Personal?" she asks, taking another bite of food. At least she's enjoying the meal. "Like what?"

"Sasha, please." I smile and she shakes her head at me, telling me not to try to charm her. But I can't help it. I want to charm her. I want her at ease and smiling. I want her to be happy with me. "Let's tether the assassin part of you, and unleash the woman."

"Oh my God, please. If you start using player moves on me again, I might throw up."

"It's a not a player move if it's genuine."

"It's not genuine," she retorts. "You're using me."

"I am," I admit. Because it's true. "But I'm interested in you as well." And that's true too. "Let's try for a normal first date, how about that?"

"Define normal."

"You know, favorite things. Vacations you've taken. How about your trip to Peru? You were hunting dinosaurs?"

She turns to look at me, but instead of the smile I expected, I get sadness.

"What?" I ask. "What did I do now?"

She goes back to her food. "It's just surprising that you used that term. Hunting. That's what my real dad used to call it back when I was a kid. Dinosaur hunters, that's who we were. We looked for bones all over the West."

"Sounds fun."

"It was. Until I realized it was just another way to fly under the radar. I bounced, as you put it. From place to place. Not home to home, because we took our home with us. I grew up in an RV."

"Oh, well, that's pretty interesting. Regardless of his motive. He did, after all, manage to keep you safe, train you to fight—"

"Kill, you mean."

"—and foster a love for ancient bones." I smile at her, but she doesn't return it. "I had some good moments in my early life as well. I mean, they pretty much all evaporated at the age of fifteen"—she looks up with interest at that, but I'm not going there yet—"but the younger years had some good times."

"In foster care?"

"Ah, well. No. I was a bad kid before I got picked up by Barlow. But I had some friends who would do anything for me as well. In a ten-year-old kind of way, at least. We did kid things. Nothing serious. But it was fun to run with them and be tight. Like a gang."

"When I moved in with Ford, that's what he gave me. A tight circle of friends. So even though you—"

"I get it Sasha. I misjudged your relationships. I insulted you. I'm sorry. Those people are important to you, so I take it back. I didn't know it was real."

She takes a deep breath and lets it out. "OK. Since you're offering me an olive branch, I'll accept it."

"Good. So... you had a bad day at school today?"

"I'm sure your spy told you already."

I throw up my arms in defeat.

"Sorry," she says. "Yes, I had a bad day. I was basically kicked out of grad school. I went to take my orals, the last step before being an official PhD candidate, and my advisor told me I wasn't serious enough about my chosen field of study and needed to take a break to think about things."

"Are you serious enough about your chosen field of study?"

Another sigh. "I guess not. Maybe you're right and I'm just passing time? I don't need money. Sometimes having more money than you need makes people try less. When you're desperate, you act differently. You work faster, have more original ideas, take things more seriously. So she's right. I don't want it bad enough to give it a hundred and ten percent."

"But you're still upset about it? Even though you know she was right?"

Sasha nods, but takes a few moments to answer. "I really thought if I did this, life would be better."

"Better than what?"

"Filled with satisfaction, maybe?" Her tired eyes look up at mine and I know this is the girl I've been waiting for. The one who feels. "I am unsatisfied. Like something is missing from my core. And maybe that's Nick. Maybe that's what I'm grasping at as I sit here with you turning into the bitch those people created. The child killer. The one who says fuck and threatens to kill people just because she can. It makes me feel ungrateful when I become that girl from my childhood. After all that struggle, I should feel like we won. I got a new family. I had a normal young adult life. I am very, very lucky. And I'm still left wanting more. I have everything I *need*. You know? I have everything required for happiness, yet it eludes me."

"Then you don't have it yet, Sasha. It's not wrong to be sad for the things they took from you. And I'm sorry that I sprang this aunt thing on you like this. I didn't know. You seemed so put together."

"I'm not, though. Am I? And my reaction a few minutes ago just proves it. I'm as lost as I ever was." She puts her fork down and places her napkin on the table. "Is there a restroom? I need a moment alone, if that's OK."

"Sure," I say, standing up as she does. "In the back of the plane."

She walks off and I have to force myself not to watch her as she does it. If she needs privacy, I can give her that. God knows, I've needed privacy before and no one gave me that courtesy. I've been an open book for so long I barely know what it's like to be alone. The FBI has been watching me since I was fifteen, every move I made scrutinized. They didn't want me. No one ever wanted me. But Max Barlow blew into my life and changed everything. His family has been with the FBI since its inception in 1908. And when Max Barlow says he wants his son to follow in his footsteps, people take note. Even if that son was adopted out of nowhere.

I suddenly had prospects. I had a future. And this is it. My future. So why do her words filled with want and longing stir me up as much as they did her?

"Essie?" I call.

"Yes, sir?" she answers, sliding the pocket doors open.

"Clear the table and bring us dessert and Tokay."

"Right away, sir."

WASTED LUST

Essie claps her hands and two more attendants appear from the front of the plane. Thirty seconds later the table is clear, there's a plate of fresh strawberries, a candle flickering under a small fondue pot, a cannoli drizzled with chocolate, a classic banana split, and a plate of cookies.

"Jesus Christ, are you trying to get me fat?"

I stand up as Sasha walks back to her seat on the long side of the leather bench. I wish she was sitting at a real table so I could pull out her chair.

"I leave the room for two minutes and you've decorated the table with calories."

"I don't know what you like, so I got you a sample. And the Tokay wine is the best in the world, so please, try everything, Sasha."

She takes a deep breath and lets it out slowly. "Where do you get your money?" She looks up at me with wide eyes, almost as if she's afraid to hear the answer.

"Where do you get yours?" I take a sip of my Tokay and then set my glass down.

"Did we get it the same way?"

I smile at her. For such a formidable woman, she possesses an innocence that I can't help but find a little irresistible. "My father, Max, has money. I use it when I need it."

"This is his plane?"

"No, Sasha."

She nods. She's a Company girl. She will figure me out very quickly. So I have two choices. Lie or tell the truth.

Only one of those is an option.

"No, it belongs to his company."

"The FBI owns a luxury jet?"

"Let's talk about kissing."

"What?" She laughs. "Kissing?"

I smile with her, both at her willingness to drop the topic of money and her pleasure at the new one. "Specifically, the kisses we've shared."

"We haven't shared any kisses, Agent Jax." But she says it with a sly grin as she lifts the glass of Tokay and takes a sip. I watch her throat as she swallows and then wish I could lick the sheen of sugar left over on her lips before her tongue darts out to swipe it away.

I scoot closer to her on the curve of the bench and while she remains seated in her spot, her upper body instinctively pulls back from my approach. "You liked it though."

"I didn't, actually," she says. Her pupils are dilating before my eyes, and her breathing picks up a notch.

"You did, Sasha." I reach out and pick up her hair, feeling the softness of her golden locks between my fingers. "But I took you by surprise, so you didn't have a chance to realize that. Most dates end with a kiss. And since we're almost to our destination, maybe we could try again?"

"And end the date before we eat dessert?" She cocks an eyebrow at me.

It doesn't matter what she says at this point. The invitation is hanging in the air between us. She can tell me no, if she wants. But she knows I'm going to try, so she stays quiet.

That's the only opening I need.

I lift up a dessert spoon, holding it up before her. "Which dessert would you like then? Ice cream?"

Her eyes sweep the presentation before her. "It all looks pretty good. Which is your favorite?"

"You," comes out automatically. In my head I cringe.

"Oh my God." She laughs. But she picks up a spoon as well, and scoops up some strawberry ice cream from the sundae. "I can't decide if you're serious or not."

"About what?" I'm truly confused.

"Are you a slick FBI agent?" she says, sliding the ice cream into her mouth. She licks her lips and says, "Mmmm." I have an urge to fist her hair and kiss her hard right now with that move. But I'm gonna make her beg for the next one. "Or are you some well-mannered gentleman? Because you're quite a contradiction, Jax."

"As are you, Sasha."

"Yeah, but you're playing a game with me tonight. Give and get. Push and pull. So which one of us is giving and which one of us is getting? Who is pushing and who is pulling?"

"Does it matter?" My fingertips get the better of my judgment and stroke her lightly on the cheek. "If we both get what we want in the end?"

"I guess that depends on what we each want."

"You want me and I want you."

"You are the definition of player, Jax. How do people trust you?"

I want to laugh with her, but not yet. So I make another move. "I'm confused."

"You're not at all confused. You're secretly giggling inside like a little girl. Do you want me for dessert, Jax?"

"Fuck, yes."

She looks down to hide her blush.

"OK," I say, pulling my hand back. "Look, I'll be honest with you. This is business. I need you. But it's my pleasure to have dinner with you tonight. I kissed you this morning because you are a beautiful woman and it just felt right. I kissed you tonight because you were sad and I wanted to wipe that frown off your face. And I'm going to kiss you again, even though you threatened to break all my fingers. I'll take my chances. Because my window of opportunity with you is short. You could end this night at any time. And if you walk out I will spend months—years, possibly the rest of my life—wondering what could have been. I won't let that happen. I won't let you ruin me and drive me mad with desire—"

She laughs at my declaration, beaming a smile. "Where do you get this shit?"

"You're not buying my heartfelt proclamation of love?"

"No," she giggles. "You're so full of it. But it's good stuff, Jax. Do you read Harlequin novels? Do you like the damsel in distress?"

"Oh," I sigh. "I very much do. Holy fuck, I love women who faint in my arms from too much passion. Heaving bosoms, breasts spilling out of their—-what the fuck are those things called? Corsets?"

"I have no idea," Sasha says, still laughing at me. "I'm not a romance girl."

"No? But you like dining with me?" I take her hand from her lap and stroke it gently with my fingertips. Her eyes dart down and watch for a second before she drags them back up to my face. "And I sorta pulled out all the stops on this date. I mean, I had planned on spooning you dessert and licking the sweetness from your lips after each bite. I can feel the cold and taste the ice cream in my head right now."

"You're pretty good," she says in a whisper.

"I really am." And then we both laugh. "I'm driving myself crazy. I'm ready to rip your dress off, bend you over this table, and take you hard right now."

She just stares at me. Silent. I can almost hear her heart beating. If she had a corset on, her breasts would be heaving. She might even faint.

"But you don't do hard, do you, Sasha? You run away from that sort of thing. So I'll control myself and be happy with a kiss."

The pocket doors slide open and the flight attendants enter. "We need to clear the table, sir. We'll be landing in five minutes. They've sent a car for you."

I sigh. So fucking close. "Thanks, Essie." And then I look at Sasha and shrug. "Foiled again. Timing is everything."

I kiss her hand and even though I might be making it up, I think I hear a sigh of regret from her as well.

CHAPTER SIXTEEN

My heart pounds as Jax withdraws his lips. When one of the young flight attendants smiles as she clears the table, I get self-conscious and snatch my hand from his. I place it in my lap and then lace my fingers together for lack of something better to do. I'd start wringing them, if I didn't feel like I was a fish in a bowl, every movement scrutinized by the man making my heart beat faster.

"Thank you, Essie, Lynn, and Mari. It was a wonderful presentation."

All three of the girls smile. The one called Mari might even have winked at my date. "Yes," I say, my Aston manners catching up with me. "Thank you. It was delicious."

Jax takes my hand again as the girls exit this part of the cabin, pulling the pocket doors closed behind them as they go. "We're not buckled in—which is against protocol. But I'll hold your hand and keep you safe." He smiles warmly at me. "If that's OK?"

I nod. I have nothing. I'm not a player. I know there are girls out there who do this kind of thing for a living. They scout out prospective husbands. Dress up, put on a show, try to hook one with the bait.

I have no bait. I'm cute—not sophisticated like my mom's friend Rook, or badass like her friend Veronica, or even smart and sassy like my mom, but cute. A Smurf, they used to call me. And those ladies are the only real role models I ever had growing up. That's it. The extent of my wily ways with men come from half-ass copy-catting people who have more game in their pinky fingers than I have in my whole body.

So I'm at a complete loss here. Because Jax insists on treating me like a woman. And I've spent a good number of years trying to avoid this kind of scenario. The kind that sweeps you off your feet. The kind that jumpstarts your heart and makes it hum in a way you never thought possible. The kind that makes you doubt all those pledges you made to yourself through the years.

I will never love again. I will never give my heart to a man. I will never have to endure the crushing reality that comes after the only person I ever wanted to be with practically begged me to forget about him.

I tried it, it just didn't work. I can't just erase my first crush. I can't just throw away the one thing I held onto after my father died. I kept the boys at bay all during high school. I didn't even lose my virginity until my first year of college. Ford made sure of that. The memory of his crazy overprotective antics as I grew up make me smile.

So I don't have much experience.

But Jax is a player, I can see that now. He's got me wound up tight. My head is pounding with the possibilities he comes with.

Sex being one of them. I have not had sex in over two years. And I'm not one of those girls who go for a toy at the first hint of a dry spell. After two years though, I'm considering that option.

But now Jax is here. Kissing me. Making my whole body tingle. Awakening the desire I've pent up for so long.

"Are you afraid of planes, Sasha?"

I look over at Jax. "What?"

"Does landing bother you?"

"No," I say, confused. "Why?"

"You're squeezing my hand so hard, you might be cutting off my circulation."

"Oh." I let out a rush of air and release my grip on his hand. "Sorry. No. I'm not afraid of landing."

"Afraid of me?" he asks, one eyebrow up. He takes my hand back for a third time, stroking my palm softly with his fingertips.

"No," I say again. "I'm not afraid of you. I can take you, Agent Jax."

"You can drop the agent part now, Sasha. Just call me Jax." And then he nods to our hands, one again intertwined. "Do you want me to let go? Am I making you uncomfortable?"

I have to take a moment to collect my thoughts. Because he is making me uncomfortable. But not in the way he suspects. I'm just not used to the heat of desire. It's a little bit overwhelming. And being with him like this is not part of my life plan. Of course, Nick resurfacing and spinning my world so out of control that

WASTED LUST

I can't concentrate on work, which leads to me being asked to rethink grad school, wasn't in my life plan either.

But I can't tell him that. So I say, "I'm nervous about meeting my aunt," instead.

And as soon as the words come out of my mouth, I realize they are not a lie. Jax has kept me occupied during the short trip, but now that we're nearing the final destination, the worry rushes back into my forward consciousness.

The plane touches down and the engines roar as the brakes are applied. I lean forward from the momentum, but Jax wraps his arms around me and holds me in place.

I want to throw up.

Do not embarrass yourself, Sasha, that inner killer tells me. *You cannot afford to let your guard down now. The game is on and you're a player, whether you want to be or not. Keep cool, be alert, and see everything the way your father taught you as a child.*

"OK," I say out loud.

"OK?" Jax laughs. "We're on the ground now so you're OK?"

"Yes," I answer quickly. Jesus Christ. He was right back at school this morning when he said I've lost my game. *Recover*, the inner voice says. "I'm always relieved when the plane is back on the earth where it belongs." Let him think I'm afraid of the landing. What do I care? The only things I need to protect are my true fears.

When we stop, Jax guides me to stand with him, and then we thank the flight attendants as they help us with our coats. They smile broadly as we exit the plane into the darkness.

"Where are we?" I ask, the nerves taking over again. I take a step, almost trip and fall, but Jax is there to hold me up.

"Are you sure you're OK?"

"I am," I say as we descend the stairs without any further stumbling on my part. "But where are we?"

"Colorado. Where we started."

"I don't recognize this airport. Which airport? This isn't Centennial." I look around and realize there are no lights. No city in the distance to give me reassurance that we are somewhere safe.

"We're in Burlington. The place we're going is not far off."

But there is nothing but flat farmland on all sides. And yeah, it's winter, so there's no corn to mark the landscape. I've been to Burlington airport with James. Years ago. But places don't degenerate, they grow. "This is not Burlington airport. Where is the freeway? The hotel? There's a dairy across the street. I don't smell any cows. And I'm sick of the secrets, Jax. Either tell me where we are, or I walk away."

He smiles down at me as we approach a black town car. "You're so suspicious. Just relax."

"Where are we?" I demand one more time. And then I plan my attack if I don't get the answers I need. Chop to the throat, chop to the back of the neck, leg sweep, stomach kick, face kick, run.

"We're at a private airstrip in Nebraska. And you're perfectly safe."

"Then why lie?" I take my phone out and pull up my map app. It pings my location and places a pin in north central Nebraska.

"Because I had a suspicion about you and a pilot who worked for your friend James. And now I know that suspicion was true."

I whirl around, breaking his grip on me. "What the hell kind of game are you playing? And why do you need to know about that pilot? He's a good man, Jax. He saved my ass a few times over the years. And if you're just using me to arrest people—"

"Calm down, killer." Jax says it with a smile, but I don't smile back. "I'm just—" He takes a deep breath. "I'm just piecing together your life, that's all. I've been trying to figure it out for months. I've been looking for someone like you for years. Someone who could help me fill in the missing parts of my own life. And then one day, there you were in my case file. There wasn't a whole lot in there except for the massacre that happened in Santa Barbara. At least the sterilized version of it. But your friend's names were in that file. Bits and pieces of that plan you put in motion to kill off the Company were in that file. And I had some lingering questions about how you and your friends got from place to place back in those early days."

"So you baited me? To get me to spill info about that pilot. Why?"

His smile falters and he takes a step closer to me, reaching for my elbow. I pull it away. He doesn't deserve my trust right now. "I just need to know, that's all. I need all the pieces of the puzzle to fit together."

"Why?" I demand again.

He stares at me for a few moments. Silent. Like he's thinking pretty hard about the conversation we're having. How it might turn out, how it might turn against him if he says the wrong thing. "Because," he finally says with a sigh, "your aunt got word that you were killed. That some assassin shot you in the chest and you fell off a boat in Newport Beach harbor. She was told your body was never recovered. She was a mess for weeks until the final shootout in Santa Barbara revealed you were still alive. But then there was another report. This time your body surfaced in Mexico. She was distressed again. All these years she's been beating herself up for not being there for you."

"So you've been reporting to her for a decade? About me?" Jesus Christ, I feel sick. He's been watching me.

"Yes." He stops again, hesitating. "No. I mean, not exactly. This is all new to me too, Sasha. I've only been on the case a few months. It all came in the file the FBI has. But I need more so I've been hunting down clues and trying to fill in the blanks."

"You have something personal against me, don't you?"

"Not against you, Sasha. You're taking this the wrong way."

"How should I take it?" I snap. "You're a spy. You're an FBI agent. You've just admitted that the FBI has been hunting me for ten years. I want to know what you're really doing. I want to know right now, Jax, or I won't get in that car with you."

"Sasha," he pleads, "listen to me. I'm not here to hurt you. I told you that when you came home last summer. I'm after someone else."

"Nick," I say.

"Yes. No. Maybe. I'm not sure, OK? You haven't told me anything. I can't know which direction I need to go until I debrief you."

"Debrief me? I don't work for you!"

"Not yet," he says, scrubbing his hand down his face with frustration. "I realize I said you have the option of walking away tomorrow, but I fully expect you to cooperate after you talk to your aunt."

"Why? What's she gonna tell me?" My head is throbbing

again. All this information is too much right now. I put up my hand to ward off his words. "Don't. Please. Just stop talking. I want to cut this *date*," I seethe that word, "short. I want it to end right now. Take me back. I don't want to meet that woman calling herself my aunt. I don't want to do any of this. I don't want to hear about the past or how you've been looking for me. I don't want to hear about that party in Santa Barbara or being shot in the chest in Newport Harbor—"

"So he really did shoot you?"

"No. Yes. Just stop, OK? Just stop!" I whirl around, trying to get my bearings as the unfamiliar landscape closes in on me. My head hurts. God, it hurts. And my world is spinning out of control. The memories come flooding back. The blood, and the explosions, and the beach…

Those are my last coherent thoughts as the blackness takes over and I slump to the ground.

CHAPTER SEVENTEEN

"Sasha?"

"My head." It's being cupped in a warm palm, but it's still throbbing. Worse than ever.

"Sasha? Can you open your eyes?"

I try, but the stars above my head are disorienting and they whirl, so I close them again. "What happened?"

"I think you fainted."

"That's stupid. I don't faint You drugged me. Or gave me some sleeper-assassin trigger word."

"What?" He laughs.

"It's not funny. You're drugging me."

"I'm not drugging you, killer. What kind of guy do you think I am? And what was that about sleeper assassins?"

I force my eyes to open to see if his expression matches the laughing tone of his voice. It does. His eyes are twinkling and his grin is wide. "Why am I fainting all of a sudden?"

His eyes narrow and his grin falls. "It's too much, isn't it?"

"What's too much? Getting kicked out of grad school? An unexpected airplane trip with an FBI agent who says he's stalking me? The revelation that I have a living relative? Talking about being shot by James and left behind by Nick? Which of these things are too much for one day?"

"I'm sorry," he says, placing his other hand behind my shoulder to encourage me to sit up. "And you're bleeding. You fell and hit your head on the asphalt. I caught you, but only by the arm. I'm sorry. I should've kept you from hitting your head."

I sit up as he removes his palm from the back of my head and wraps me in his arms. He's warm. And I'm cold, even in this fancy fur-lined coat. There's a little bit of wind tonight and it chills me to the bone.

"Do you really want to go home? Because if that's your decision, then we can go now. I'm not going to force this on you. Especially if it's going to continue to bring on these panic attacks."

"I don't have panic attacks."

"You don't faint, either," he chuckles. "You can call it whatever you want, but the fact is, you're overwhelmed. So just say it again. Tell me to take you home and I will. No more questions."

"But what about Nick?"

"I'll find out what I need without you. It's OK."

"No, I mean, we had a deal."

"We did."

"And if I refuse to go with you to meet my aunt, then I don't complete the date?"

He looks at me hard for a moment, studying my face. "If you need me to force you to go forward by holding that over you, I will. But you're the one calling the shots here tonight, Sasha. And I think you'd start processing all the changes that are happening better if you take control and accept that you want to meet your aunt. You want to know the truth about your family and your place in it."

I feel the lump in my throat forming, the one that signals the tears that will soon follow. Tears I refuse to show anyone, least of all this man. So I cover my face and start breathing in and out, over and over. Counting my breaths like they teach you in meditation. And when I have things under control again, I lower my hands.

Jax is waiting patiently.

"What can she possibly have to say? What excuse can she have for walking out of my life?"

"They think she's dead, Sasha. She was only a half-sister to your mother. Your grandfather had an affair. Lots of Company men do this, thinking they can have secret children. Children who won't have to live by Company rules. But there's no such thing as secrets in the Company."

"Not true. I was a secret."

Jax smiles at me, and then he scoops me up in his arms and stands up like I weigh nothing. We start walking to the car. "You were a damn good secret too. We didn't know about Ford Aston. He was a wild card. Of course looking back, it all makes sense. You're connected to Ford through James Fenici, who did a job in Fort Collins where you finished growing up the year after you were supposed to have been killed out in that harbor. Someday you'll have to tell me how Assassin Number Six managed to shoot you in the chest in front of a dozen people and you survived."

"He really did shoot me."

"I believe you. And your aunt believed all the reports of your death for weeks. She was so relieved when you turned up at that party."

"I can't think about that night right now. I really can't. It was the worst night of my life. Even worse than losing my father. Because the night my dad died, I was sorta expecting it. He was acting so weird leading up to that job. But the night Nick Tate decided that working for a drug lord in Honduras was better than spending his life with me… well, nothing prepares a lovestruck thirteen-year-old for that kind of rejection."

"For someone who can't think about it, you sure did explain a lot about you in a few sentences."

He's right. So I shut up.

We reach the car where a man is holding the back door open. Jax sets me down on the gray leather seat and waits for me to get settled before closing the door and walking to the other side. He exchanges a few words with our driver, who gets in the front, and then Jax joins me in the back, his arms wrapping around me protectively, the same way he was holding me outside. The opaque black glass slides up, secluding us from the eyes and ears of whoever it is at the wheel.

Pressure on the back of my head makes me gasp.

"It's a pretty good gash, but the blood is clotting well. You shouldn't need stitches." He pulls a handkerchief out of his coat pocket and applies it to the wound.

"I still feel dizzy."

"Come here," he says, pulling me into his lap and repositioning me so my head is cradled in the crook of his arm. "Put your feet up on the seat and just rest. It's a good hour drive to where we're going."

I could resist. He's not entirely trustworthy. And he's a stalker. That's pretty creepy. I wonder how deep that obsession goes. I wonder if it's safe to even be in this car with him.

But his embrace feels too good to make him stop.

My dress was not made for being cradled in a man's arms. Or maybe it was? Because the slits up each side bare my thighs, and the heat of his hand on my skin stirs up the longing I've been pushing away for years, making me shut my eyes.

His fingers stroke me gently, back and forth across the top of my thigh. It feels so damn good, I lose myself in the pleasure. I lean into him and his hand drops down between my thighs, making me gasp.

"Sorry," he says, removing the offending hand.

I reach out and place his hand back where it was. "Don't stop touching me. Please. It feels good. I don't get a lot of intimate interaction anymore."

My eyes are still closed when I say this to him, but the ensuing silence and the tenseness of his hand on my skin—his hesitant touch—forces me to open them. It forces me to seek him out.

And I guess he wins, doesn't he? He's got me right where he needs me. Wanting more as I gaze up into his eyes.

"Pull your dress up, Sasha."

I wasn't expecting that command. But it absolutely *is* a command. He'll give me what I'm asking for, but he won't give it away for free.

"Do it," he says. "You've been pushing me away all day. You've complained about my kisses and threatened to break my fingers. And now you're here in my lap. Vulnerable and needy. So if this is what you really want, you need to participate. I won't force you to succumb. I won't take advantage of your longing for Nick, or your very bad day, or the panic that seems overwhelming. If you want me, show me."

So I do. I do it without thinking or rationalizing. I just want it. My hand reaches for the silky fabric of my dress all bunched between my legs, and I pull it up. Inch by inch, until the coolness of the air sweeps across my lace panties.

He licks his lips as he watches.

The heat I feel is immediate.

"What should I do now?" I ask.

His hand slides up my inner thigh and the wetness gathers in a pool between my legs. "Open your legs."

I swallow hard as the request sinks in. I want to obey. So badly. I want him to fix everything that is wrong with this day, erasing the shame of my failure at school and the haunting regrets I have from the past by fucking me in this car.

"I'm scared."

"We can stop if you want."

"No," I whisper as my thighs inch open. More cool air sweeps in, passing over the wet spot of my panties. "I'm not scared of you. I'm scared of giving in."

"Then don't give in. I'm not in a hurry. I mean"—and the familiar grin is back, along with the light in his eye—"since I found you at the airport last summer, I've been daydreaming about what it would be like to make you mine. But I don't want to win you by default."

"Can't this be casual?"

"Casual. Hmmm." He pauses for a moment to think about it. "This time, I guess. It can be. I want you too bad to say no. You've got me where you need me, don't you?"

I let out a small breath of air. "I was just thinking that exact same thought about you."

"So maybe we're both right where we need to be?"

"I want to be loved and I know this isn't love. You're here, you're handsome and polite. You know more about me than anyone outside my small circle of family and friends. And I'm dying, Jax. I'm dying of loneliness. I'm drowning in a sea of shattered dreams and wasted lust."

He leans down and kisses me on the lips. It's soft and tender. No tongue. Nothing harsh about it. It's not a request or a command. It's just… a kiss.

I kiss him back, but he withdraws. "Open your legs wider, Sasha."

It's my move. If I do as he asks, I'm giving him permission to break through the walls I've set up. But I want it so bad, there's no chance of me saying no.

My legs inch open again. One foot drops to the floor of the car and my thigh rests on the leather bench seat. The other leg lifts higher, bending at the knee and pressing into his chest. His hand is warm as he slips it under my leg and strokes my inner thigh.

Touch me, I whisper to myself in my head. *Touch me*. I'm ready to beg him.

His hand dips lower into the v of my legs, as if he can hear the silent plea. His thumb presses against my wet panties, and then begins to stroke it in a circular motion.

More. That's the only word on my mind. *More.*

His other hand finds my breast and gives it a hard squeeze. He tugs at the low neckline of the dress and my bra, and drags them down until my nipple is exposed.

Then he stops.

I open my eyes, seeking the reason behind the pause. "Please, Jax, don't stop."

"I want to watch you watch me," he replies in a husky voice. "I want your eyes open, on mine, and every second I'm touching you, I want to see it."

"See what?" I whisper.

"The longing. The desire. And when I make you come, the relief."

No lover I've ever had was quite like this man here. There was no talking. No demands, no expectations beyond finishing.

But even though it was so much easier to have those kinds of relationships, it's so much better to have this kind of sex.

"OK," I agree.

The second the words are out of my mouth his hands are working. The one over my panties fists the fabric and pulls it aside, while the other hand slides down the length of my body, coming to a rest on the mound of my pussy.

His fingers begin a dance. Some desperate to get inside me, others deftly strumming my clit like an instrument. I hear the moans coming from my mouth, and then a sharp, "Open your eyes, Sasha," that brings me back to reality.

But this cannot be reality. Nothing in my life has ever felt quite like this. I'm losing control and I don't care.

His finger slips inside me, stretching me as it seeks to go deeper. And then another finger is there, doubling the sensations.

His other hand is busy caressing all the sensitive folds surrounding my clit. A pool of desire collects there, his fingertips sweeping through it, before withdrawing.

He removes his hand, but he's got a grin on his face, like he's got a surprise for me. So I stay silent.

"Open your mouth, Sasha."

I part my lips and a second later his wet finger is inside, pressing on my tongue. It tastes like shattered dreams and wasted lust.

"Suck," he says, slowly moving his finger in and out of my mouth. "Suck my finger and imagine it's my cock as I fuck your pussy with my other hand."

I wrap my lips around his moving finger. Between my legs he pushes inside me with more force. Everything is in and out, moving together like a dance of back and forth. Give and take.

My back arches over his knees, and then he repositions himself, sliding down a little to flatten his lap and give his growing cock more room. I can feel it pressing against my spine. I imagine how big he is, how he would fill me up.

"Open your eyes, Sasha."

I didn't realize I'd closed them. My desire is growing quickly, and pretty soon it will be impossible to keep them open, even if I concentrate. But I do as he asks and I'm rewarded with burning lust in his gaze.

"Come," he says. "Come on my fingers so I can make you

suck it off before I fuck you for real."

His words make me breathless. No one has ever talked to me like that. No one has ever made time slow down or my heart speed up quite like this.

He pumps me harder. Both in my mouth and my pussy, making my back arch. I suck his finger as it slides across my tongue, wishing it was his cock. I picture myself on my knees, looking up into his eyes. His fingers entwined in my hair as he encourages me to take him deeper.

He curves his finger inside my pussy, finding my g-spot, and a few strokes later I'm writhing. The shudder of release forces me to close my eyes so I can enjoy it. And then he takes his finger out of my mouth, slips his arm behind my head, and brings my lips to his. His kiss is the last thing I expect, but the perfect ending to my climax.

"Sasha," he moans, his words caressing my tongue, his breath mingling with my own panting. "Sit up."

"I don't want to," I say. "I want to lie here in your arms a little longer."

The hand still between my legs rips at the thin strings of my panties, breaking them and pulling them away from my still quivering body. "Sit up," he commands. "And take my cock out of my pants."

I open my eyes, understanding. He helps me sit up and I maneuver in the small space so I'm straddling his lap. I am too shy to meet his gaze. The reality of what we're doing is replacing the heat of desire. So I concentrate on undoing his belt buckle and unzipping his pants. He's wearing black boxer briefs, and he's hard and big under the thin fabric. I can feel the heat coming off his cock.

I pull at the waistband, freeing him, and his full length springs forth.

"Pull your dress aside and ride me."

I get up on my knees a little, positioning myself over the top of him, and then I grab his shoulders and ease down.

"Oh, God," I moan. He is thick and rock hard.

"Look at me," he says. "I want to see your face."

I slowly raise my chin and find his gaze. His eyes are half closed. His mouth is open, and his breathing is rushed. Small moans escape his lips as I lift up and slowly lower myself over and over. He cups my face and stares into my soul.

"I'm not even done yet and the only thing on my mind is doing this again. I want to fuck you everywhere, Sasha Aston. Every. Where."

I don't know what to say to that, so I lay my head on his shoulder and continue my movements. They are slow and the pace is steady. He doesn't rush or force me to go faster. He doesn't ask me for anything now. He just moves his hips with mine in a circular motion, rubbing himself against my clit. My only thoughts are of making him feel the same relief as I just did, and I'm surprised when my desire begins to build again.

"I'm going to come again," I whisper into his neck.

"And again, and again, and again," he whispers back as his hand finds its way under the silky fabric of my dress and he fingers my asshole.

The pressure is slight, not even close to entering, but I've never been touched here before, so the sensation is new and exciting.

WASTED LUST

Everything about Jax is new and exciting.

We come at the same time. We moan softly together as he shoots his semen inside me.

Rational thought invades my pleasure for a moment as I realize what we just did. "I'm on birth control," I say though my heavy breathing. "And I haven't had sex with anyone in years."

He turns his head and kisses me, his tongue twisting together with mine for a few moments before he pulls back and says, "You're safe with me, Sasha. Always know you're safe with me."

I savor his words as we rest in our post-coital embrace. It's an unexpected relief to hear them, even though he might just be hinting that he has no STDs for me to worry about.

But I'm not worried about that. Jax strikes me as a cautious man. I'm thinking up hidden meanings in his declaration. Things like he will protect me from harm. He will be there to catch me if I fall. He will get me through this night in one piece. He will surround me when the past comes rushing back to slap me in the face.

When was the last time I felt safe?

I think about this for a few moments as he softly strokes my hair.

Never, I decide.

I can't recall living a single moment free of fear.

CHAPTER EIGHTEEN

She rests her head on my shoulder, a weary sigh escaping her lips. "Tired?" I ask.

"Very. I'd rather go home than go meet some long-lost aunt."

"Just give her a chance, OK? I know it's weird and I know she needs you more than you need her—you have a great family already. So just know your worth when you walk in there."

Sasha sits up straight, rubbing her pussy against my cock in a way that makes me instantly hard again. "Worth?"

"Jesus, Sasha," I laugh. "Don't squirm like that while you're sitting in my lap."

"What do you mean she *needs* me?"

"She's got her warm moments, but I've known her a long time. She's not a woman who wastes an opportunity."

Sasha squints her eyes down at me. "I don't want to meet her. Can't you take me home? Didn't I keep my end of the bargain already? We had a date. We had sex, for fuck's sake. I put out. It should be enough."

"You did not *put out*," I growl up at her. "I don't want to hear you refer to sex with me like that. It's offensive. If you didn't want to—"

"I did, Jax. That's not what I meant. I just don't want to meet her. And I don't think you'll make me if I push it. So I'm pushing it."

I sigh as I play with her hair. "I won't make you do anything. But it's always better to be over-informed than under-informed. You should meet her so you can formulate a decision about her. That's how you do the job, right? You gather information, evaluate it, and then form an opinion."

"I'm not working for you and the FBI, Jax."

"Not yet," I joke, poking her in the ribs. She squirms away from me and rubs against my dick again. "Holy hell, you need to get off me or I'm going to attack you." I reach for the handkerchief I used to dab the blood on her head and hold it up for her. "Sorry, I know I made a mess inside you. It's all I have."

"And you ripped my underwear. Now I'm wearing this stupid dress with no underwear."

I can't think about that. I'm ready to give in too. "I'd much rather have you to myself tonight than spend the night—"

"I'm not spending the night!"

"It's a big place, Sasha. You'll have your own room. It's practically a hotel."

"No, no way. I think we need to turn around."

"Sasha," I say, cupping her face in my hands. "Didn't I just tell you you're safe with me? Relax. It's already almost eleven o'clock. It will be one informal introduction, a little chatting, then they will show you to your room and we'll leave first thing in the morning."

She hesitates. My words hang in the air with no answer. And then she gets off my lap and starts wordlessly putting herself back together. Her hair is tousled and her face is flushed pink. I'm suddenly hot as well, and then I realize what just happened. We had sex in a car with our winter coats on. I had sex with Sasha Cherlin, former child assassin, Company secret, and all-around badass chick.

I let off a little laugh.

"What's so funny?" Sasha asks, trying to see herself in the dim reflection of the dark windows lit up by the moon outside.

I can't answer that without offending her. So I just shrug. "The way things change so fast, ya know?"

"You mean us." She drags her eyes away from the window.

"Is there gonna be an us?"

She gives me a shrug back. "Who knows? I'm not exactly in a good place right now. My whole life seems to be up in the air."

"That's not always a bad thing."

"Pfft. Speak for yourself. I'm OCD about this kind of stuff. I like planning things. I hate being spontaneous. I like clear goals with measurable metrics. And a few hours ago I had to clean out my office, and you know what?" Her eyes are fixed on me now.

"What?"

"The only personal thing I had in that office was a dinosaur Chia Pet."

"Sorry I broke it."

"No," she says, swiping a stray strand of hair from her face. "That's not what I mean. I didn't care about it. Not really. After two years of practically living at that school, my office should be like a bedroom. Filled with crap, trash, remnants of life. But my office was spotless."

"So your OCD carries over into your professional life."

"Why didn't I notice that I was so uninvested?"

"Does it matter who notices first? You or your mentor?"

"Yeah, because I'm super-competitive. And I found out I lost a prized internship and got kicked out all in the same hour. I mean, that's one hundred percent total failure."

"Or," I counter, "it's a chance to take a second look at what you're doing and why." I'm about to say more, to ease her mind about what happened today. It has to feel like failure and I don't want to end this conversation like that. But the car comes to a stop and she looks at me with pure panic in her eyes.

"You're fine," I say, squeezing her hand.

"What if they are panic attacks?"

"What if they're not?"

The front door slams as the driver gets out, and then he's pulling open Sasha's door and offering her his hand.

She looks up at him, takes his offering, and steps out of the car like a professional.

I get out on my side and offer her my arm as the driver hands her off. She accepts it and we walk forward, her head tipped up to take in the entire four-story estate.

"Holy shit," she says. "It really is like a hotel."

"You don't get out much, do you?"

"What makes you think that?" She laughs.

"You're a billionaire's daughter. You have a ton of money stashed all over the world, I'm sure. And yet this country estate in north central Nebraska impresses you."

"I've been lots of places..." She trails off as we walk up the front steps. They are massive, like the manor, and built of stone, also like the manor. In fact, it looks like something from the French countryside. You can't see it well at night, but the bricks are light-colored sandstone, there are wings on either side of the main house that seem to go on forever, and there are turrets to give it character. It looks a little like a castle to the kids who come through here. "But I'm a simple girl, Jax. My childhood home was an RV. And Ford's house isn't big. Not like this. I even shared a room with my sister Kate while we remodeled the main floor one year."

The door swings open before I can remark on that insight into her childhood, and then the doorman is there, bowing and extending his hand in a wave that signals we are to come inside.

Sasha tightens her grip on my arm and I give her a reassuring pat on the hand.

"Your coat, ma'am?"

It's a simple question, but Sasha just stands there with her mouth open.

"Here," I say, slipping her coat down her arms. "I'll help you with that." She nods at me, but I can see the panic in her eyes. Has she been like this all fall? I don't recall seeing her so disoriented. Of course, she's practically been a recluse. Staying home most nights, unless she was working. "Are you OK?"

She looks around to see if anyone is watching, and then gives me such a small shake of her head, I almost miss it. "No. Let's go, please."

"Shhh," I say, taking her hand. "You're fine, I promise."

CHAPTER NINETEEN

But I'm not fine. Everything about this feels wrong. The house is pretentious. The doorman is subservient. The entrance is massive, and all the doors I can see from here are closed.

"I want to go home," I whisper.

"Ten minutes, Sasha. Just ten minutes. Meet her, we'll go to our rooms—"

"I don't want to sleep alone, Jax."

He sighs down at me. It's an opening to some joke about being more than willing to let me sleep with him. But he knows I'm serious right now. He reads me well, and I'm not kidding. This place is creeping me the fuck out. "Sasha," he says in a discreet tone, "nothing is going to happen to you. Your aunt is responsible for—"

"Saving more than twenty-five Company kids from their pre-determined fate," a woman's voice says from behind me.

My heart, holy fuck, my heart. It's beating so fast I want to pass out. I take a few deep breaths and force myself not to place a hand over it and let everyone in on my panic.

"Sasha Cherlin, meet Madeline Haas. Your aunt."

"Call me Auntie," Madeline says. "Everyone does."

"Jax didn't," I quip. "So I'll just call you... Ms? Haas? Since I know that's my mother's maiden name, that would make you an unmarried spinster or a divorcee with pent-up hate."

Oh my God, what the fuck did I just say?

"Sasha," Jax whispers.

"Sorry." I seriously don't know what just came over me.

"I see the reports are true," Madeline says.

"What reports?" I snap.

"Your reputation precedes you, niece."

I sigh heavily. Annoyingly, in fact. "Well, it was great to meet you, but Jax and I were in the middle of having fun before we pulled up here. So"—I turn and look up at a stunned Jax—"can we go now?"

"I'd like to have a few words, Sasha. Explain what it is we do here. What my plans are—"

But I stop listening at plans and just start shaking my head. "Nope. No way. I'm not part of your plans. I have no plans with you at all, in fact. I'm ready to hit the road." I turn around, searching for a coat closet.

"Can you give us a minute, Madeline? We'll meet you in the greeting room."

I glance over my shoulder, since the doorman is blocking

the coat closet with his large, very large—like bodyguard large—body. My aunt is scowling at me, like she had some vision of what kind of person I was and that's just been shattered.

"Fine," she says through gritted teeth. "I'll have the servants bring drinks while I wait."

The stress on the word wait seals the deal and as soon as she's out of earshot, I lean up to Jax's ear on my tiptoes. "She's a bitch."

"What the hell is going on with you?" Jax asks. "It's like you just flipped into Bizarro Sasha before my eyes."

"I didn't flip into Bizarro Sasha, Jax. I went from Sasha Aston to Sasha Cherlin in two seconds flat. I. Don't. Like. Her. I can feel it in my bones."

"Just stop, OK? She's not what you think."

"What is she? Some do-gooder saving kids from the Company? I don't see it."

"Well, she has. She still does, Sasha. She's known me most of my life. I know her."

"I hate her. It's not even dislike, it's *hate*."

"That's not even rational."

"I do not care." I even cross my arms for good measure.

"Sasha," Jax says in that FBI voice of his. "Consider the possibility that you're angry at her for not being in your life. That you were left homeless and orphaned after your father and grandparents were killed. That is rational. But blind hate is not."

"Blind hate seems pretty rational to me. I've felt it before. I had an uncle from this side of the family as well. He was a total dick. I never liked him. And that was a good call. He tried to kill Harper once."

"Just give her ten minutes. OK? Ten minutes. That's probably all the time she scheduled for this meeting anyway, she's incredibly busy."

"Yeah, busy running this... this... what the hell kind of place is this?"

"She's gonna tell you. If you let her."

"I don't like this, Jax. I'm telling you, the inner assassin in me is screaming, *Get out*. I want to leave."

He sighs. "OK, fine. I told you it was your call, and it is. So just wait here. I'll go tell her we're leaving."

The relief floods through my body. "Thank you." I grab his arm before he walks off. "And I'm sorry, OK? I am. But I just can't be here."

He nods at me, feigning understanding. But I know he thinks I'm irrational. Regardless, I got my way. He walks off down a long hallway in the same direction as Madeline—which was not the way she approached—and I watch him until he disappears around a corner.

I hug myself, chilled to the bone. Something is wrong here. I can feel it. I'm not sure what it is about this place that has me on edge, but—

"Giving up already?" I whirl around to find a man about the same age as me, standing under an archway with open double doors. "I figured you'd bail. Auntie had higher hopes, but I know your kind."

"Who the fuck are you?"

He's wearing a black suit. Like, all black. Shirt and everything. "Just another broken promise."

"Excuse me?" *Heart rate, Sasha*, I have to tell myself. *Control your heart rate.* Because it's beating so fast, my chest might explode.

"Tell me, Sasha Cherlin," he says, walking towards me slow and deliberate. "What would you do if I attacked you right now?" He nods to the hallway Jax disappeared down. "He's out of range, believe me. Madeline took him outside."

"Why in the world would you attack me? I thought she was all benevolent and she just wanted to talk."

"She does. But I have other plans for you."

"Is that so?" Cocky motherfucker.

He lunges, striking me in the face with the back of his hand.

I react, diving for his legs and sending him to the floor. He puts a leg up and kicks me in the chest, sending me reeling backwards on the shiny floor.

I taste blood in my mouth from his hard slap and then jump up to my feet. He's on his as well, circling me like a predator.

"Come on, asshole," I seethe through my teeth. "I'm ready."

"You sure about that?"

I attack this time. I take two steps forward, duck to the left a little too slow, allowing his fist to connect with my cheek, and then grab his throat and his arm and swing myself up into a flying armbar. The momentum slaps him down on the hard travertine-tiled floor, and I sit on his back for a few seconds of rest before he bucks me off, sending me flat on my ass, my dress hiked all the way up my legs.

He stands over me laughing. "Next time you pick a fight, trying wearing panties."

The next thing I know, he's face first on the floor and Jax is standing in the spot where the new guy just was. Blood is spilling onto the expensive polished floor and my attacker lets out a groan.

"You OK?" Jax asks, breathing heavy and extending his hand to help me up. "I'm sorry, I didn't know he'd be here, or I wouldn't have left you alone."

"Damn right," new guy says. "You know I've a score to settle with her."

"That's enough, Julian." Jax says it with authority and Julian bites his tongue. "Get the fuck out of here or I will handcuff your ass right now and take you in."

"Do it," Julian challenges. "See how far that gets you with Auntie."

"I cannot believe you call that bitch Auntie."

"Watch your mouth, Sasha," a voice from behind me says.

I whirl around to see Madeline back in the entrance. "You people are crazy."

"I asked for one conversation. Ten minutes of your time. And you treat us like we are unworthy of your company. What's that say about you?"

"I was brought here against my will."

"Then Jax misunderstood. He was asked to set up a meeting. If he went about it using less than honorable ways, that's something you need to take up with him."

I shoot Jax a look.

"It's ten minutes, Sasha. Hear her out and we'll leave right after."

"He attacked me!" I say, sounding like a child as I point to Julian with one hand and touch my lip with the other. "I'm bleeding!"

"She's rusty," Julian says to Madeline. "She needs to be

retrained all over again if I agree to take her on."

"Take me on for what? Someone better start talking or I'm gonna lose my shit!"

"I practically begged you for a conversation, yet you—"

"Fine," I yell at Madeline. "Five minutes. Start talking."

"In private," she demands. "And while you're waiting," she says to Jax, "maybe you can find her some undergarments."

I glare at her. "If you think you can shame me, you're wrong, lady. I'll strip naked and kick your ass right now."

Jax chuckles.

"And you," I say, whirling around. "What the fuck? You bring me to these crazy people after I spent the last ten years squeezing the psycho out of me one drop at a time? Just what the actual fuck?"

Jax's face gets serious. "Julian was not supposed to be here. He knew better than to approach you tonight."

I open my mouth to ask what that means, but Madeline has my arm. It's a gentle grasp, up near my elbow. Meant to guide, not threaten. But I shrug her off. "Fine, lead the way, Auntie," I sneer the word. "But the next asshole who attacks me will not get back up when I'm done with them."

"Duly noted," she says with a swish of her long gown as she turns. "Please follow me to the library."

I don't look back at Jax as I make my way after her. But if my paranoia was piqued when I got in that black jet with him earlier, it's off-the-charts manic at this point. I have to take deep, cleansing breaths in rhythm with my steps to calm myself down.

I made a huge mistake back in that car. I should not have had sex with him. But it's easy to come to that conclusion after two orgasms. Not so much when you've been in a two-year dry spell.

I need to get my head on straight because he's hiding something. All these people here tonight are hiding something.

And I have a feeling they're about to tell me everything. But there's only one thing worse than not knowing about secret shit, and that's knowing more than you should.

CHAPTER TWENTY

We end up in a room I would assume is the library but for the fact that it's lacking books. It's more of a sitting room filled with butter-colored leather couches, overstuffed chairs, and a grand floor-to-ceiling window that must have some stunning views during the day to warrant such a prominent place in the room.

Madeline waits for me to enter first and then quietly closes the double doors behind us and walks over to a couch. "Please, sit. Make yourself comfortable."

I walk to one of the chairs, still looking for the books in this library, and take a seat.

"It's all digital these days, right?" Madeline says, waving a hand at the room in general. "Everyone reads books on a device.

I resisted for years, but technology. The future cannot be denied, no matter how hard we try to rebel."

I shrug.

"Besides, we move too often to have collections of anything."

"Move what?"

"Places, Sasha. Residences. I don't own any homes in my own name. They are all purchased or leased under company names."

I know what she means. I understand that the word company has a generally benign definition to most people. But we are not most people and my spine goes stiff at the mere mention of the word. "What is it you need to say?"

"You're not the least bit interested in me?"

I have nothing for that. She's serious. "Why would I be? You show up in my life after all these years and expect—what? I'll run into your arms and give you a hug? I'm so over that."

"Over what?" she asks, reaching for a tea set on the large oval coffee table. "Drink?" she offers.

I ignore her offer. "Over wishing my life was anything but what it is. You could've found me at any time after my birth and you didn't. You left me to figure all this shit out for myself."

"You did a remarkable job. You turned out much better than most."

"I was lucky."

"You were taught well."

"And that has nothing to do with you."

"True. But your hostility towards me is misplaced. I'm not part of the problem. I'm part of the solution."

"I don't need your solution. My problems were solved a long time ago."

"Is that why Nick Tate is on the hunt?"

"I have no idea. I haven't talked to him in years. But I'm sure if he wanted to find me, he'd find a way."

"That's his number one priority at this very moment, Sasha. He's looking for you. And he's broken away from his handler in Central America. Matias is just now figuring it out, but Nick Tate was never part of his gang. He was always one of us."

"Define us."

"Company."

Once again the word shuts me down.

"I have a simple request, that's all. And I'll get right to the point since you are so eager to leave. You can think about it overnight, but I need an answer in the morning."

"I'm not staying here, so I'll just give you my answer now. No."

"Not even if it means you can prevent dozens, if not hundreds of other girls from having to navigate the world like you? Hmmm? You're so selfish that you'd turn your back on your Company sisters who need help?"

My thwarted plans the day Jax found me at the airport hit me in the chest like a bullet. "I have no idea what you're talking about."

She gives me a funny look and I squirm in my seat. *Shut the fuck up, Sasha.*

She drags her stare from me and concentrates on filling a tea cup and adding two teeny-tiny spoonfuls of sugar. "I'm well-loved around here. I have over twenty-five saved souls on my list of accomplishments."

"Excuse me?"

"All boys, so far. As you well know, they are much easier to save." And then a small chuckle erupts from her lips and I get that chill again. "Jax might disagree, but his situation is unique."

Jax? He said he wasn't Company. If he lied to me—

"We did our best in that case. But the Company, as I'm sure you are aware, has legions of assassins on staff. You yourself are one of them."

"I wasn't. I have no number."

"Zero? That's a number, isn't it? Last I checked."

"Zero means nothing."

"You're wrong. Zero is the number that when added multiplies everything by ten. Add two, and you multiply by a hundred. Three, a thousand."

"I get it, but it's bullshit."

"It's not, Sasha. It's the one thing they've tried that actually *works*."

"What are you talking about?"

"Sleepers. The girls. The child killers. You were one of them. Your father didn't follow protocol and that's why you're still alive, I think. But none of the others survived, aside from Harper Tate, and she barely counts, since the Admiral never seriously had her in the sleeper program to begin with. It was all for show. To make everything equal. You know, an example. None of the other Company girls had protection like the two of you did. But Nick, on the other hand, he was properly indoctrinated. He's made quite a name for himself down there in Miami."

"Miami?" Shit. I have no clue. I'm so out of my element here. I used to be the girl who knew everything but lately I feel like the last to know anything.

She waves a hand at me and takes a sip of her tea before setting her china cup down on its pretty matching saucer. "Never mind Nick for now. I can handle him. But the girls I've found, they are another matter. They are wild. Have you met any of them?"

"No," I lie. "Just Harper."

"Hmmm," she says. Not quite calling me out. So maybe she doesn't know about Sydney, Merc's girlfriend. She was a Company girl. And she was a sleeper assassin too. As dangerous a girl as they come. Maybe even more dangerous than me under normal circumstances. But her mind was fucked so hard, she might never be normal.

No, I'm the one who kept her head. I'm the one who made it out intact.

"At any rate, you're angry at me for not saving you. But now that I'm offering you a chance to save other girls, other *Company* girls, you want to run away from the offer."

"You never offered me shit."

"I'm offering now, Sasha. Help me reach them. Help me undo the years of training and abuse. Help me steal them back, if necessary."

"You want me to steal baby girls." This bitch is nuts.

"And retrain the older ones."

I really might throw up. Just what the hell is she asking? "You can't just steal children."

"Why not? The Company does. They stole you. They stole your mother."

"And yet you managed to escape."

"Your grandfather—my father—went to extreme lengths to

save me."

"But not my mother?"

"She was a full-blood Company girl. He had no chance. But tomorrow there will be a very important meeting here. A meeting that will change the tide for these girls. And I need you to be there. I need your support. Because my associates have it in their heads that you are the only one capable of this job and I have it in my head that I am the only one with enough knowledge to see it through. I need your help to secure that position."

"That makes no sense. Who would follow you? Not me!" I laugh. "And I'm just a grad student in anthropology. I have not seen action in a decade."

"But Julian's attack proved that you still have skills."

"So that was planned. You people are sick. And I think I've heard enough." I get up from my chair and turn away, walking briskly to the door.

"You can leave, Sasha. I can't force you to cooperate. It would never work unless you're a believer. But those girls, they're counting on you. Their fate rests in your hands."

I stop for a moment, but I don't turn to face her. "I'm not the savior of Company girls, Madeline. I'm just a recovering Company girl myself."

"You were never a Company girl, Sasha. You were a Company assassin. There's a big difference. You had it better than most. You and Harper both had it better than all the others. You have no idea the torture they endure. You were a very sheltered child in that respect. And now you're a very sheltered adult. But I know you've met Sydney Channing. Now that is what a Company girl looks like. And Nick is out there now, killing them as fast as I can save them, Sasha. Did you know he's been killing Company kids for years? Hmmm? You're on the wrong side."

Nick? What? I try my best not to react and spit out my words. "You're a liar and my answer is still no." And with that I grab the handle of the door and pull it open.

"The fourth door on the left is a washroom, Sasha Cherlin. You should wipe that blood off your face before you leave. Makes you look like a fighter. Best to keep up your high-society appearances."

"Fuck you."

I exit, slamming the door behind me on my way out. But I touch my bleeding lip as I walk towards the door she was referring to, and open it up.

Julian is standing in front of the mirror. He looks my reflection in the eye as he messes with a tie around his neck.

But when he turns I realize it's not a tie. It's a white collar. I have to let off a laugh. "A priest? Are you fucking kidding me? You're like twenty years old. There are no twenty-year-old priests."

"Twenty-four, Sasha. Just like you. And celibacy was my only option after Nick took what was mine."

"That's enough, Julian," Jax says from behind me. "The car is ready, Sasha. Let's go."

"She'll find out eventually, Jax."

"Go home, Julian. You've done enough damage tonight." And then Jax takes me by the arm and guides me with his other hand on the small of my back.

"What's that mean?" I ask, as we shrug our coats back on. "What the fuck? He's a priest because Nick took... what? His promise? Did Nick kill some girl he was promised to?"

He ignores my question until we exit the mansion and head back towards the car. "Forget Julian. He's never been entirely sane. Let's get out of here. I had no idea she set this up."

I sigh as I climb back into the car. So tired. So ready to just go home and sleep in my bed and try to forget this day ever happened. Everything about it was bad.

Well, I think as Jax climbs into the car on the other side of me, *maybe not everything.* I know I should be fuming at Jax, but the comfort I felt in his arms earlier… that was unexpected. It was nice, actually. And the sex was amazing.

I've always tried to find the good in the bad. Even back when I was a kid, I was known for making the best of things. Knock me down, I get up. That's how it's always been.

So I make Jax the reason I get back up tonight.

I want more of that. But I need to figure out what his role is in all this before I let him touch me again. I can't afford to lose myself to lust.

CHAPTER TWENTY-ONE

I have a bad feeling I fucked up.

Madeline, Julian. The empty estate. I shouldn't have given in to Madeline's demands to meet Sasha tonight. I should've waited until the house was full. Even one child in there would've been better than none.

How will Sasha trust me when everything she saw tonight pointed to Company? And I have to admit, looking at it with Sasha's eyes, that's exactly how it appears. She has no idea what Madeline has been doing all these years.

Fucked. Up.

"So," Sasha says as the car pulls away to begin the hour-long drive back to the airport. "Did you find me some underwear?"

My laugh bursts out. I look over at this girl who surprises me at every turn. She is brave and smart. She is funny and real. She is the only woman I've ever been obsessed with. "I didn't," I say, controlling my smile as best I can. "My mission was a complete failure."

She stares at me, and then scoots closer, wrapping her hands around my bicep. She leans her head on my shoulder and I have the purest moment of happiness because of this small gesture. "Well, Agent Jax, that's OK. I only put them on to impress you. I'm a commando girl."

I smile into the darkness of the car's backseat.

"And I'm sorry I was such a childish bitch back there, but that woman… she's bad."

"Why do you think that? This is not the general consensus, Sasha. And I'm not saying you're wrong, I just need to understand where that impression comes from."

Sasha shrugs against my coat. God, I love this moment. I love having her trust me. Cling to me. "The estate and grounds remind me of the house in Santa Barbara. The one where all those Company people died because I brought a legion of fucked-up people there to get revenge. The one where Nick made me leave without him. Get on that boat with Merc and James and Harper and never look back."

I know she warned me about talking about this stuff earlier, but I can't help it. I need to know everything about her and if she's in a chatty mood I'm not gonna pass this chance up. "He *was* your promise, wasn't he?"

"He was," she sighs. And then she's silent. This goes on for so long I start wondering if she's asleep. But then she says, "I know it's stupid. I mean, I get that. I've had ten years to come to the realization that having an arranged marriage is not the ideal. But it's all I knew. He started coming around when I was almost eleven and he was fifteen—"

"Why?" The peaceful moment I was just having is gone. Nick, man, he does that to me. And the last thing I want to talk about with Sasha is that asshole. But I promised her. I told her I'd show her what I had. So this reveal is gonna come crashing down sooner or later. Might as well get it over with.

"My father was an arms dealer for the Company. He used to be an assassin trainer too. Which is why I was trained to kill as a small child when my place in the Company was supposed to be like any other girl's. Brainwashing, torture, and servitude. But he changed my future by teaching me to kill. It kept me alive, it made me brave, and it got me through."

"So Nick was there to buy guns and he decided he wanted to marry you when you were ten?"

"No." She laughs. "No. He was chosen for me by… his father, I guess. And my father too, since it takes two to make a deal."

The word *deal* hangs in the air. As many times as I've heard about the deals, it has never become normal. No amount of conditioning will ever make me think that bartering your daughters off in the name of global corruption is normal.

"So Nick was coming around for about a year and we became friends."

"So he was sixteen and you were going on twelve."

"Yeah, I guess so. That's when he told me the Company was in trouble. My father was in trouble. And Nick was my promise."

"Did it make you happy? To have him as a promise." I dread the answer, but I already know what she'll say.

"God, I don't even have words. I felt like the most special girl in the world. The Admiral chose me to marry his son. Back then, I didn't know what they did with the mothers who refused to obey the Company brainwashing. James told me they kill them when I was thirteen. Just before we brought the whole thing down. "

"And what did you think of Nick? Did you think he'd save your daughters from the fate you barely escaped? That you'd never be bound by those same rules if you just kept fighting?"

"It didn't sink in." She sits up a little and turns her head so she can look me in the face. "I heard the words coming out of James' mouth, but it didn't sink in. It took so many years for that concept to become reality for me."

I nod slowly as I study her face. She is so pretty. And she doesn't need makeup to be that way, either. Her skin is fair, with just a hint of color in her cheeks. Her eyes are a deep blue. Like I'm looking at the sky when thunderstorms are approaching. "She's too Company for you."

Sasha nods, instinctively knowing I switched the conversation back to Madeline. "Families don't organize. Companies organize. Governments organize. Madeline is Company, even if she's not."

"I get it." And I do. I can't blame this girl for her first impression. She's far more worldly than she seems.

"And…" Her words trail off and I wait a few seconds to see if she will pick her thought back up.

"And?" I finally ask.

"I have a lot of things hidden in my head, Jax. I'd like to tell you about them all, I really would. You have no idea how bad I want to be unburdened. I want to spill every secret I ever had.

But..."

"But you don't trust me yet."

"Right. I'd be very stupid to trust you. You took me to that woman. You've been kinda pressuring me to join the FBI and help you hunt down Nick. And even though I have no idea how I feel about Nick these days, I do know I'm not ready to turn him in."

"Fair enough. You've more than lived up to your end of the bargain today. So I think I owe you. I'd like to show you, though. So can you be patient?"

"Sure." It comes out with a long breath of air. Like she's exhausted.

"You should sleep. I'll wake you when we get to the airport."

I get silence again, but a few minutes later she's breathing heavy as she begins to drift off. And I have to hand it to her. She says she doesn't trust me, but if falling asleep cuddled up to my arm is not trust, what must it feel like to have her completely?

Nick is an idiot.

But I can't fault him for it. If he had realized Sasha's true worth—aside from killing and secret information—she'd still be his. She'd probably be dead because of it too.

My hatred for him dims a little. I will never like that man. Ever. But he left Sasha for a reason, I think. He left her because she was too good for him. She was pure and he was corrupt. I have a feeling that leaving her behind was as purposeful a move as any of the others he's made throughout the years.

But why?

Does he love her? Is she the missing woman? She can't be. Sasha freely admits she has not heard from or talked to him in a decade and I believe her.

So who is the woman who lured him back to the States six years ago? Sasha would've been just graduating high school. Her passport shows she was in New Zealand with her family that summer after graduation. So if he didn't come to see her, then who?

This mystery has plagued me for years. Why does one of the FBI's most wanted criminals leave Central America and come back to the US when he's got a powerful position in a Honduran gang to protect him at home?

Why risk it?

For the job?

No. It can't be that simple. Nothing about this guy is simple.

Did he lie to Sasha? Was he really her promise? Because Julian has said some interesting things over the years about his lost promise. It's convenient that Sasha's father and Nick's, the only two men who could substantiate the claim he made, are both dead.

I ponder this until we reach the airport. And by that time, Sasha is sleeping so deeply, she doesn't even wake up when I pick her up in my arms and walk her up the stairs. I take her to the back of the plane and place her on the bed. "Sasha," I whisper softly in her ear.

"Hmmm?" she moans back.

"Let's take off your coat."

"Mmmm." She moves just enough for me to get her coat off, and then she turns over and falls back asleep with her hands bunching the pillow up to her face.

I stand there and smile down at her. Just smile. She's so

fucking adorable. And I'm starting to regret that rash decision to have sex with her in the car. You only get one first time. This one was pretty good as far as first times go. But still… I should've waited. Made it more romantic and less primal.

I lean down and kiss her on the head and then I walk out, leaving the lights off so she can get some rest. I go all the way up front to the business end of the plane and take a seat at the table.

"Drink, sir?" Essie asks.

"Sure. Brandy, if you've got it. You the only one on staff tonight?"

"No, the other girls are chatting in the galley. But if you want them, I can get them."

"No, let them chat. I've got everything I need and I can use the quiet time."

"Very good, sir," she says, placing a snifter with two fingers of brandy in front of me on the table. "Just call if you need anything."

I need a lot of things. But nothing Essie can help with. So I won't be calling for her. I just drink my brandy and think about Sasha. I think about picking her up again and carrying her to the car that will be waiting for us when we land. I hope she doesn't wake up.

Mostly because I want to carry her again. I loved that feeling. Her soft body against my hard one. But also because I'm not taking her home. And when she figures that out, she's gonna be pissed.

CHAPTER TWENTY-TWO

I wake up screaming.

"Sasha," Jax says next to me.

"What the fuck?" I look around the room wildly. "Why are you in my bed?"

"Sasha, you're fine."

"Where am I?" It's dark and I am in bed. But even in the dim light I can see I'm not in *my* bed. "Whose room is this?" And then I look down at my clothes. Which are not my clothes. "Whose clothes are these?" I jump up, slipping out of Jax's firm grip on my arm, and bounce out of the bed, my feet hitting the floor.

"Sasha, please. Listen." Jax gets out of the bed on his side, ready to come towards me, but my instincts kick in. My eyes find the door, and before I can even make a conscious decision, I'm through it—running down a hallway. It leads to a small living room and my socked feet slide on the polished hardwood floors.

Front door. Check.

I'm unlocking the chain and pulling it open before Jax even makes it to the living room behind me.

"Sasha!" he yells.

But I'm already out into the cold night air. There's a steady drizzle coming down and even though I'm in full-on get-the-fuck-out-of-here mode, all I can think of is why the fuck is it still raining in December?

"Sasha! You're getting wet. Come back inside."

I stop about a hundred feet from the house and look around. "Where the hell am I?"

"Just come inside and I'll tell you."

"No." I whirl around. "No. You drugged me again!"

Jax laughs, just like he did the last time I accused him. "Where do you come up with that shit? I didn't drug you. You were obviously exhausted. You fell asleep in the car, remember? After we left Madeline's estate?"

I do remember that. "Why am I here when I should be home?"

"I can explain, OK? Just give me a chance. You're gonna freeze out here. Come inside."

I look down at my clothes. I'm wearing men's black boxer briefs and a man-sized black t-shirt. "Where the fuck did these clothes come from?"

"You were sound asleep when we got here, Sasha. I swear. I woke you up as best I could and I told you to change."

I stare at him dubiously.

"I swear to God, Sasha. I did not drug you. You're just disoriented. And if you calm down and come back inside, I'm sure you'll remember."

I look around and take it all in. There's a half-moon. Just enough light to see that there are no lights anywhere surrounding this house. I force myself to take deep, deep breaths to calm my racing heart. "Where are we?"

"Nebraska."

Farmland. That's all I see. Flat, fallow farmland. And a few dark splotches in the distance that might be trees. "Why the fuck am I still in Nebraska?"

"Will you come inside?" He's wearing the same thing as me, I realize. And we were sleeping in the same bed. And I had sex with him in the car last night.

Jesus Christ. What the hell am I doing here?

"Sasha," Jax says, reaching behind the door to grab something. My heart kicks it up another notch as I picture him grabbing a gun. But he comes back into view sliding an umbrella open. "Come on," he says, taking a few slow steps outside towards me. "You're getting wet. Let's go inside and talk about this."

"Take me home, Jax. Right now." I eye him as he carefully makes his way out towards me. "I want to go home."

"I will, Sasha." He's only a few paces away when he stops walking. "I will. But I told you I'd show you everything I had on Nick. And this is where I have it."

I shake my head. "No, it's a trick. You're tricking me."

He takes those final few steps and places the umbrella over my head. The cool prickles of rain stop misting my bare skin and I realize just how cold it is. "You're all wet now. Come on, let's go inside and I'll show you why you're here. This is my safe house. It's FBI-sanctioned. It's only a secret to outsiders. I swear," he says, crossing his heart with his free hand. "They know you're here with me. I called it in last night. I'll show you inside."

"You turned me in?"

"Sasha," he says, blowing out some air like he's getting frustrated. "I already explained to you. Months ago. We don't want to arrest you, we only want your help. They're not gonna come take you away. No one is going to hurt you here. That's why we call it a *safe house*. This is where I keep all my reconnaissance on Nick. And if you come inside, it will take one flip of a light switch to prove that everything I just said is true."

I stand still as I consider this.

"Come on," he insists, taking my arm and pulling me back towards the house. "It's wet and cold out here. Let's go back inside and I'll explain everything."

I allow him to lead me back to the house. What choice do I have? I'm half-naked and in the middle of buttfuck nowhere.

When we get to the door I hesitate for a moment, but he doesn't ask me again. Just tugs me back inside and closes the door behind us.

"Just..." He hesitates, making me look up at his face. I can't see much since there are no lights on, but I can tell his reluctance is due to what's coming.

"Just tell me, Jax."

And then his fingertips find a light switch on the wall and the room illuminates.

Everywhere I look, there is nothing but Nick.

CHAPTER TWENTY-THREE

"What the fuck is this?"

It's a stupid question. I know what this is. A full-fledged case study on Nick Tate. The wall in front of me is filled with pictures of him. It starts on one end, the corner nearest the front of the house, and fills the entire wall. There are even a few pictures and notes pasted over the corner on the far end of the room.

He ages in the images on the wall. They start out with Nick as a young teen, before I met him. Then Nick the same age as I remember him from when we were working together, the golden-haired, brown-eyed surfer boy. And then, at less than a quarter of the way across the montage, he begins to morph in appearance. Head shaved almost bald. A scar across his cheek.

One tattoo. Spanish lettering arched across the front of his chest with the words *Mara Perro* in old English calligraphy.

Then slightly longer hair. More tattoos. Skulls and crossbones. Dogs snarling, their teeth dripping with saliva. Chains encircle his neck and arms. His wrists have thick links inked on them, like he's a prisoner.

My eyes move on, taking in the next set of pictures. His hair is long now, past his shoulders. And it's the same bright yellow I remember from when we were kids. The tattoos are more religious. There's a picture on his back, a man with his head illuminated like an icon. The word *Santino* rides the space between his shoulders. This one in a pretty script writing. There are flowers and children sitting at his feet.

The two sides of his body couldn't be more different.

I walk over to that image and touch his back. Tracing a line down his spine.

"That's him."

I figured.

My eyes leave that image and move on to the next set of pictures. I take it all in as he ages before my eyes. More or less hair. More scars. More tattoos. And when I get to the end, he is nothing but ink. Every question I had about him is laid out on this wall. A decade's worth of answers.

"When I said I had more information, I meant it." Jax is frowning. "You said you wanted to know, right?"

I nod.

"Well, then let me walk you through it."

I hug myself as my body begins to tremble.

"I met Nick Tate when I was fifteen. He was fifteen too. I

guess, from what you said earlier, that was the same year you met him?"

"Probably."

Jax clears his throat. "I knew him as a teen in the Brooklyn neighborhood I was living in as a foster kid. My foster brother and I came out of juvie together, escaped social services, and both ended up getting adopted by Max. We were friends with Nick for a couple months. He appeared out of nowhere. But I was young and didn't have any idea what lurked beyond my small world. I had no idea powerful people might use children to do the dirtiest work imaginable."

I shake my head. "No, he was with Harper back then. She told me. They're twins and she said they were inseparable. He was never away from her for long because she had panic attacks and she needed him. It was a big deal when she left the Company and went out on her own. And that wasn't until she was eighteen."

"I have no idea what he did when I wasn't with him, Sasha. If he was with his family, it was sporadic. Because I'm telling you, he was a regular fixture in my neighborhood for months. He'd appear for days, then disappear for a week or more. He was almost never in school even though he was registered. So maybe he was going home."

"How could he just go home? They lived on a superyacht on the ocean, Jax."

"I don't care, *Sasha*," he says back, sneering my name. "I'm fucking telling you something. So stop trying to make excuses for him and listen."

I force myself to shut my mouth. Mostly because I'd rather look at the pictures on the wall than argue. Nick. Finally I get to see what became of him.

"My brother Jacob and I had another little brother too. Michael. We were all fostered with Max Barlow. Jacob and I found Michael in the youth center one day. This was before we knew Nick. Before we even knew Max Barlow existed. And we were a team, ya know? Jake and me and Michael. Michael was just a little kid, but he was tough, man. Like super fucking tough. Jake and I latched on to him because of it. We were orphans, street kids. Nothing to look forward to, nothing to dream about. Life sucked.

"Max came into the picture not long after the three of us teamed up. He wanted to adopt Michael, and Michael said he didn't go anywhere without his big brothers. So that's how Jake and I got the luckiest break a foster kid can get. A permanent home."

"What happened to your brothers?" I'm stuck in his story now. Picturing his life as a kid.

"Jake is..." He hesitates. "He's..."

"What?"

"Never mind Jake. It's Michael I want to tell you about. Because a little while after we all settled into our new lives, Nick appeared. Nick Tate. He didn't even use a fake name. And I have to wonder now why he did that."

"We have no birth certificates. Harper never had one either. She didn't really exist, she said. I already had fake papers but we had to get fake papers for her. An ID, a passport. Everything."

"I guess that makes sense," Jax says. "But I've come up with my own theory over the years. And I think he used his real name because he wanted us to know who he was."

"Why?"

"Pride? To boast?"

"Boast about what?"

"Assassinating Michael in his own bed."

My stomach turns as I process those words. "What?"

"He came into our house as a friend. He cased us for weeks. Got to know us. Played with Michael. Sucked up to Max. We had him over for dinner. And then one night, he came inside, shot my little brother assassination-style, and disappeared."

"No." I say it forcefully. "Did you see him?"

"No, but it was him."

"How you do know? Because Nick Tate is not that—"

"Kind of guy?" Jax laughs. "You have no idea who Nick Tate is, Sasha. None. But I'm gonna spell it out for you right now. Because we've had someone on the inside of *Mara Perro* for decades. Ever since that gang's inception, there has been a rat watching every move. That's what Max Barlow does. He's the king of infiltration. He's got men in every Westernized gang in the US, Mexico, Canada, South America, Central America, Russia, Moldova… you name it, if it's not Islamic, Max Barlow runs the rats. The only organization we haven't been able to infiltrate is—"

"The Company." I say it like a dead person. My world was dark, but this room sheds a new light on everything. I'm not sure I like the light.

"That's right."

"You need a rat in the Company?"

"No, Sasha. We don't want to waste time infiltrating them. Why? Why bother doing that when we have you?"

I hear the words, but I ignore them and concentrate on Nick's scars. What happened to him? Did he get them fighting? Was he tortured? Did they make him do these things?

Or was he in on it from the beginning? Did he lie to me?

Jax takes my hand and places something in it. I look down at the gold badge encased in leather. There's a beaded chain and plastic credit-card type ID attached.

"For you," Jax says.

I look at the badge for a moment. Then the ID. It's got my picture on it. My full name—Aston, not Cherlin—and some fancy, authentic-looking symbols. "What the hell?"

"You don't have to accept it, Sasha. Yet. But think about it. You could make a difference."

I look up at him. My whole body is freezing now, and I start to tremble. "You want me to get Nick for you, don't you? To get revenge because you think he killed your little brother."

"I know he did."

"You don't know, Jax. Unless he tells you, you don't know. And what the fuck happened to innocent until proven guilty?"

"Whatever happened to a man's home is his castle? Didn't my brother have a right to life, liberty, and the pursuit of happiness? Nick Tate took it away. Nick Tate has killed hundreds of people—"

"So did James, Jax. So when I'm done with Nick, do you want me to go after James? Is Harper on your hit list as well? Merc? Did you really bring me here to try to talk me into selling out the people who almost died for me?"

"As far as I know, they are all retired."

"And you have no personal grudge against them, right?"

"True," he admits. "But they got out of the business, Sasha. You got out. Nick didn't."

"We're *all* ex-Company, Jax."

"No," he seethes. "You're not. Because Nick never left them, Sasha. He's still in."

"He's part of a Honduran gang, not the Company."

"They *are* the Company. Nick knew that going in. They are the Company, Sasha. You think you got them all?"

"I never said that. We knew we only got some of them. But that guy, that Matias guy who took Nick—"

"They didn't take him, Sasha. He left with them. It was a setup."

"By whom?"

"By Nick."

"Where the fuck do you get your information?"

"From Nick." And then Jax walks over to a desk and pulls out a stack of letters. "Nick sent me these every year on the anniversary of Michael's death. He justified it, Sasha. He said he'd do it again if he had to. He admitted it, he took credit for it, and he believed in it."

"Why would he want to kill a little boy?"

"Why would people want to kill you, Sasha? Or should I say, twelve-year-old you?" He waits for it to sink in.

I turn away. "What the fuck?"

"Michael was someone's Zero, Sasha."

"What?" I whirl back around. "What did you just call him?"

"The Zero. The new breed of Company assassin. Nick was one, too."

I turn back to the wall and stare up at the golden boy of my childhood.

"So were you."

But my head is shaking out a no. "My father never put me in the program. My father—"

"Taught you how to kill as a child."

"No."

"Yes. I brought you out here to show you the truth. You wanted me to give you all the information I had about Nick. And here it is." Jax walks up to the wall and starts pointing at the pictures. "Age fourteen—this is him. Just a kid in a low-income classroom. Some inner-city school where politicians go to make up feelgood moments. The next day that government official was poisoned. Didn't I once hear that the Company assassins had to use poison for personal jobs? What kind of personal job could a fourteen-year-old boy have, Sasha?"

No.

"Age fifteen. This picture was taken in my own fucking house. That's Nick sitting between me and Jake. That's Michael on the far left. He was shot in the head as he slept less than two weeks later."

No.

But he goes on and on and on. Sixteen. Seventeen. Eighteen. Jax pulls out an envelope with pictures of me and Nick together at the antiques mall in Cheyenne where my father ran his business. The same place I dreamed about the life Nick and I would have together. Where I sat reading *Little House* books, lamenting over my stupid braces and hoping against all hope that things would turn out OK. That Nick Tate might save me.

No.

"After he left you crying in that boat, he went down to Honduras for his final phase of training. Before Nick Tate came to town there were between two and three homicides per day in

San Pedro Sula. After, it averaged four."

"So that's all Nick? Please." I laugh. "You cannot be serious."

"He brags about it, Sasha. We've got video. I told you we have informants. We have plenty of video. And I've got it all queued up for you on that laptop right there." He points to a computer.

I swallow hard.

"I'm not lying. I swear to God, everything I just told you is true."

CHAPTER
TWENTY-FOUR

S he processes the information I just dumped. Her face is tight, her emotions controlled. No tears from this girl. None.

"I have you too."

She turns to look at me and I pan to the wall behind me. There are far fewer images of Sasha. Long stretches of white space reflect the trouble I had finding her. "I wasn't sure you were real. I mean, we heard rumors of a little girl, a Zero, as they call them, leading the way during that year the Company went defunct. But they were just rumors. No one really thought you were real."

"I'm real," she says in a whisper.

"I know, Sasha." I take her trembling body in my arms. "I know you're real. And I'm sorry I have to be the one to show you this stuff. But he's back, OK? He's back for you. And no way in hell is he gonna get what he wants again. No way."

"He would never hurt me."

"You have no idea how bad he can hurt you."

She sighs in my embrace but she doesn't pull away. It's something. More than I could've hoped, probably. I mean, I just shattered her reality. And how many times has this happened before tonight? How many times has she had to suck it up and accept the truth about who and what she is?

"That's my middle school." She points to one of the pictures. "And my high school."

"I found them much, much later. I have your yearbook pictures from that time, but that's it."

"And me at graduation two years ago."

"Found on the web. I wasn't there. The day at the airport, that was the first time I ever saw you. Everything came after that meeting."

"So this is what you've been doing all these months?"

"Yeah," I say flatly.

"Cataloging my life. Building a timeline."

I can see where this is going, but she has every right to be pissed.

"I don't want to hunt people for a living, Jax."

"I understand," I say, pushing her away a little so I can see her face. "I do. But hunting with a badge and hunting with a gun are two very different things. And I'm not asking you to decide today, all right? I just want you to think about it. Make it an option. We could use your help, Sasha. We really could. With you we could bring the Company down once and for all."

"But there's Company people in the FBI."

"I know. Why do you think Max Barlow's division is black ops? It's been black ops since the Seventies when he figured out the Company existed. We don't have any infiltrators in that area, Sasha. I promise you. There are only four people in the whole department."

"You?"

"Me and Max. And two others I can't name unless you sign on."

"I don't know what to think."

"Don't think anything yet. OK? Just… let's just go to bed. Get some rest. And then we can discuss it again over breakfast and I'll take you home if you want."

She turns to look at the wall of Nick again. "I need to know what he's been doing. All of it. Even if it's bad."

"Not now. Tomorrow. You've heard enough tonight." I take her hand and lead her towards the bedroom. She resists for a moment, but then she's walking with me. "I'll sleep on the couch if you want."

"No," she says. "The last thing I want tonight is to be alone in a strange bed."

I smile into the darkness. "I told you, you're safe with me. I meant it."

We walk into the bedroom and she starts to climb under the covers. I put a hand on her shoulder to stop her. "Wait. I have some dry clothes you can change into."

I grab her a new t-shirt and boxer briefs and point towards the bathroom. She shoots a shy grin towards the floor as she takes them from my hands and that just kills me. I imagined her a million ways as I gathered information these past few months, but finding out she is soft and so very, very sweet is a complete surprise.

"Thank you," she says, walking into the bathroom and closing the door.

I watch her shadow change the light seeping out from under the door for a few seconds, and then climb into bed, leaving the covers open for her.

She comes out a few minutes later, flipping the light off as she passes through the door. And then a few seconds later her small body is next to me. "You know a lot more about me than I know about you."

"Sorry about that. But if you have any questions, just ask. I'd love for you to know me better."

She turns her body and I can see her shadowed face in the dim light from the window. "Why me?"

"You're special." It comes out easy because it's true.

"I'm bad too. I'm just as bad as Nick."

A strand of hair falls over her cheek and I reach over and tuck it behind her ear so I can continue looking at her face. "I know you think that thirteen was old enough to call the shots, Sasha. I can tell. You're independent and strong. You're well-educated and logical. But that's not logical. You were a child. They killed your whole family. You responded the way they trained you. You didn't choose to continue that path like Nick did. You allowed someone else to take charge and you left it behind. I'm stunned that you don't see yourself as a survivor."

"I do," she says, her defenses up. "I've always seen myself that way. I kicked ass back in the day. And I can still kick ass now."

"As Julian is now aware. And that's not what I meant. I meant that you allow yourself to be a product of your environment. And you're not. You rose above it. You're out. You can stay out."

"If I join you."

I lean in and kiss her gently on the mouth. She responds in her soft way that has had my full attention since I saw her outside her school yesterday afternoon. She is on the edge of something. A discovery. About Nick, for sure. About herself, I hope. About the world, unfortunately. And tomorrow it's only going to get worse. I pull back a little and whisper, "Let me erase those doubts."

"With sex?" Her eyes are searching mine. Longing for more, I can tell. But afraid to ask for it.

"You can call it that if you want. But I'm not gonna."

"What's it called?"

"I don't know," I answer truthfully. "I just got you, ya know? I wanted you so fucking bad, you have no idea."

"You don't even know me. You know Nick better than you know me. And I don't know you at all. So tell me something real, Jax. Because every day I feel like a fake. I'm not real. I'm that illusion you thought I was. An apparition of that girl the Company made me. I have no idea what I'm doing. And I feel like I'm suffocating. I feel like my past is back to strangle the life out of me. I feel like I've been walking around wearing a costume for ten years and it's so much a part of me, I'm afraid to take it off. I think I'll lose myself for good if I take it off, Jax. So tell me something real. Or this ghost version of me might float away and disappear. I might never pull myself back from that. I was young when I killed those people. I was scared and I didn't know any better. But now I know. What I did was wrong. What I became—"

I stop her words with another kiss. This time I cup her face with both hands, afraid that she really will float away and disappear. She opens her mouth, her tongue seeking me out. One hand slips up her shirt and I find her breast and twist her nipple.

Her moan makes me instantly hard. "That's real," I say, placing her hand over my erection. "That's real. And last night when I was inside you, that was real, Sasha. I like you. Not because of who you were or who you might be in the future. I like you for the person you are now. I'm hard for you now."

She squeezes my dick in her small palm. I flip her over on her back in one swift motion, and then hover myself over her body. "Say no if you want me to stop."

I stare into her eyes as she thinks about my words. And just when she's about to answer me, I put a finger to her lips.

She moans.

And then she opens her mouth and my finger slips inside. The wetness of her tongue sliding up and down my finger as I pump it in and out drives me insane. I would do anything to keep this girl. Anything.

She bucks her hips upward, driving into mine. Rubbing against my hard-on. "I want you on top," I say, withdrawing my finger.

"Put me there."

I reach underneath her back, hold her close to me, and then flip us over. Her knees immediately slide up next to my hips and she rises up on them as she pulls her t-shirt over her head.

"Holy fuck," is the only thing I can manage as I stare at her perfect breasts. "You want something real? If you walk out on me tomorrow, Sasha, I will never recover. That's something real."

"I've never been naked in front of a man before."

The change of subject is seamless. And it stuns me. "Never?"

"I have never let a man look at my body." And then she rolls on her back, balancing herself on top of my thighs, and slips my boxer briefs down her legs. She gives me the most perfect pussy shot in the history of lust.

"Jesus fucking Christ."

Before those words are out of my mouth, she's back on top—knees at my hips, pussy over my hard-on, and her breasts pushing into my chest. "Fuck tomorrow. I always thought that was my motto. But I'm a fraud, Jax. I've been afraid of tomorrow my whole life. And just once I'd really like to give tomorrow the finger and not think about the consequences."

"I am happy to help you flip off the future."

She laughs. "I'm serious."

"Me too."

"Then why are you still wearing pants?"

"Sasha—"

"Please," she begs. "Make it stop. Make this loneliness go away. I'm so fucking tired of being alone."

I pull my shirt over my head and toss it into the hazy darkness and she lifts up her hips to allow me to get out of my boxers. They go flying into the void with the shirt. "You're lying, right? About never being naked in front of a man?"

"I'm not. I spent every night I ever spent with a man trying my best to hide who I am. I never took off my clothes in the light because I thought they'd see through me." And then she reaches over to the bedside table and flips on the small lamp. She bares her body to me in the glow. And when I look up into her eyes I see nothing but fear.

"Come here," I whisper, wrapping my arms around her back and pulling her into my chest. "We don't need sex, Sasha. I'm not here to take advantage of your confusion."

"I do need it, Jax. I really, really do. And I need it with you. Because I believe you when you say I'm safe. And I've got to be honest, safe is something I've never felt before."

God, that is sad. "You're safe now. OK? And maybe you *should* say no tomorrow. You can say no and I'll still want you. I don't care about the job, Sasha. Really. I don't. I was so persistent because I thought I'd get to keep you around. I thought I'd get to see you every day. We might become friends. And then maybe more than friends."

Her chest hitches for a moment and there's a split second when I think she might cry. But she draws in a long breath of air and gets it under control. "I thought we were flipping tomorrow the finger?"

"We are," I say, rolling us over again. She lets out a small squeal and I take that as encouragement. I want her to be happy. I don't want her to feel used by me tonight. I don't want to take her. I want to feel her.

I inch my way down her body, kissing the soft skin of her breasts as I go. I squeeze the nipple of one and suck gently on the other. She moans and brings a leg up. Just the sensation of it brushing against mine is erotic.

"It's all about you right now, killer. All about you." I continue my journey south, my tongue dancing along her belly, then her hip. I nip her skin and she buckles her back, urging me to find my final destination. "Fuck, you're so goddamned sexy." My tongue flirts with the tip of her pussy, easily finding her sweet spot. I lick small circles around it and then nip the inside of her thigh.

"Keep going," she urges softly. Her fingers are threaded in my hair, grabbing tight fistfuls, like she's holding on for dear life. And then she pushes me into her folds, her hips doing a little dance along with my tongue.

I grab her clit gently between my lips and then suck. Not hard—she is far too soft to make this hard—but just enough. Just enough flicking of my tongue. Just enough movement of my lips. Just enough of my fingers reaching between her legs to find her opening before sliding in.

Everything tonight is just enough to make her come.

And she does. She contracts her muscles around my finger and she comes on my face with barely a whimper. But I know that giving herself to me like this is surrender. And letting me take control of her body this way is a gift.

"Fuck," she moans, once the contractions stop. I kiss her once more and then roll off to the side and scoot up to her face. Her eyes are closed, so I surprise her with a taste of herself. Never knowing what to expect from this woman, I have a moment of fear that she will push me off and call me disgusting.

But she doesn't.

She takes my offering and reaches down for my cock.

"We don't have to go any further," I whisper into her mouth.

"Yes," she says, opening her eyes, saying it back just as softly. Like we're keeping secrets. "We do." She climbs on top of me and holds my cock in her fist. Her hand is small, barely arching around my wide girth. And then she lifts up and flicks it across her wet opening before easing back down. She slumps towards me, resting her head on my shoulder like we are lovers.

I wrap my hands around her back and hold her tight as I sit up straight, leaning against the headboard. She moves her hips, rubbing herself with each back and forth motion.

I cup her face again and tilt her head towards me so I can kiss her. And then, just as she really begins to move, I grab her ass with one hand and place my finger over her lips one more time.

I fuck her mouth as she moves on my dick. Our motion is synchronized, like we've done this a million times before. Like we know all the small movements, all the tiny gestures that will make each other climax. The motion of her lips. The friction of our bodies. Her long hair gently caressing my chest.

We are love in slow motion. We move as one, leaving the darkness behind, where it belongs, and become the light.

This is the moment I realize we are in this together. No matter what it takes—I don't care what the sacrifice is—Sasha is mine. She deserves me. She deserves a man of truth. She deserves loyalty and love. She deserves to let her past go, embrace her present, and find her future. I will do whatever it takes to keep her safe so she can find that future, even if it means putting my own life on the line. I will die for her.

"I will die for you too," I moan as she sucks on my finger. Tasting herself. Embracing herself. What she was, who she is, and what she can be if given the chance to live out her destiny.

She pulls away and frowns down at me. "Please don't die, Jax." She says it with such emotion, I feel her sadness flow through me. "Please don't die. I won't be able to live if I lose another person in my life. I won't be able to go on. Promise me, Jax. Promise me you won't leave me. And promise me you won't kill Nick."

"Sasha…"

"I can't lose him, Jax. I know he's not the boy I thought I knew, but I can't lose him. I need to know he's alive. Even if it's in prison. Just the thought of him dying makes me want to shrivel up into a tiny ball of sadness."

Fuck. "I can try, OK?"

"No, Jax. I need you to promise that the only way you will kill him is if he's trying to kill you. Promise me that much, at least."

I stroke her hair and kiss her mouth, but she ducks away and hides her face in my neck. I give in. I can't help it. It's the mission objective anyway. Bring them in alive is always better than dead. "I promise, then. I promise. I will do anything to make you happy again."

She lets out a long breath, like she was holding it in until she got my answer. And even though every rational person on this planet understands that life and death don't obey the law of promises, she believes me. I know she believes me because we climax together. And once again I find myself coming inside her. I hold her close and moan into her neck as I fill her up in every way possible. I don't care one bit about the consequences. I don't care that I made her a promise that I can't keep or she accepted it on misplaced faith.

I do not care.

She is mine and I'm going to keep her forever.

CHAPTER TWENTY-FIVE

"Yeah," Jax growls into his cell phone. My eyes are refusing to open, even though I can tell by his ensuing silence something is wrong on the other end. "When?" More silence. "Where'd they take him?" He breathes out a long breath of air and I manage to open my eyes in time to watch him rub his hand down his face and swing his feet over the side of the bed so he can sit up. "I'll be there in two hours."

He doesn't turn to me, just puts his head in his hands and rests his elbows on his knees.

"You OK?" I ask.

"I don't know." No emotion in that statement. Just blank.

"You gotta leave?"

He finally turns a little to give me a sideways glance. "I do.

I know it's bad, Sasha. I know I should stay here with you. But I have to go."

"Should I go with you?"

He smiles then. Like big. And then he lies down and pulls me up to his chest. "God, I wish. See, if you take me up on that offer we could be partners. Wouldn't that be fun?"

I picture it in my head. "Am I Scully or Mulder?"

"Definitely Mulder," he says with a huff of laughter.

"I think so too. Can we look for aliens and take on weird X-Files cases?"

"For sure."

It's my turn to smile big. I think I might really like Jax. He's nice. "I'll think about it."

"Will you be OK here?"

"I'm OK everywhere, Jax. Don't worry about me."

He leans in and kisses me on the lips. It's a little kiss. Not meant to be spectacular. But for some reason it feels amazing. "I gotta go. That call was about my brother."

"Oh, did something bad happen?" Jesus, I hope not. I can tell his brother means everything to him.

"Very bad. Very, very fucking bad. But he's OK, so I can't ask for anything else without being selfish."

I prop myself up on my elbow. "Are you religious?"

"What?" He shoots me a confused look.

"Do you have guilt for wanting more out of life, even when you have plenty?"

"A bit."

"And you think asking for too much makes the bad luck come?"

"In a way, I guess. I just try to be grateful for the small things."

I lie back and think about that as Jax drags himself out of bed and starts to get dressed. "Do you think we bring our own bad luck? Or do you think sometimes our luck mingles with the luck of someone else, and gets tangled up in it?"

He's pulling up his pants when I ask this question, but he stops with his fingers on the zipper to look at me in the approaching dawn. "I never thought of it, I guess."

"What time is it?"

He points to the bedside clock. "Four-thirty. I don't know when I can come back, Sasha. It'll probably take me all day just to sort out what happened. So if you want to go home, it's only a two-hour drive. There's a car in the garage. The keys are in the kitchen drawer next to the fridge."

"Is someone coming to pick you up?"

"Yeah," he says, grabbing a white dress shirt from the closet and sliding his arms into the sleeves. "The jet. There's an airfield about a half a mile away. By the time I get over there, the jet should be landing."

He buttons his shirt and grabs a tie. I watch him as he dresses and feel... like I should not ask for too much more right now, either. If he's right, and we should be satisfied with the little things that makes us happy, then I'm way overdue for some bad luck. Because I really want more with this man.

"Next time," he says, leaning down to kiss me as he ties his tie, "I'll make you breakfast. I promise." Another kiss, this time with a little tongue, and then he's gone. Dashing down the hallway. A few seconds later the front door opens and closes.

And I'm alone.

WASTED LUST

I'm used to being alone. But now that I've had a taste of Jax, I don't like it.

I weigh my options. I could stay here. But I'm not sure I can stand looking at all those pictures of Nick all day. And what if Jax can't come back at all? What if his job just swoops him off to DC or something?

I could go home. But what's at home for me? An empty house? A non-existent career in academia?

Or… I could go to my real home. My mom and dad are gone. I know that. But Five said today is Sparrow's birthday and she was having a party. How hard could it be to find the party?

I don't want to be alone anymore.

I get up and go searching for my coat. My phone is in there. I have a moment of panic that I left it in whatever vehicle brought us here, but when I open the coat closet, there it is. My phone is even in the pocket, right where I left it.

Can Jax be any more perfect? It's like he thinks of everything. He's the guy who just takes care of shit. Like, I bet if he came into my house and saw the leaky faucet in the first-floor bathroom, he'd just fix it. Or if the car needed an oil change, he'd take it to get it done on his lunch break.

Jax is reliable.

I like reliable.

Plus he's hot.

I like hot too.

But right now I need to be grounded. I need to go home. So I search my contacts and find Harrison's name. I've called him dozens of times for the favor I'm going to ask for. But not since the abduction. I haven't gone anywhere since the abduction.

I press send and it rings. Just twice.

"Yeah," Harrison says, clearly asleep.

"I need a ride."

"Sasha," he growls at me. "It's three-thirty in the morning."

I say nothing. I know what time it is. And he's on Mountain time, so it's an hour earlier than here.

"Is it an emergency?" he asks.

"No. But I need to go home. Sparrow's having a birthday and I need to be there."

"She's not having a party at three-thirty."

"I know, but you hate last-minute trips. So I'm calling ahead."

He laughs. "Your idea of calling ahead kills me, kid."

"You love me though."

"I do. But not enough to come get you now. I'll be in Lawrence at—"

"No, I'm not in Lawrence. I'm in… hold on. Let me find my map app." I page through my phone until I get to the maps, and then open it up and zoom in. "I'm in a place called Falls City, Nebraska. And there's an airfield there. You know it?"

"I know it. Be there at noon your time, and not a minute earlier."

"I love you, Harrison."

"I know, kid."

And then I get the three beeps that say he's ended the call.

Harrison was the pilot we used to pull that last Company takedown. He's really a friend of James, but he always liked me better than James because James is a crazy asshole.

A lovable crazy asshole, though. I'd love to see him and Harper again. But they almost never leave the yacht they live on.

But seeing Rook and Veronica is just as good. Better, probably. I can talk men with them.

Jax is just as good a catch as their husbands. I bet they'd approve of him.

I set the alarm on my phone for ten AM, and then climb back in bed to daydream about Jax. I'd like to get to know him better. I don't know if I want to take that job he's offering, but he said he likes me either way. Maybe I don't need to work or go to school at all? Maybe I can sit around and be lazy and live off my money?

I don't have to decide now, though. So I drop it and drift off to sleep thinking I haven't felt this happy in years.

CHAPTER
TWENTY-SIX

"What are you doing?" Harrison asks as we settle into the short flight to Fort Collins.

"What do you mean?"

He shoots me a dubious look. "I'm not stupid. You call me when you need to get somewhere fast. So what's going on today?"

"Just Sparrow's birthday, that's all."

"You sure about that?"

"Jesus, Harrison. I'm not a kid anymore. I do grown-up stuff and I don't have to explain myself."

He sighs. "I know that. But I don't want you taking any risks."

I squint my eyes at him. "I swear to God, I'm just dropping by for a visit."

"So you want me to wait around and take you home?"

"Uh…"

"Or back to that town that is not your home?"

"No. OK, look. I'll tell you something, but don't tell anyone else. It's my thing and I'll deal with it, OK?"

He gives me a conspiratorial nod. "OK."

I take a deep breath and let it out with my words. "I got kicked out of grad school."

"What?"

"My mentor said I wasn't serious about anthropology as a career and I needed to take a sabbatical to think through my options."

"That's it?"

"What do you mean *that's it*?" I know what he means. This man has been with me through some pretty fucked-up Company plans. But I'm not about to tell him Nick is back or the FBI is asking me to join up with them. "That's a big deal, you know. I've been working my ass off for years for this and it all gets taken away in one afternoon."

"When did this happen?"

"Yesterday."

"Who lives in Falls City?"

"My boyfriend," I huff. "Any more questions?"

"Where is he now?" Harrison's squinting his eyes even more. He knows I'm hiding something, but what I'm saying makes sense, so what's he gonna do about it but ask more questions?

"He left for Denver last night. For business."

"So you're lonely."

"I guess. But more importantly, it's Sparrow's birthday."

"Hmph."

I win.

So I smile. But I look out the window as I do it so he'll stop with the interrogation. We talk about other stuff the rest of the ride and then when I'm on the ground and I figure I'm gonna get away with no more discussion, he gives it one more try.

"I'm serious about the ride home. If you need one, just call."

But I'm ready for it. "I'm gonna stay at home and think about my options. There's no reason to go so far away when all my family is here. But if I do, I will call, believe me. Driving home to Kansas is not my idea of fun."

"I'm gonna drive down to Boulder to visit my brother then, OK? I'll be here for the weekend if you need me."

He thinks I'm in trouble. And I might be, but I'm not sure yet. So I accept his offer of help with a kiss to the cheek and then exit the plane and make my way to the terminal.

The local airport is small, but they know me. I called ahead and asked them to find me a rental car, so it's ready for me when I get there.

Ten minutes later I'm on my way into town.

I check Spencer and Veronica's bike shop, Shrike Bikes, first. It's right in the small downtown, and I need to drive by it to get to Rook's or Veronica's house.

I hit the jackpot there, because there's balloons flying in bunches near the side door. I park the car next to Spencer's red truck with his shop logo on it, and as soon as I get out I hear the squealing of little girls coming from inside. Ronnie used to be a tattoo artist at her family shop a block down the street. But she retired after she got pregnant. Now she body-paints in the back of the bike shop.

I open the back door and there are kids running everywhere. It looks like tattooed princesses threw up in here. Five wasn't kidding when he said Sparrow was having a biker party. Every little girl is wearing those fake tattoo sleeves, jeans with tutus on them, and tiaras.

God. I have never seen anything so adorable in my whole life.

"Sasha!" Princess Rory squeals. "Look, Mommy! It's Sasha!"

Veronica stops painting a little girl's face and beams up at me. "Hey! I wasn't sure you'd come."

"Hey, Sasha," Rook says, her younger little girl, Starling, on her hip. She likes to name her girls after birds. "Wanna help me out for a second?" She holds Starling out to me.

"Sure," I say, taking the baby. "What's up, little cutie?" I ask as I nuzzle her nose. Her gummy smile brightens my whole life. I miss having babies around. Both Five and Kate were very small when I moved in with Ford and Ashleigh. Five was a newborn and Ashleigh was glad to have help since Kate had just turned one.

Rook goes off to help Sparrow open her presents, and I take my attention back to Ronnie. "When Five said Sparrow was having a biker theme, I thought he was kidding."

"Don't ask. But these girls are crazy for tattoos and bikes right now. I blame Spencer. He made mini-Shrike Trikes for them, and they think they're in a motorcycle club now."

"Oh my God. I might die."

"They want patches and leather jackets. And Rory asked me for Frye boots like mine."

I'm smiling so big as I picture this pack of princesses dressed up like Spencer. "Does their club have a name?"

Ronnie rolls her eyes. "Spencer calls them the Shrike Sisters."

"Damn, I miss all the good stuff living so far away. I should move home."

"Home?" Ronnie stops her face-painting and looks up at me. "What about school?"

"Oh, I don't know. Maybe I'm not cut out for school."

"No? Well, you should talk to Rook. Remember when she dropped out?"

"Yeah, and it all worked out for her. She won that indie film festival prize three times now."

"Yeah, so you know, if you want to dig dinosaur bones—"

"What if I don't want to dig dinosaur bones?"

"What?" Ronnie is really confused now. "But that's always been your dream."

"I know, but don't you think it's a little childish? I mean, what kind of job is that?"

"It's not a job, Sasha," she says, going back to her face-painting. "It's your passion."

"I guess."

She looks up at me again, her brush in mid-stroke, painting flames up the side of the little girl's cheek. "Unless you're just over it? Like me. I always wanted to be an artist. I used to think I was above tattoos and lament about how all I wanted was to be taken seriously as an artist. But you know what my passion is?"

"What?"

"Being a mom." She smiles down at the girl as she finishes her design. "OK, Jenny, you're done. Go watch Sparrow open presents." Little Jenny, who must be a new friend because I've never seen her before, jumps up and runs off squealing for the other girls to look at her face. "And don't touch it," Ronnie calls, "or you'll smear it all over!" She stands up and walks over to the sink to wash her hands. "Yeah, I wanted to be an artist, but this shit is just fun, Sasha. I mean it. This party is not even for my kid and I couldn't do enough to help Rook plan for it. I always wanted to be Spencer's wife, but I had no idea how much joy having his children would be."

"Wow."

"You're not like me though, I know that. So if you're thinking you'd like a different career, then go for it. You can change your mind any time you want, Sash. You're so young."

"I'm the same age you were when you got pregnant with Rory, though."

"So? You can't live your life on someone else's timeline. Find your passion, like I did. And then give it all you've got."

I nod, but then Rory and her three other girls are yelling for her to come watch as Sparrow opens her presents. Rook and Ronnie have been friends forever, it seems. They are raising their kids together as a team. Ashleigh too. But Ash and Ford are their own best friends. They mostly hang out together.

I want all of that. I want a guy like Ford and friends like Ash, and Rook, and Ronnie. And when I get out my checklist for happiness, I have none of those boxes ticked off.

I watch the presents being opened, then the singing, and the cake. But it's too much for me today. It's too much to sit here and take in all the things I don't have. It's heartbreaking to realize that I'm twenty-four years old and I have nothing to show for it but a long list of could've-beens and failures.

So I kiss all the Shrike Sisters, and hug their mommies, and get back in my crappy rental car so I can go spend the night alone at my parents' house.

I drive slow down Mountain Avenue and pull the car into the driveway. I cut the engine and sit there in silence for a few seconds, pondering what I should do next.

I have no school to go back to. I'm sleeping with an FBI agent who wants me to rewrite my life plan and join him in hunting the lingering Company assholes. And the man who broke his promise to me is back in the picture.

Crossroads.

I feel like a kid back out on the prairie waiting for James to come kill me or save me.

It was a toss-up. My future was up in the air and it could've gone either way. But it went this way.

So here I am. Alone, lonely, and wishing so bad I could do it all over again, it hurts my heart.

Because I fucked up. Somewhere along the way, I fucked up.

And even though Jax is fun and makes me forget all the mistakes I made, I want to remember. I want to remember every single one of them so I can set them right.

And there is only one person alive who can help me do that.

Nick.

CHAPTER
TWENTY-SEVEN

"**C**ome on in, Jake. Just sit down and relax."

My brother is... gone. This guy, I have no idea who he is. He makes his way across the safe house Max keeps in the Denver suburbs and collapses into a chair. He's been chain-smoking since I picked him up at the Federal Center.

I wish I could make it better but I don't have any words. So I just take a seat in the chair opposite him and lean back to wait him out.

He takes a long drag on his cigarette and blows the smoke into the room. It took me all day to secure his release and convince the entire fucking FBI satellite office that he is absolutely not under arrest. I don't care how many dead bodies they found in his apartment.

"I hate my life," he finally says after we've been sitting in the depressing room for ten minutes. "I hate my fucking life."

"I'm sorry, man. I am. I'm so fucking sorry I didn't answer when you called. I'm in the middle of recruiting this girl, Jake. She's Company, man. She's the Zero everyone was talking about years ago. I have her at the safe house in Nebraska."

"Fuck that girl." And then he drags his tired eyes up to mine and snarls, "Fuck you too."

"Look," I say, "I get it. You lost someone—"

His look alone is enough to cut me off. But he doesn't stop there. "Lost someone? That's what you're calling this? Did we just lose Michael when Nick Tate came into our house and shot him in the head?"

I have nothing for that. But I have to try. If I don't, he's gonna walk out of here and never talk to me again. And I can't let Nick Tate take away this brother too. He took Michael, he can't have Jake. "No," I say. "No. But listen to me, Jake. Everything we've been working for is in reach right now. I've got this girl ready to give up everything she knows."

"Bullshit," he says, looking up through the hair hanging across his face. "Bull-fucking-shit. If she's Company, she's the one playing *you*."

"You don't know her."

"I know her well enough to know she can lie. She can kill. How much more do I need to know?"

"She's not like that, man. I swear to God, we're so fucking close to the win. She was Nick Tate's promise."

These words finally get his full attention. "Bullshit."

I sigh and shrug my shoulders. "She was. And she was there

that night it all went down in Santa Barbara. The night Nick got away, he used her too, Jake. He used her to do his dirty work and then he left her behind. She's only twenty-four. She was only thirteen when that shit went down. And she's assimilated really well into post-Company life."

"There is no such thing and you know it." He takes another long drag on his cigarette and blows some rings out of habit. "You never walk away from the Company. Just look at Nick. That motherfucker has been running shit since the day he walked out. All they do is reorganize, Jax. That's all they do. We lost, man. We lost Michael and..."

He can't say the other names. There are too many dead friends from the first time we tried to infiltrate the Company back in Miami several years ago. That ended the same way. Him in custody and Max and me saving his ass. And I really don't want to play this card, especially after he lost two people last night. But I have no choice. "You made a deal with me, Jake. You made a deal and that's why you're not rotting in federal prison right now. So let's make a new deal."

"Fuck you," he yells, standing up. His fists and jaw are clenching in unison. "I gave up four fucking years of my life for what? Those people they arrested last night weren't Company. The whole thing was a bust. And I lost *again*." He stresses the word. Hard.

He knows I can't argue about that. He's the one who takes the fall. It's been that way since he made his choice to ditch the FBI and work alone. "It doesn't matter. You got a lot of bad people off the streets of Denver, brother. You did your job and now you're done."

"Yeah," he says, walking over to the terrace door and sliding it open. "I'm done." He turns back to me, the cold wind from outside blowing past his face and catching his hair. "I'm out of here. You can do whatever you want with that Company girl, but I'm officially retired. I want everything you promised back in that interrogation room. Everything. I want that kid I told you about who went missing four years ago and I want my name erased from all the police reports they're writing today. I'm not taking the fall for this, Jax. I won't do it."

"Hey, I said it's done. And it is. It might take time to get the kid—"

"Fuck you and your time." His eyes blaze as he walks back into the cold room. "And I want access to everything you took out of my apartment."

"That's FBI evidence, Jake. You know this."

He sweeps his arm across an end table and shit goes flying. A lamp crashes against the wall and shatters, a plant lands on the coffee table, the dirt spilling out all over it. "Get it back!" he roars. "Get it back or I will turn your ass in. I will tell them, Jax. I will tell them everything we've been doing. I'm not even fucking around."

I let out a long sigh. "I'll get it back. I will. But I have to work on this case. I have to get back to that girl in Nebraska. Like today. I can't leave her alone for too long."

"Put a babysitter on her."

"I will. I mean, I have. My street partner is watching her Kansas house right now, but my partner's not one of us, so she doesn't know about the Nebraska safe house. So if this girl walks out on me, there's no one there to follow her. It's a critical moment, Jake. Nick Tate is in the picture. He's probably making a move right now. So I need to get back to Nebraska and work this shit out."

Jake walks back to the chair, takes a seat, and pulls out another smoke. He draws in deep as he lights it, and then blows it out into the room already thick with haze. "I just lost everything."

"It wasn't yours to lose." It's a low blow, but someone's gotta say it, and since Max isn't here, I'm the only one who can.

"I don't know how to get past this, Jake. You have no idea what was happening in my life the past few months."

"I have some idea."

He shoots me a look.

"And I'm not judging, OK? I'm not. But do you really want to throw away twelve years of waiting and planning so you can mourn?" I wait for an answer but he stays silent. "Or do you want me to get the fuck out of here and go find Tate? Because this is the decision, Jake. Nick Tate's time is up. But that guy is like a cat. He's got spare lives tucked away in hell. So it's possible he gets to Sasha first and turns on the charm. We both know what an accomplished liar he was when we were kids. Just imagine how good he is at this game by now."

"Sasha?" he sneers. "You're on a first-name basis now?"

But I stay silent. He can't know how conflicted she makes me. He can't know.

Another drag, more smoke, and then finally a sigh that says I give up. "What do you want me to do?"

"Nothing."

He shoots me a sidelong look that says, *Try again.*

But I'm not lying. "You're done, brother. It's over. You're

free. Full pardon for all that shit that happened in Miami and no responsibility for what happened last night. I got the girl, she's gonna help me, we'll get Tate, and you just have to stay out of the way."

"I want to go talk to my boss in Denver, Jax. I need to talk to Ray and figure this shit out. I need to know what I should do next."

"No. No fucking way. The FBI is all over that motherfucker. You can leave town, hell, you can leave the country for all I care. But you're staying the fuck away from that case. You do not talk to anyone about anything we had going. You don't know that those guys last night weren't Company. You have no clue. So we're handing it over to FBI, I'm going back to get Sasha so she can tell me where I can find Nick, and you're gonna..."

He shakes his head. "I'm gonna what?"

"Recover. You just go recover."

"Get over it, then?"

"Dude, I get it. You lost your friends—"

"I lost two fucking *lovers*!" He yells it. His words echo off the high ceilings. But at least he finally admitted it. "I want Nick Tate *dead*. Do you understand me? I know he's behind this. I know he's pulling all the strings like some kind of twisted puppetmaster. He just took everything from me, Jax. Everything. And he's gonna take everything from you next."

Fuck. Up until yesterday I didn't have much left for him to take. But now I have Sasha. And like it or not, she's officially his. So this threat from my brother hits me hard. A lot harder than he knows. But I have to keep him contained. I have to keep Jake out of this or he might lose his shit and start killing people. This whole case might end up like Miami.

So I keep my calm. I keep my fear for Sasha tucked away. And I give him good, solid, rational advice. "I know. I get it. But we took an oath to Max Barlow and that oath said we're professionals, Jake. So you have to be a professional this time. Leave town. Spend money. Be patient. And I promise you, I will get enough revenge for both of us. I swear on Michael's life."

Jake scrubs his hands down his face and breathes deep as he considers my offer. "I trust you, Jax," he finally says. "I do. So I'll wait it out." He takes his hands away from his face, revealing bloodshot eyes filled with pain and heartbreak. "I know you'll make it right. You have to make it right."

I swallow hard and nod my head. "I will." I stare him in the eyes and say it again, and again, and again until he believes me. "I will. I will. I will."

Now I have two promises—kill Nick for Jake and keep him alive for Sasha.

The only question left is… which of them do I keep?

CHAPTER
TWENTY-EIGHT

My parents' house is dark and empty, but it feels light and full the second I walk through the door. It's weird to be greeted by silence, since we've had at least three German shepherds in this house since I came to live with them. But my dad takes them with the family on long trips. The cats stay with the neighbors since they don't care for nineteen hours of flying across the world.

I head to the kitchen and drop my keys on the table, and then continue into the family room and flip on the TV. The couch is old and comfy, so I flop down and slide the spare laptop out of the drawer in the coffee table. Ash and Kate use this one when they feel like going online. Ford and Five have an entire room devoted to computers upstairs. But I don't have the code for the security lock on that door.

I only need to check my email, anyway. So it's not like I'd ever need it.

I flip through the channels until I find something mindless to watch, and then open my email.

Fuck. Seventy-two emails in two days.

I scan down the list to see if any of them need to be opened and sure enough, there's one from Professor Brown. I feel sick just looking at her name. But she might be kicking me off the email server altogether, since they won't let you have a university email if you leave school.

I open it and take a deep breath.

Dear Sasha,

> *I wanted to make sure you understood exactly what I was saying yesterday. I went up to your office to see if you had any questions and found your desk cleared out. Does this mean you've made a decision to leave school? Or, as I fear might be the case, you think I kicked you out of school during our talk?*
> *I hope you don't think that. It was not what I was saying at all. I love having you as my student. I think you are bright and motivated. I'd be proud for your future research to be a reflection on my career.*
> *If you truly do not want to continue to study under my guidance, I will understand and I will wish you good luck and happiness. But if you misunderstood me and packed your office up on the assumption I was kicking you out—please, please reconsider. Come talk to me*

when you have time. I'll be in my office for a few more days finishing up grades.

Your friend and mentor,
Dr. Janet Brown

Holy shit. I am a total idiot. I stare at the screen for like five minutes. I'm not kicked out!

"Woohoo!" I jump up and do a little dance. "She believes in me!"

Oh my God, I am so happy. And to think I was depressed all day yesterday thinking I was a total failure. I look around, wondering who I should tell my good news to. But I never mentioned it to my parents and Ronnie and Rook will still be pretty busy with the birthday party.

So hmmm. I had a crisis and victory and I have no one to share it with. That sorta sucks. I guess being anti-social and having no friends is only fun when you're a failure and don't want to share news. But success, that's a good time to have friends.

And I have none. Boo.

I could try Jax. That makes me smile.

But then he would start in on me about that FBI job. And I really don't want to think about that right now. I'm not sure I want to be an FBI agent. I spent the last ten years trying to get away from a life like that. What possible reason could I have to go back into it working for the other side?

Nope. Jax doesn't need to know. I'll just check the rest of my email, then call for pizza delivery. My mood has done a one-eighty in five minutes and I'm starving.

I go back to perusing my email and then gasp out loud when I see one a few lines down from Professor Brown's.

It's addressed to Smurf.

"No," I say, shaking my head. "It can't be him. Not now. Not when my life just got back on track." It could be James, he's the one who gave me that name. But James does not email. And Merc wouldn't address it to Smurf. He calls me Sash.

I know before I click the screen who this is, but the face in the video message brings it home. He's wearing a gray hoodie with a black beanie covering up his golden hair. The chain tattoo around his neck peeks out from the collar of a black thermal shirt. The video message that starts playing as soon as the page is displayed makes my heart stop.

"Got you," is all he says. Five seconds long.

But it's not *what* he says that's disturbing.

I press replay and it starts again.

"Got you."

Replay.

"Got you."

He's holding a cell phone up to the computer monitor as he says the words, *Got you*. But the disturbing part is the barely audible sound of a camera shutter just before he speaks.

Got you.

My stomach starts to churn as things become clear. He's taking a picture... not of the computer monitor, but of me. My face is being displayed on his computer monitor.

I slap the laptop closed.

What the actual fuck?

I swallow hard and try to keep my cool, and then I open it

back up so I can see when the email was sent. Yesterday afternoon. Before I even got home from school. He hacked into my webcam at home and then waited until he saw me on his screen—when was the last time I used my computer? Two days ago.

My phone rings in my purse. "Ahhhh!" I scream, my hand over my heart. "Jesus Christ, Sasha. Calm the fuck down!"

I get up and walk slowly to the kitchen table, but the phone never rings again. Instead I get a voicemail alert.

This is it. He's back. He's made contact and he's gonna—

Another alert. This time it's a text. I fish my phone out of my purse and read the message flashing across the home screen.

Come outside.

CHAPTER TWENTY-NINE

I can't see anything through the peephole, so I stand there for several seconds debating internally. What if it's not Nick? What if it *is* Nick? Am I ready to see him again? What does he want?

I hear Merc's voice in my head. *Just open the door, you little brat. You're a trained killer. They are more afraid of you than you are of them.*

Which is most likely true in this case. I'm not afraid of Nick. He would never hurt me. So I punch in the security code and swing the door open.

"Took you long enough."

A hooded figure is sitting on the second stair of the front porch. His hands are stretched out behind him, palms down, and his legs are kicked out in front. He hasn't got a care in the world, that pose says.

I take a deep breath and let it out. "I'm mad at you."

"I know."

"Why are you here?"

He turns his head a little and I catch a bit of his face under that hood in the lights coming from City Park across Mountain Avenue. We are at the end of a cul-de-sac, so there are no cars, and the park is empty in the winter, so it's just us. "I was in the neighborhood."

I smile, recalling our first conversation at the antiques mall in Cheyenne back when we were still kids. I asked him what he was doing in Cheyenne all dressed up like a surfer.

"It's a nice neighborhood," I reply, changing the answer from the past when I told him he could do better.

"You deserve it, Sash. You really do." He pats a hand on the stoop and says, "Come sit next to me. Let's catch up."

I reach back inside and grab my coat off the hook near the door, then shrug it on before slowly walking towards the steps. My heart is beating so fast, I put one hand over it and feel the thumping. I take a deep breath when I get to the steps and then sit down. "I missed you."

He turns to me, fully illuminated now. And none of the photographs back at that safe house can prepare me for what I see.

The scar on his cheek that looked small and superficial is... not. It's thick and speaks volumes about the life he's been leading. The tattoos on his neck are so realistic, I have to take a second look to make sure the chains are not real.

"Nick."

He looks me in the eyes, his brown ones meeting my blue ones, then shakes his head. "No. Nick's been gone a long, long time. They call me Santino now." He talks with an accent and that kills me almost as much as the scar. "How have you been?" He manages a smile, but I can tell it's forced.

"OK." I search his eyes for a moment, but then he turns his head and he's hidden in the shadows of the hoodie again. "I want to know how you are too—but I'm afraid to ask."

"You don't want to know." It's not sarcasm. It's truth. He doesn't want to talk about his life because he's got nothing good to say about it. I put a hand on his shoulder and he reaches up and gives it a squeeze. "I loved you. I just needed to tell you that. I've been practicing this speech for ten years and I had so much planned. But"—he sighs—"the only thing that matters is that I loved you."

I feel the tears, but I've locked them away for so long, I squeeze them back out of habit. "I would've gone with you, ya know."

"I know. That's why I was mean to you that night. I knew you'd do anything to stay with me and it was wrong, Sasha. I'm not sorry for the way it ended between us that night." He stops to swallow down his sadness and then he turns his head again and looks me straight on. "I'm not sorry. You'd have grown up in hell if you came with me."

"You planned it, didn't you? You always knew I'd go to Matias for help."

"I knew." He smiles at me then and I find the old Nick in that grin. It comes back easy. I see him as a teenager when we first met. How golden he looked to me. Like a movie star. And his life was something out of a movie too. The good kind. The kind where rich kids live on superyachts and play in paradise growing up. "Your father gave you an exit strategy."

"My father?"

"Yeah. When I used to come see you guys in Cheyenne, he told me about Matias. He told me all the secrets he gave you. And when I left you at that hotel and told you I'd be back, I lied."

"I know."

"No, I mean I lied about everything. I was never coming back. But I knew you'd never let me go. I used you to bring Matias because I had to go find Harper and I didn't have time to set it up myself."

"How could you know it would all work out that way? I mean, was I that stupid and transparent?"

"So fucking transparent." And then he laughs and so do I. "I had you pegged as a sappy romantic from the first second I saw you. And you know what?"

I smile at his laugh. "What?"

"I knew back then that you believed in that promise. I knew you were the only person on this whole fucking planet who would go the end of the earth to save me."

Oh, God. I bite those tears back again. "I would," I squeak out. "And I did my best, Nick. I really did."

He puts his arm around me and pulls me close. He smells different now. I used to think he smelled like the beach, but now he smells like the cold. "I know you did." And then he laughs again. "You're fucking spectacular, you know that?" He turns his head and his hand slips behind my neck to pull me closer to him.

He's about to kiss me, but I turn away. "Sorry," he whispers. "I can't help myself."

I rest my head on his shoulder and lean in. God, how many years have I wished for this moment? How many ways did I imagine him as he professed his love to me? And now I don't want it.

"Are you in love with him?"

I know he's talking about Jax. I'm not sure how Nick knows we've been seeing each other, but I know that's who he's talking about. "I'm not sure what love is."

"You like him, though?"

"I do. He's so nice. He's one of those guys who holds doors for old ladies. And every time I find myself stuck in the rain, he's got an umbrella over my head."

"You deserve nice."

"Do you know him?"

"Yeah."

"Did you kill his little brother?"

"Yeah."

"Was it an order?"

"It was." And then he hugs me harder. "But it's no excuse."

"I killed people too, Nick. We didn't have a choice. We had to back then."

"I still have to now, Sasha."

I let out a long sigh. "I know. But you're not gonna kill Jax, right?"

"No. He's not on my list."

My back stiffens at the mention of a list.

"Don't ask me if you're on the list, Sash. Because if you do, my heart will break completely in half."

I want to hug him so hard right now. I know the pain and desperation I feel inside myself, and when I'm close to him like this, I think I can feel his too. We are promised. No matter how it turned out, we are promised. Nick may not be my soulmate, but he's part of my soul. "I know you'd never hurt me."

"I hurt you so bad back then. I hurt you so bad I wanted to cry when I watched you disappear on that boat."

I want to cry right now just picturing him fading into the foggy night. But once I start, I will never stop. I can't let this be the night I fall to pieces. I'm not ready yet. "I went to the hotel room and waited for you. I waited until those two weeks you paid for were up and James made me leave."

"I figured you would. That's just the kind of girl you are. Loyal to the end."

We sit in silence for a few minutes after that.

"So," he says after the quiet goes on too long. "What did you think of your aunt?"

"You know I went to see her?"

"Did you like her?" he asks, ignoring my question.

"Not really. The whole place seems weird. Too... I dunno how to explain it."

"Too Company?"

"Yeah," I say. "That's how it looked. Secret shit and big houses and some guy named Julian attacked me."

"He's her... James, I guess."

"A killer?"

"Yeah. Did you kick his ass?"

I laugh. "What do you think?"

"I heard you did."

"From who?" His knowledge is bugging me. "How do you know all this?"

"I have rats too."

My back straightens again. *Rats.* That's the word Jax used to describe what his father does in the FBI. He runs the rats.

"Julian, the priest," Nick says with an air of contempt. "They run a school, Sasha. Or they did until I got here and put a stop to it. A school for girls. Julian was in charge of it."

"Who would send their children to a school with that creep running it?"

"Who do you think?"

I close my eyes. "No. No. Please." I let out a laugh that is so far from laughter, it strikes fear into my heart. "No. They aren't allowed to do that shit, Nick." I look him in the eyes as the pieces start to fit together. "You—"

"Don't get paranoid on me, Sasha. It's my job to know what they're doing. I'm still the Admiral's son, after all. Did she tell you some story about the Zeros?"

My chest hurts. I might be having a heart attack.

"Sasha," he says, turning his body so he can face me full on. His scarred face is hard for me to look at, but I force myself. He deserves to be seen. He earned it. I owe him. "That program they had to raise Zeros, it's all true. You were one of the first, but there were more. Michael, the foster kid Jax loved so much. He was one of them too. Your father—"

"No."

"Yes, Sasha. Your father was in on it with your aunt. They started that program but they never had a boy who didn't go crazy. And all they had to do was look at James to see what the future of that program would bring. He was, I guess, the pilot kid. The one they tried everything out on first. Including his capture and imprisonment in Honduras back when he was sixteen. But the girls were different. They were trainable, but they didn't snap like the boys. They've been breeding them for more than twenty years now."

Breeding them? That's how they think of us? *Offspring*? What the fuck is wrong with people? How do you do that to your kid?

"She said you were one too, ya know."

"I was Number Eleven, Sash. You know that. You were always a Zero. Harper, she was a Zero, but my father set her up to fail on purpose. And I helped him. There was no way we were giving Harper up to that sick program."

"But your father, the Admiral, he was a bad guy."

He looks at me sideways, one eye peeking out from his hoodie. "We're all bad guys, remember?"

"We can't all be bad, Nick. Someone has to be good. The whole world isn't bad. I mean, I get it, there's shades of gray and all that good shit. But seriously, I need to believe in something right now. I have no idea what's happening. And then you show up and spill this shit on me. I can't take it anymore, Nick. I swear to God, I want to scream, that's how confusing this is."

"Whatever Madeline told you, she lied. She's gonna use you, Sasha. To train more Zeros. She's gonna use you to bring the Company back to life, only this time she'll be in charge. Matias is the *de facto* leader at this moment because I made that deal with him back in Santa Barbara. It was planned that way, Sasha. I've been plotting this moment for more than a decade. But he's meeting with Madeline tonight at that estate. They are forging a new relationship—"

"Matias is Company?" Jax was right. How many other things was he right about?

"Why do you think he let me live?" Nick grabs my hand and squeezes hard. "Think, Sasha. Why me? Why did he want me?"

"You're a killer? He needed you?"

"Why did he need me?"

I know where he's going with this line of questioning, but I can't bring myself to say it. Because if I do, then I have to admit that my life was planned for me as well. That I am just a pawn in a game. I am offspring.

"I'm the Admiral's son. I'm the next in line. I'm the only thing left of the Company leadership."

"You're not still Company. You left. We *all* left. That was the whole fucking point of killing all those people ten years ago. We set the kids free—"

"I am the Company heir, Sasha." He says it hard. In a way that leaves me no doubt that everything Jax said about him was true. "And the kids aren't free. Just ask Sydney if the kids are free. Ask her about the kids she found two years ago. It's bullshit what we did. The Company never died, it just went underground and regrouped with me as their promise for a new future. I did a lot of shit down in Central America, Sasha. With kids, the new Zeros—"

"Those kids on your back, that tattoo…"

"I make Zeros down in Honduras. That's my job. I've been doing it for years. But in order to keep them from succeeding, I have to fuck it all up. I set them up to fail." He grabs me by the shoulders and squeezes so hard I wince. His eyes dart back and forth, looking into each of mine like he's desperate for me to see what's happening. But I'm not sure I want to know these things. "I kill them," he says in a flat voice. "I save them by killing them. I am responsible for the death of every single one. I kill. That's my only purpose. And I'm not sorry about any of it. Every death was a sacrifice that needed to be made."

I feel vomit coming up in my throat.

"And the only reason I came back tonight was to tell you the truth about me."

"Why?" I'm so angry. "Why do I need to know? Why now? Why not just leave me alone? You're the one who told me to move on, love someone else, live a normal life. So I did. I did my best, Nick. And now you're back, fucking it all up! If you hadn't started looking for me, I'd still be in school. Jax would've never found me. I'd be safe and living my stupid life as a PhD wannabe."

"I only came back to make sure you understood. I can't do this anymore, and I need you to understand."

"Understand *what*?" I want to scream so bad.

He cups my face in both of his hands and forces me to look him in the eyes. "That you're the only one I can trust. So when the time comes, all I'm asking is that you do your job."

And then he stands up and walks down the stairs.

"Hey!" I yell after him. "Where do you think you're going? You don't get to show up here and fill my head with all this shit and just leave!"

But he keeps walking and then gets into some stupid little car parked on the other side of the street. I run after him, but his door is closed and the engine is already running before I get there. I pound on the window, but he puts the car in gear and drives off.

"Motherfucker!" I yell. Dogs start barking down the street and then a porch light goes on. I back away, all the way to the sidewalk in front of my house. Afraid that the neighbors will come out and ask me what's wrong.

And I can't even begin to explain.

I can't.

Because this is history repeating. Nick came, he wrecked me, and he walked out.

Again.

CHAPTER THIRTY

My phone is ringing when I walk back inside. I pick it up, read the number that says Unknown Caller, and tab accept on the home screen. "Yeah."

"Sasha," Jax says, sounding a little breathless on the other end of the phone.

"Jax," I breathe. And then I cannot say anything else. My throat closes up with my desire to cry. I want to cry my heart out.

"Sasha? Are you OK? I've been calling for like ten minutes. I called the safe house landline, but you didn't pick up. And Madrid said you never went home."

I gasp in some air.

"Sasha? Sasha? Where are you?"

"Ford's house," I choke out.

"Are you OK?"

I shake my head no as I sniff away the building tears. But I say, "Yes," because that's all I know how to do. I only know how to be OK because if the day ever comes when I'm not OK, I will die. I know it. I will drop dead on the spot from loss, and pain, and fear. And there won't be some promise of salvation on the other side either. It can't be that simple. It. Can't. Be. That simple.

Because if we get salvation after we're dead, then what's the purpose of living?

"Sasha, stay where you are. I'm forty-five minutes away."

If we can't find salvation in life, then why should we be rewarded in death?

"Do you hear me?"

"I'm dying, Jax."

"What? Sasha?"

"We're all dying. Me, Nick, James, Harper. There's no saving us. Ever. Because those people will never let us go. And it's not fair. OK? I never asked to be born. It's not fucking fair!"

"Are you inside?"

"Yes," I sniffle out. And then I realize there's a tear streaming down my cheek. "Oh, God," I sob, drawing in a hitched breath. "I'm dead."

And then I end the call, throw the phone down on the couch as I run past, and take the stairs two at a time as I race to the bathroom. I turn the shower on and step inside fully dressed. I wash away those tears under the cold water as I hug my body.

Make them go away, I say to myself over and over. *Make them go away.*

My teeth start chattering and before I know it, my whole

body is shaking. I slump to the bottom of the shower and pull my knees up to my chest.

It's over.

I can feel it. Everything that's happened in the past two days feels like the trumpets of Revelation for Sasha Cherlin. My life is over and I failed. Because no matter how hard I try, no matter how fast I run, how many times I change my name, or how many degrees I get to make myself legitimate… I still belong to *them*.

I am property.

CHAPTER THIRTY-ONE

Ford Aston's front door is unlocked, and knowing that Sasha learned everything he knows about security, this concerns me.

"Sasha?" I call out as I enter. "Sasha?" I have a very bad feeling as I move through the front room and into the kitchen. She sounded very distressed on the phone. "Sasha?" I ask again, making my way towards the back of the house. I stop at the bottom of the stairs and listen as I identify the sound of water coming from upstairs. I take the stairs quietly, not sure what to expect.

The bathroom door is open, and for a moment I come to terms with the worst-case scenario.

She killed herself.

No, my rational mind says. Sasha is not a girl who gives up. She's a fighter. If she wanted to kill herself, she'd throw herself in front of a bullet to save someone else. She would not slit her wrists in a bathroom.

But that fear takes over again as I approach the shower. She's fully dressed in clothes I recognize as my own, slumped on the tiled floor.

"Sasha," I whisper.

Her head raises, just enough for her thundercloud eyes to peer up at me through her wet and stringy hair.

"Sasha," I say, opening the glass door and reaching for her. The water is freezing cold, and when I touch her arm, it's ice.

She tilts her head all the way up to me and whispers, "I already died, Jax. I can't stop crying. I can't stop crying and it scares me."

I pull her up out of the puddle of water on the floor. She doesn't resist, but she doesn't help much either. "Come here," I say, lifting her off her feet and cradling her in my arms. "Let's get you out of these clothes."

She buries her head in my chest and the sobs start. Long, hitching breaths of sadness.

"It's OK, killer. You can cry if you want." I need to know what happened, but she needs me to take care of her first. So I carry her into the hallway and she points to a room.

I take her in there and stand her up in the center of a black rug that covers most of the dark hardwood floor. It's her childhood room, I realize, and just the fact that I have an opportunity to get a little glimpse of this part of her life makes things just a little better. "Lift your arms," I say as I tug her wet shirt off. I have her lift each leg so I can take off her shoes, and then I tug the wet sweatpants over her hips.

She stands there in the black boxer briefs I gave her last night, shivering uncontrollably. "He left me, Jax." Her teeth chatter to the rhythm of her shaking body. "He left me."

"Shhh," I say. "We're not talking about anyone else but us right now." I reach behind my head and take off my shirt, throwing it on the floor. And then I kick my shoes off and drop my pants.

I stand there in my black boxer briefs and we stare at each other. Not at our bodies. We look each other in the eyes.

And then I hold out my arms. "Come here," I whisper. "Come here and I'll warm you up." She takes a step forward and crumples into my arms, sobbing hysterically. "It's OK, Sasha. It's OK. You're always safe with me, remember?"

She nods into my chest.

"But you're cold. So let's get you a hot shower this time, warm up, and rest for a little bit. The world can wait until we're done." I lead her back into the bathroom and then turn the water on hot, checking the temperature until it's warm enough to motion for her to get in.

She takes off her underwear, and steps under the spray of water. I watch as she goes through the motions and when she's done I turn the water off and hold up a towel for her.

We go back into her bedroom and she shuffles through some drawers until she comes up with night clothes and then I lead her over to the modern low-profile bed and pull back the black down-filled comforter. She climbs in without me asking and then I lie down next to her, pulling her into my arms. "Just relax." I stroke her wet hair, then her cheek. "Just relax. You're not dead and you're not dying. I'm here now, and there's no way I'm gonna let you drown yourself in tears."

She nestles her face into my neck and lets off a long gasping sigh. But her crying slows, and after several minutes, her breathing evens out.

I just hold her as she drifts off, thinking about what she said on the phone. She's right. It's not fair. Nothing about her life has been fair. She was born into the very definition of unfair. Lost her whole family as a child. Lost the one man she thought was gonna be with her forever. And then she lost herself to the new family that took her in.

There is no doubt in my mind that Ford was the answer to all her problems back then. But when you have to pretend to be someone else for ten years, there's no way that doesn't have consequences.

"I have never needed saving."

"You're silly, Sasha Aston. You have always needed saving. And I'm here now. So it's OK to admit it."

She starts crying again. Harder than before.

"Shhh." I pet her hair. "Please don't," I whisper. "Please don't cry because I want to help you."

"I can't take it anymore, Jax." She shakes her head against my chest. "I can't do it anymore. I just want it to be over so fucking bad. For ten years I've tried to convince myself that we won. But we didn't. We didn't do anything but change the game."

"That's not so bad, you know. It's better than giving up and doing nothing."

"It feels like nothing. Every moment of struggle feels worthless right now. I just want to curl up and give in."

God, she is so sad. I can't stand it. "Give in to me, then," I say. "It's the only answer I have right now. Just let me take care of you and I promise, I can help you. I will be your friend. Like those other friends you have, Sasha. I will die for you too. Just trust me. Give me that and I'll do everything in my power to make it end."

She pulls away from me, her chest and head back, trying to see my face. She sniffles, and then she reaches up and touches my face with her fingertips. "I'm falling for you, Agent Jax. I'm falling for you and your promise. And that scares me. Because every time I find something good in this world—Nick, or James and Harper, or even Merc—they take them away."

"No, they're still here."

But she shakes her head. "James and Harper have been running for ten years. They can't even come visit us here because of Kate. My little sister Kate is half Company kid, Jax. And James was afraid if he came around to watch his niece grow up, they'd find out about her and kill her."

Fuck. I didn't know about the little sister. Why the fuck didn't I know?

"And Sydney keeps Merc away. If he comes around too much, she might lead them to us both. So even though they all get each other, I am left with no one who understands the fear I live with every single day. My secret is out. And that means my days are numbered. They're gonna come get me, so if I trust you and your promise, you'll break it. They'll make you break it. They'll kill you to get to me, and I'll still be here. That's my curse. I'm a survivor, remember? I'm a survivor. But it's no fun being the only survivor, Jax. It's no fun being the only one left."

I place my hand on her cheek, mimicking her tender gesture.

"I won't let that happen, Sasha. I won't."

"I went to a little girl's birthday party today. Sparrow, her name is. She's the daughter of one of my mom's best friends. And they all had babies together, ya know? Like best friends do when they all get married. And it hit me while I was watching all those little precious girls play and laugh and have a good time. It hit me that I will never get that opportunity. I will never have children, Jax. Because every child who comes from my bloodline will be Company property."

"Sasha…" But she's right. She can't escape her fate. She is who she is.

"I can't bring a girl into this world and risk them being stolen away and turned into me, or Harper, or God forbid, Sydney. And I can't have a baby boy without wondering if they will make him crazy like James or Nick.

"My mom has no idea what they really do. She didn't listen to Sydney tell her story from beginning to end, like I did. They treated her like an animal. Trained her like the dogs my dad keeps for protection. Only our dogs are family members. They are loved. Sydney's humanity was… discarded. She went crazy and lost touch with reality. She tried to kill me and Merc. Two years ago I was abducted by her handler. He poisoned me with drugs and almost—"

Her words drop off, and my rage builds as the understanding of what he almost did sinks in.

"When Sydney was being controlled, she held a gun to my head and threatened to kill me if Merc didn't drop his rifle." Sasha looks at me and shakes her head. "And he did, Jax. He dropped that rifle without a second thought about what would happen to him. And maybe the Company didn't succeed with me. But they have so many opportunities. Because when people fall in love, they want to express that love by having children. The Company will never run out of opportunities, Jax, because people will never stop falling in love."

"We can't let them win, Sasha. We can't."

"They've already won. You remember when I came home early from my trip to Peru last summer? And you thought I was seeing Nick?"

"Yeah," I whisper.

"I wasn't seeing Nick, Jax. I was setting up a safe house of my own. Only not for me. For Company girls. I have a house in Golden, Colorado. Up near my old school. And I have it stocked and ready. I even have a girl who lives there full time. Her sole purpose is to take care of these girls we find."

"Oh, God. I'm so sorry for accusing—"

But she stops my words with a shake of her head. "No, you don't understand. We have the house, the supplies, everything. But we have *no girls*. We can't even find them. We have no idea where to start looking. And it's like fate is spitting in my face, Jax. It's telling me to give up. Because I can't ever succeed. I can try and try and try. I have millions of dollars from when we stole the Company's money and all I want to do with my life is help those Company girls. Harper and Sydney and I talked about it once. We said we'd never let it happen again. That we'd find a way. So I set up that safe house. But none of that matters in the end, because I have no idea where to find the girls. They are everywhere, I know that. And that's so much worse. Because they're nowhere at the same time. I'm a total failure. I'm a fraud.

I'm a killer masquerading as an academic. Hiding behind a new name and a new life. But none of it is real. Sasha Aston isn't real. Only Sasha Cherlin exists. And she's dead, Jax. She's a ghost. So what's left for me?"

I lean down slowly and cover her lips with mine. I kiss her and she tastes like tears. It hurts my heart when her sadness melts into my mouth. And then I pull back and whisper, "Me, Sasha. I'm what's left. I'm here. I'm not going anywhere. I will keep my promise. And your aunt—"

"She's one of them, Jax. Nick came here today. That's why I didn't answer my phone. I was outside with him. And he said she's bad. I felt it as soon as I met her. She's bad. They keep kids too—"

"It's not the same, Sasha. Nick doesn't know what she's been doing."

"You're wrong. Nick knows everything. He always has. Nick pulls strings and makes mountains move, Jax. He's the leader of the Company now. He said so himself. And I know you want revenge for your brother, but I want him alive, Jax. If you want to save me, then you have to let me save him."

"Fuck that," I say. "Fuck that. You don't need him to save yourself, killer. Because you have me now. So fuck him. Just fuck—"

She puts her fingertips over my lips and says, "Shhh. I have this moment with you. And if there's one thing I've learned, it's to take your moments as they come." Her hand slips down to my shoulder and then her mouth is on my neck. Her soft kiss sends a shiver of pleasure up my spine. "Love me, Jax. If you really want to save me, then love me. Make our moment count."

CHAPTER THIRTY-TWO

"I need more, Sasha. I need more from you than begging. I need some truth."

I kiss his neck again, moving up, gripping his hair. "I'll tell you anything you want to know about it, Jax." I breathe those words into his ear. "Just ask." He slides his fingers into my hair and pulls my face into him. I inhale his scent. He smells like freedom, and truth, and the rain.

"Why did Nick risk everything?" I bow my head, but Jax tips my chin up to make me face him. "Just tell me why, Sasha. Why a man like that would leave the gangs and come back to America just to have a few words with you."

"He needs me," I say.

But Jax is shaking his head. "No, that's not why."

"I have secrets, and skills, and these are all things—"

"No, Sasha." he says firmly. "That's not why. Tell me why he came back."

I can only shrug my shoulders. "I don't know. I don't know. He's done some bad things. He left me and he has regrets. He wants to be forgiven."

"That's not why." Jax's mouth is in a severe frown. "Can't you say it? Or can't you believe it?"

"I don't understand, Jax. Just tell me what you want—"

"To hear? Is that what you think this is about? Telling me what I want to hear?" He closes his eyes and sighs. And then his hand drops from my face and finds the dip of the muscle of my upper arm. He caresses my skin for a few seconds before nipping my shoulder.

I inhale sharply, the slight pinch catching me off guard.

"You're real," he says, inching his body down. His lips find the center of my breast, and then he nips again. This time I'm ready for it, but my back arches because it feels so good. "You're real," he repeats.

He turns me so I'm flat on my back and takes my hands in his, entwining our fingers together. And then he lifts them above my head and holds them on the pillow for a moment, so he can look into my eyes. His face dips down to mine. "You're real," he breathes into my mouth. "Say it back, Sasha."

"I'm real," I mouth back, almost no sound escaping.

He lets go of my hands. "Trust me now."

"I do," I say, closing my eyes.

He sits up, straddling my hips, the muscles of his legs pressing against my outer thighs. And then he leans down and kisses my stomach. The soft pecks turn into little nibbles and then he sweeps his tongue straight down between my legs, licking the fabric of my panties. "Why am I here, Sasha?"

"You want me," I answer, filled with sadness and longing.

"No," he says. I open my eyes and find him looking up at me from his position over my stomach. His blue eyes are bright from the dim light of the clock on my beside table. "I already have you. Tell me why I'm here."

"You need me."

He lets out a soft puff of air in a laugh that floats across my skin and gives me a shiver. "I do need you, but not how you think. Now stop being tough for a minute and think, killer." He licks my belly button and then bites the tender skin that surrounds it. I let out a little gasp at the new pinch. "Just tell me why I'm here. I promise, you will feel nothing but relief after."

I shake my head at him. "I don't even know you."

"And yet here we are."

"I just met you."

"We've been together twice already. And both times it was your idea."

"I don't know why I did that—"

"Don't," he says, reaching up to squeeze my breast with one hand.

I whimper a little, but not because of the pain. At least not the pain from his hand. The pain of what he's asking me to say.

"Don't do that. Don't run anymore. Just stay here with me. You're safe. I told you that. Every word you say. Every feeling you accept. Every fear you let go. You're gonna be safe with me. I promise. And I'm not Nick, Sasha. I don't break my promises. So just say it. Tell me why I'm here."

I feel the tear slip out and roll down my cheek. "You think you love me," I sob.

He smiles. "Yes."

"You don't even know me."

"I know you, Sasha Aston. I know you." He reaches up and swipes that lone tear away. "You're brave, and smart, and so fucking beautiful." He whispers the last few words. "And even though I've tried to show you, I don't think you know me at all. You're my partner now. Whether you accept my offer or not, you're my partner. And I will not walk away. Do you hear me?"

I nod.

"I will not walk away. So tell me, now that you understand that. Tell me why Nick is here."

I take a deep breath and the words spill out with the air on the exhale. "He loves me."

Jax smiles. "And why did your friend James drop you off at this house back when you were thirteen?"

"Because he loves me."

"And why did your friend Merc drop his rifle for you, Sasha?"

"He loves me."

"Yes. You're very, very fucking real to those people. They love you. You told me this yesterday with such confidence, but I don't think you believed it. And maybe I'd do it different, but maybe not. Maybe this end is the only way all the wrongs can be righted."

I nod, lying there on the bed, spread open before him. Helpless because I choose to be, and not because I'm tied up, or being threatened, or fear for my life or the life of others.

And looking up at him, I realize that even though he's on top of me and my hands are above my head, he's put me in a position of control. He looks up at me, waiting for acceptance, knowing I can find a way out of his hold on my mind and my body. Trusting me to give in and be still. To listen to his words and think about them in my own way. On my own time.

The tears start again. "I'm so fucking sad," I sob. "I'm so fucking sad, Jax. I've lost everything and still they find new things to take from me. And if they take Nick, that will just be the final nail in my coffin. Because if they can take the things that they already took, over and over again, then when will it stop? When will it end?"

"I don't know, Sasha. But the thing is, no one does. No one knows when the pain will stop and the joy will begin. My brother walked away from a murder scene yesterday. He lost everything he had built up over the past few years. I guarantee, he feels just like you do right now. But who knows how he'll feel in a year? Who knows how many good things will happen if he lets them? You're not any different than the rest of us, Sasha. You're not any more or less in control of the future than me or him. But each step you took to leave Sasha Cherlin behind was one step forward into the life of Sasha Aston."

"I don't know who Sasha Aston is, Jax. She's this thirteen-year-old girl who got a new name and a new life. She went to school and got good grades. She has a bazillion dollars and not one penny can buy her happiness."

"So stop trying to buy it. You don't need to buy it, Sasha. Happiness is free. You just have to accept it."

"Will you love me?" I ask, another sob escaping. I have never asked anyone this question before and it makes me feel so naked.

"I already do," he replies back. "I already do."

"Show me, Jax. Show me how you'll love me."

His grin makes me laugh through my tears. He moves off of me and lies flat on his back beside me. He takes my hands down from above my head and pulls me on top of him. And then he holds my face and kisses me deep. Our tongues twist together, picking up the dance we started yesterday.

I break away first and inch myself down his body, kissing and nipping him the way he did me a few minutes ago. He places his hand on my head, urging me to keep going. So I find the edge of his boxers and pull them down. His cock is hard and ready. His breathing picks up and becomes louder. And when I touch the tip of my tongue to the top of his head, he fists my hair and pushes me down. I open my mouth and take him in, sucking, then withdrawing so I can lick the side of his shaft. He throbs with anticipation. I place his cock back on my tongue and close my lips tightly, making him moan.

I give in to him. I give myself *to* him.

He reaches down and grabs one of my hands and brings it to his mouth. I look up at him as he kisses my knuckles. And this is when I realize I've never been with a man like this. I've never let anyone see inside me before. The sex I had was mechanical. A release and nothing more.

But making love with Jax is like a celebration.

I suck him harder, massaging him as I move my face closer and closer with each dip. His cock penetrates my mouth like his words penetrated my soul earlier. We float there together in some ethereal ecstasy. I lose time with him. I lose track of everything as I make him moan. He begins to thrust his hips up to meet my face. I know he's close, so I take him as deep as I can.

He comes down my throat and instead of being disgusted, I swallow all of him. He's warm, and safe, and mine.

"Fuck," he growls. "Come here, Sasha." He pulls me up by my hand, so I crawl up his body. He tugs on my underwear until he gets them to my knees and I have to maneuver to get them off my legs.

"Get on top," he says, anxious to keep going.

"No," I say, lying down beside him. "You get on top. I want to feel your body covering mine. I want to feel every inch of your skin in contact with me."

His smile is like sunshine as he slowly moves to grant my wish. He reaches down and lifts my thigh, hiking it to the side, up next to my stomach. And then he eases himself between my legs, his cock already hard again, gently rubbing against my entrance. He cups my face, and my lips part as his thumb gently caresses my lips. He enters me both ways, making me arch my back against his hips as he fills me up.

We find the light in the darkness that way. We see each other for what we really are.

Not secret-keepers. Not hunters. Not parts of a whole.

But just us.

And for the first time in my whole life, I feel... real.

CHAPTER THIRTY-THREE

"**Y**eah?" I mumble into the phone. This middle-of-the-night shit is getting old.

"Jax." Max's voice on the other end of the line is hesitant and subdued.

I sit up in bed, the warmth of Sasha's body retreating as I snap to attention. "What happened?"

"It's Madeline. I'm… sorry." He stops to draw in a breath. "Nick Tate blew the whole compound up last night. She's dead. All her servants are dead. And there was a meeting last night, Jax. Very important people were there. They're all dead too."

"What? How? I mean, how the fuck did he know where to find her?"

"We're still trying to piece that together, but we're pretty sure it was Sasha. You were there the night before last?"

"Yeah, but it wasn't her."

"I need you here heading this investigation. Now. Madrid is going to take Sasha in, so get her ready."

A hand traces down my back and makes me jump. I look down and Sasha is staring up at me. "I'll call you back," I say.

"You have dragons on your back," Sasha says.

I sigh at the memory. "I do."

"What's it mean?"

"It was a promise. My brother and I made it together. We're the dragons and we were gonna take over the world. He's got the same tattoo. Two fire-breathing beasts with the world at our mercy. We were so angry after Michael was killed." I stop talking and look at her for a moment. "It's nothing. I mean, it was something, obviously. A promise that we'd see this through to the end together."

"Get revenge and kill Nick."

"Not just Nick. Everyone. But he wins again, I guess." I gesture to the phone in my hand.

"What happened?" she asks, propping herself up on her elbow as I end the call.

I scrub a hand down my face and scratch the stubble on my chin as I think of how to word this.

"What, Jax? Tell me, dammit."

I shake my head and just let it out. "How bad did you hate your aunt?"

"I barely knew her. It was just a gut reaction. Why?"

"She's dead, Sasha. Nick went there last night and blew the place up. You said it reminded you of the house in Santa Barbara.

Also blown up by you and Nick."

"Whoa there. Also? I didn't have anything to do with last night! I was here with you!"

"I'm not saying that, obviously. But Nick was here. You talked to him. Did you tell him where that compound was?"

"No! He never even asked, Jax."

My phone rings again. I grab it off the bed and thumb the accept button. "Yeah."

"You motherfucker!" Madrid's voice booms out of the speaker so loud, I have to hold the phone away from my head. "We are partners, asshole! That means you tell me everything. And I've been sitting here for two days waiting for this girl to come home, and ain't nothing goin' on at her house. Now where is she?"

"She's with me."

"And just exactly where is *with me*?"

"Classified."

"Classified my ass! I have my orders and so do you—"

I end the call and turn my phone off as I look at Sasha.

"Um," she says, holding the sheets up to her naked torso, shielding her body. God, that almost kills me. "What's going on?"

"I have to go head up that investigation. I'm supposed to hand you over to Madrid so she can keep an eye on you."

"Keep an eye on me? Like I'm your prisoner? Jesus Christ! You did sell me out!"

"No, Sasha. I'm not handing you over to Madrid. But I need to figure this shit out. Nick killed your aunt last night. She was working with Max. Has been working with Max for years. This is not going to sit well."

"Well, you better start questioning your loyalties to Max, then. Because Madeline was bad. I believe Nick. He knows what's going on. Your father isn't Company. He has no idea and neither do you." She gets out of bed, still hugging those sheets to her body, and points to the door. "Get out of my house."

"Sasha, look—"

"No. I'm not listening to you. Not after that accusation. Not after that justification. I trusted you with the secrets Nick told me last night and you turn around and blame me? Accuse me of working with him?"

"Look, I don't think you're working with him." But I stop and take a deep breath. Because that's not true. I've always thought she was working with him. And even Jake said she might be playing me. But last night felt so real. "I just need to know what's going on. What exactly happened last night?"

"I told you. He came here."

"How did he find you?"

"How should I know? I've been with you for the past two days!"

"Just walk me through it, OK? There has to be a logical explanation, but right now it all points to you." Her face turns red with anger and I put up a hand. "I don't think it was you, OK? But he's clever. He has ways of making people do his dirty work. So just tell me what happened before he showed up."

"I was checking my email. And I got a message from my mentor at school saying I wasn't kicked out and she wanted to talk to me. And then I found a message from Nick—"

"Wait," I say, stopping her. "You never told me that part."

"I never had a chance! You showed up here and my world

was falling apart!"

"What did the email say?"

She takes a deep breath and then points to the door. "I'll show you." And then she quickly dresses and says, "Follow me."

I get out of bed and tug on my pants, then follow her out the door and downstairs. We end up in the family room behind the kitchen where she opens a laptop and brings up her email account.

"Here," she says, thrusting it at me. "See for yourself."

I look at the video of Nick and press the play button. *Got you*, he says. "What am I looking at?"

"Wow. You're not all that bright for a guy who works for a secret black ops department of the FBI. Listen carefully, Agent Jax. There's a shutter click just before he starts talking."

I play it again. And again. And again. "Holy fuck." I look at her. "He hacked your webcam?"

She nods.

"From where?"

"I don't know, Jax. I swear to God. We never even talked about the email. He said, *I have rats too*. And I think he was talking about how your dad thinks he's infiltrated Matias' gang."

"Matias."

"Nick said Matias and Madeline were working together."

"No."

"I'm just the messenger, Jax. I have no idea. But Nick came here to ask me to help him and then he left without telling me how to do that. So I'm in the dark just as much as you. But here's something you need to understand. Nothing is ever what it seems with these people, OK? Nothing. So I'm sorry you fell for

Madeline's bullshit, but I believe Nick. I know in my heart that what he said was true. And if you think I will let her take me down from beyond the grave, you're insane. I will not go down because of that bitch."

I look at the video again and try to make sense of things. And then I hit the forward button and send it to Adam.

"What are you doing?" Sasha asks, trying to grab the laptop away from me.

I yank it back and hold it up high, out of her reach. "I'm sending this to Adam. He's not just a driver or a pilot. He's my security, remember?"

"How do you know you can trust him?"

"I don't, OK? But we've been working together for a long time. If he's a traitor, it's better to find that out now." I hand her laptop back. "He can at least find out where that message came from. It's a place to start. And there's nothing incriminating in that video. If anything, it shows Nick was playing you."

"He's not playing me, OK? He's my partner. He wouldn't do that. Whatever he's doing, he won't hurt me."

"He's your *partner*? Really?"

She nods. "Really."

Fuck, that stings. "You're wrong about him, Sasha. But I truly hope you're right. Because if you're not, he's gonna take you down with the rest of us."

CHAPTER THIRTY-FOUR

"Where are you going?" I yell as Jax walks out of the room.

"I gotta go head up this investigation." He turns around when he gets to the stairs and points to me. "You stay here. No matter what, you stay here until I get back. I'll tell Madrid you're driving home and you have no clue what's going on. That will buy me a day as she waits for you to show up. But you do not move. Do you understand me?"

I want to scream at him. I want to tell him to fuck off so bad. But I don't. I just nod. "Fine." Because that's the easiest way to get him out of here so I can try to piece together what's happening.

When he comes back downstairs, his suit is crumpled, his hair is a mess and his gun holster is crooked as it hangs underneath his jacket. But he still looks fucking hot. "Be careful,"

I say, meaning it, and fight the urge to cry as he holds me tight for a second. But what did I expect? I mean, really? Did I actually think I'd get a happy ending? "And keep your eyes open," I add. "Something is very wrong, Jax. And you promised not to die on me, so I'm gonna hold you to that."

"Stay here," he commands again. "No matter what."

I nod and he kisses me quickly before heading out the front door. I hate having to lie to him, but it's not my fault I'm a player. I've kept my head down for ten years. I didn't ask to be part of this game. But now that I am, I have to see it through to the end.

I grab my phone from the couch where I threw it last night and it's already got a message on there. Just like I knew it would.

Meet me at the safe house, it says.

There is no name attached to that number, but it's from Nick. It's in the same message stream as the one he sent me last night telling me to come outside.

I page down through my contacts and find the number I need and press send.

Harrison answers on the second ring, just like he always does. "I knew you'd need me," he says in a somber tone.

"I need you," I say. "I need to go back where you picked me up."

"Meet me at the plane in an hour." And then I get the hang-up beeps.

I have about three hours then. Three hours before whatever's gonna happen out there in Nebraska happens.

And all that depends on Nick. This is the endgame we all thought happened ten years ago. The final roll of the dice to see who comes out ahead and who loses big.

CHAPTER THIRTY-FIVE

"Hey," Adam says as I walk up to the jet at the Fort Collins airport. He looks just as ragged as I feel. His suit coat is missing, his white dress shirt is untucked and hanging down like he just threw it on, and his eyes are wild. "Dude, what the fuck was that?"

"What the fuck was what?" I'm still caught in the web of Sasha Cherlin. Distracted and unsettled. Something is wrong.

"That video, dude. I don't understand."

"Yeah, it's fucked up," I say, taking the steps to the jet two at a time. The inside of the cabin is empty, so I make my way to one of the chairs and sit. My head hurts. "Where's Essie? I need a drink."

"She's not here," Adam says.

"Why not?" Jesus Christ. All I want is a drink.

"I sent all the girls back to their hotels."

I look up at Adam and actually see him. He's one of us. One of the four Taxmen—we come to collect. Me, Jake, Max, and Adam. Adam came a year after Michael's death, a foster kid like Jake and me, but way smarter. Sasha has Ford, I have Adam. "You want to tell me why?"

He shakes his head. "Not really, dude. Because I have no idea what it means."

"What what means? It's Nick, taking a picture of Sasha using her webcam. All I want to know is where it came from. Maybe he's still there and we can head him off?"

"That's the problem, Jax. It didn't come from Nick. It came from Max."

"What?"

"Nick's not taking a picture of Sasha. He's taking a picture of Max. This video came from Max."

"Why the fuck would Max send that to Sasha's email?"

Adam just shrugs. We stare at each other for several seconds before I can even think of something to say. "Why do you think he sent it, Adam?"

"Dude, do you realize what you're asking me?"

"Do you think Nick is setting him up? Sending that to Max's email and then forwarding it on to Sasha? To make it look like it was from Max?"

"Well…" Adam laughs. "OK. I get the fact that her father is some genius hacker or some shit. But how the fuck would *she* figure that out, Jax? Why would Nick do that if there's no way it would mean anything to Sasha? All she'd think was that it came from Nick. And all he says is, *Got you.* But when I looked close at the end of that video, it's been cut. There was more, but someone cut it off."

My mind is racing with possibilities. "What if Max was just trying to scare her? You know, make her afraid of Nick? Make that motherfucker even creepier than he is?"

Adam huffs out a breath. "Hey, if that's what you believe, I'm OK with it."

"Dammit, Adam, that's not what I'm asking you."

"No, you're asking me to ignore the obvious. Max did this, OK? I know that's true. If Nick did this, then why cut off the end of the video? So the question you need to be asking is what did Max hope to gain? And scaring Sasha? Sure, OK. But why?"

I roll the only logical possibility around in my head, trying it on for size. "I don't like it. I don't like a lot of this. Nick is telling Sasha one thing and I'm telling her something else. So I guess the first question is who's calling the shots for Nick?"

"Nick calls the shots for Nick, Jax. We all know that now. He never worked for Matias. He's fucking blue-blood Company, man. There is no one above that dude. No one."

"Right," I say. "And who calls the shots for me?"

Adam gives me a shrug using his hands. "Max. He's lying, Jax. You know he is. None of this shit makes sense. Did you ever ask yourself why Max wanted kids?"

I get where he's going, but if these suspicions are true, then what the fuck have I been working towards all these years?

"And did you ever ask yourself why Nick Tate was so hell-bent on killing people? Why make killing Company kids your life's mission? It's so fucking sick, right? It's insane. And that guy is a lot of things, but insane is not one of them. And furthermore, why not kill us too? He's never even tried to kill *us*."

I look Adam in the face and let that sink in. "Because we're not Company."

"We're just employees. We do what we're told. We work for the FBI, and yet we don't. We're hidden away, compartmentalized. No one can touch us. Madeline says she's there to help get these Company kids out, and yet every one of them ended up dead or missing. Where the fuck are those kids, Jax? Where the fuck are the kids she saved? And don't say we're right here, because we don't count. We're nobodies."

"So you're convinced Max is Company? And Madeline?"

"Look, I was just as happy as you to ignore all these warning signs. But not anymore. Not after that video. Max sent that video to Sasha to make her think Nick was hunting her."

"But Nick came to her house last night and then left. Why didn't he kill her if he was hunting her?"

"Because he's not hunting her, Jax. He's hunting Max. He already got Matias and Madeline last night. Now Max is the only one left. And Max wants Sasha for something. That's why he sent you to get her. He wants her with *him*. And Madeline wanted her too. But they both wanted her alive. Why?"

"Why?" I ask myself out loud.

"You have a gift," Adam says, pointing to a box on the chair opposite me. "I don't know who it's from. It was sitting there when I came on board this morning."

I stare at him for a few seconds and then he walks off to the cockpit. "We'll be there in an hour, so you better come to some kind of conclusion, Jax. Because I can't do my job if I don't trust the people around me. And we all know what happens to people who don't do their jobs."

I look at the box on the ground and open it up, thinking of all the brothers I've lost over the years. I think of Jake, the brother I almost lost the other night, the only one left aside from Adam. What was the point of all that shit in Denver with Jake? Max sent him there, but why?

I'm not sure.

I'm not sure about anything right now.

The white card on top of the white dress shirt says, *Put it on. You can thank me later.*

CHAPTER THIRTY-SIX

The estate is still smoldering from the explosives that went off last night. It's nothing but a shell of those beautiful sandstone bricks.

Max is pacing in front of me, screaming as he counts off the dead. "Julian," he yells. "Julian is dead!"

"Who gives a fuck about Julian?" I'm barely listening. I can't get Sasha out of my head. I can't get that video message out of my head. And now it all comes down to who I should trust.

"Where is he?" Max screams, leaning down into my face. "Where is Nick Tate? I gave you one job," he roars. "One. Fucking. Job. Get that girl so we can get Nick Tate. And this," he says, panning his arms towards the rubble. "This is what you delivered?"

"I'm doing my best to figure it out, Max."

"Madrid says you sent the girl home in a car. A car? It's a nine-hour drive to her home from Fort Collins, Jax. Just what the fuck are you doing?"

"It was the safest way I could think of to get her there." And if I was really sending Sasha home, that's still the way I'd do it.

"One phone call to Madrid and she'd have picked her up."

Right. Madrid is another unknown I don't understand.

"But the girl is gone, Jax. And she didn't take the car."

"What?" I look up at him. He's got my full attention now.

"Madrid got a message from Nick saying he sent her to the safe house. Sasha called her pilot friend the minute you left."

"*What*?"

"What?" he says, mimicking my reaction. "Are you stupid? That girl played you, goddammit."

"Look, I'm sorry about Madeline, but Sasha was pretty dead set that she was Company, Max. And why the fuck was Matias here? None ever told me Matias and Madeline were working out a deal."

"Who gives a fuck about Matias and Madeline! I needed them dead, so Nick Tate did me a favor. But Julian," he chokes out a laugh. "Julian was not supposed to be part of that."

"What the fuck does Julian have to do with this? He's some scumbag who's been whining about losing his promise for years. I'm glad he's—"

"He was my true-blood son!"

I don't react. My life depends on how this plays out. "You told him Sasha was his promise, didn't you?"

"She was," he growls. "Her father made a deal with me,

long before he made a deal with the Admiral and Nick Tate. I sent you to get her. One job, after all I've done for you, Jackson Barlow. One job and you fucked it up. So if you can't do your job properly"—he pulls a gun out of his coat pocket and points it at the ground—"we'll do it for you. Madrid is already on her way."

"You're gonna have Madrid kill Sasha?"

"If I wanted her dead, Jax, I'd have killed her a long time ago. I need her alive. Everyone needs her alive or we lose our only remaining path to victory."

I have no choice but accept the truth in front of me. He's spelling it out, clear as day.

"Put the pieces together, Jax. You're smart. You know what I'm doing. You've always known, you just wanted to be the hero so bad you were blinded. But you're just as mixed up in this as I am, son. You know the only way to defeat the Company is using their own weapons."

I just stare at him. And then I shake my head slowly. "No, Max. I've never believed that. And if that's your endgame—to use Sasha to make those killer kids like the Company did—well, you're on your own."

"Either you're in or you're not, Jax." He raises the gun and points it at my chest. "And since you just admitted you're out, then I have no choice, do I?"

The deafening crack of a gunshot hits my ears the same time the bullet hits my chest and the pain is so intense, I barely register the fight that follows. I expect it to be over soon, but I can hear Adam screaming between bursts of gunfire.

Get up, Jax! But that's not Adam, it's me. I'm screaming at myself to get up. I roll over on my side, my whole body on fire with the agony of taking a bullet to the chest. I reach under my jacket for my weapon and open my eyes just in time to see Adam go reeling to the side, hitting the ground face first.

Max walks towards him, his gun raised, his mouth moving a mile a minute. I hear nothing but gunshots as they echo through my mind.

He set me up. All these years, that fucker set me up. I spent my whole adult life seeking revenge. For what? So that this asshole could swoop in and take over what's left of the Company?

I force my upper body up, propping my weight with my elbows, and hold the gun out in front of me. I don't waste time telling Max to stop or put up his hands.

I just shoot him the only way he deserves. In the back.

He stumbles forward one step, squeezing the trigger on his gun out of reflex, and then falls down on top of Adam.

I close my eyes, giving myself this one moment to let the sting of betrayal wash over me. And then I roll back on the ground, blindly reach for my phone, and press the speed-dial app for 911.

CHAPTER THIRTY-SEVEN

I don't know what I thought I'd find at the safe house, but four dead people in the front yard didn't even make the top one hundred.

I take in the scene like the professional I used to be. Three unmarked government cars haphazardly parked in the driveway, all with engines running. The front door to the house wide open. And complete silence within.

"Sasha," Harrison says, tugging on my coat. "Let's call James."

"No," I whisper, crouching in the cover of some trees near the road. "No. James finished his job a long time ago. Now it's time for me to finish mine."

I don't even have a gun, so this is one hundred percent nuts. But so many people could have killed me already so many times.

This can't be about killing me. They need me alive.

So I straighten myself out and walk down the driveway. My feet are crunching in the frozen gravel and the wind is blowing my hair in front of my eyes, making me more nervous than I already am because no amount of wiping it away will make it behave.

It's dark inside, but I can see bodies before I even make it to the threshold. "Jesus Christ. What happened?"

"The Company happened, Sasha." Nick's voice from within.

I step forward into the house and a hand reaches out and makes a futile attempt to grab my pant leg.

"Help," Madrid says, one hand holding the hole in her stomach and blood gurgling out of her mouth. Her fist isn't strong enough to stop me, so I just walk past and it slips away. There's no help for her. I know what a gunshot wound to the stomach means.

"Are you surprised it's gonna end this way, Sasha?" Nick is sitting in a chair on the opposite wall. He's bleeding too, and there's a 9mm revolver at his feet and a cell phone in his hand.

"What are you doing?" I ask. "Just what the fuck are you doing?" I look around me, counting up the bodies. Three people dead in here, including Madrid, and four outside.

"Just sending someone a text, Smurf."

Seven FBI agents dead and he's texting? "They're gonna kill you, Nick. They're never gonna let you walk away from this. So just what the fuck?"

Nick stands, wincing in pain from the wound in his thigh. He's got a belt cinched tightly, just below his hip, in a makeshift tourniquet. And his head is bleeding pretty good too.

"You need help," I say, not sure if I mean he's gone batshit crazy now for sure, or if he needs medical attention. Both, I guess.

"He missed so much, Sasha. But I didn't."

"What the hell are you talking about? What the fuck are you *doing*? You're ruining everything! They're gonna kill you now, you asshole! They are never gonna let you get away with this!"

He laughs, but it turns into a cough. "Oh, but I will, Sasha." He laughs again, even though I can tell it hurts him. "I always get away. Everyone knows that. But you're here now. And you're the only person who can save me." His laugh turns into a hitch, and then a sob escapes as a tear slides down his cheek.

I step forward, not knowing what to think about this Nick. I've never seen him cry. Ever. Not even when he told me to go live my life without him and I was blubbering like a baby, begging him to love me.

"Don't cry, Nick, please." I can't take it. I really can't. Nick is a rock. Nick is the man who moves mountains. I walk forward quickly and pull him into a hug. "We're gonna be OK. I'll save you, Nick. I swear. I'll save you. Just please don't give up."

He sniffs and wipes his face with the back of his bloody hand, leaving a streak of red across his cheek. "I didn't miss anything, Sasha. I swear." And then he points to the wall that holds all the pictures Jax has of me. I look off to the side and Nick reaches for my hand as it sinks in.

The white spaces are gone. Every inch of that wall is filled up with me, starting with the day I sat out on Ford Aston's front stoop on Christmas Eve holding a kitten in my lap. The one-year anniversary of my dad's death. The first day of my new life.

"I saw everything, Sasha Aston. Everything. I never left you,

WASTED LUST

I watched you from Honduras." He leans over and kisses me on the head. "I had dozens of people watching you. I was always there, even when I wasn't. They sent me updates every week. No matter where you were, no matter what you were doing. I did it with you."

There are hundreds of pictures of me. My beach vacations in New Zealand with Ford and Ash and the babies. My first year in a real school, dressed up in a Catholic girl uniform. Me and Five's face-eating dog, Jimmy, who latched on to me like I was his best friend, when really he was all I had back then in the way of friends. My private high school in Denver, when we moved to my new grandma's house next to City Park so all five of us could stay together and keep me safe at the same time. Running the steps with Ford at Coor's Field. Me pushing Five and Kate in a stroller in Japan that summer Ashleigh went back to school to finish her master's and I played mommy. My first date. Ford catching that boy trying to kiss me on the porch when he brought me home. College at The School of Mines. The day I met my first serious boyfriend at a baseball game, and the day after we broke up when I made myself go home and cry to Ashleigh.

I look over at Nick and he's smiling. "It wasn't a bad life, right?"

I shake my head and feel the tears fall. "It was good, Nick." I have to hold in a sob before I can finish. "It was better than good. Just like you said it would be. You saved me. Just tell me what to do and I'll save you back, OK? I'll save you back. I'll do whatever you say. I'll find a way to give you as good a life as you gave me."

"My life is over, Sasha." He holds me by the shoulders as he turns me around to face the wall that holds the pictures of him.

There were already hundreds of images on that wall before. But now there are hundreds more. "Those are the pictures Jax didn't put up." He leans his head on mine as I take them in.

Bodies.

Dozens and dozens of pictures of dead bodies. Piles of them. Blood, everywhere.

And Nick. In every bloody photo there is Nick holding a gun. Small handguns. Rifles. Shotguns. AKs.

"I'm already dead, Sasha." He puts something cold in my hand and I hold it up to see what it is. The FBI badge that Jax made for me. It dangles on the beaded chain. Nick takes it from my hand and slips the chain over my head like a necklace. "But not dead enough."

He looks me in the eyes as I stare at him, shaking my head.

"Save me, Sasha Cherlin." And then he pulls out a FN Five-SeveN from the waistband of his jeans and places the weapon in my hand. "Save me, Sasha. I'm begging you."

"No." I start to cry. "No."

He places my finger on the trigger of the gun and lifts it up to his forehead. I try to pull back, but he wraps my hand in both of his and holds it in place.

The *womp-womp* sound of helicopters thunders over the house and we both look up at the ceiling, like we can see through it. Like we can see the future that is unfolding before us.

"Shoot me, Sasha. I'm begging you. If you love me—if you ever loved me—kill me now. Before they come and take me away and make me continue living this hell my parents sentenced me to twenty-eight years ago."

"I won't do it," I sob. "I can't do it, Nick. Don't make me do this."

"Shhhh," he says, taking a deep breath and stopping his own crying. "Just listen," he whispers. "Just listen to me. They take the girls, Sasha. They take the girls and turn them into monsters. And I did my best, kid. I did. But they train them as fast as I can kill them. Right now, I'm winning. I have killed so many fucked-up Zeros, I lost count. But right now, Sasha, this moment in time, I'm winning. I got so many kids. I got twice as many parents. I have literally killed thousands of people, even if it wasn't by my own hand. I'm winning. They're all dead."

He stops holding my hands on the gun and holds my face instead. "They're all dead except for us. But if we don't change the game in a big way, they'll just keep doing it. I'm the leader, Sasha. I am the Company. And if you end me, that's something they won't ignore. If you end me, it sends a message that you'll end them too. Whoever is left will get that message loud and clear. We won, Sasha. We won. And will always win because you, and James, and Merc, and Harper, and Sydney... and Jax. You six will do whatever it takes to make it *stop*."

I stare at him, not even knowing what to say to all that.

"Kate. Think of your little sister. They'll come take her, Sasha. Some nobody will get big ideas and they'll come steal her away in the night and ruin her future, just like they ruined ours."

The helicopters are louder now, and then a wind blows in through the front door as they try to land nearby.

"They'll be here in a minute or less, Sash. And if you let them take me, they'll lock me up. But one day, because of what I do and who I am, I'll get out." He squeezes my face to make this point. "I'll. Get. Out. And then I'll come for Kate myself. Because that's my job. I am the Company. That's who I am, Sasha Cherlin." He holds up my badge, dangling from my neck, and puts it right in front of my face. "And this is who you are. So do your job, Sasha Aston. Do your job or I will come back one day and get her."

Men are shouting out in the yard now, and I hear boots storming for the door.

"I'll torture her, Sasha. The way Garrett tortured you two years ago. I'll find her, take her, drug her, rape—"

I squeeze the trigger just as the light flooding through the front door is masked with men in Kevlar vests and riot gear.

"Drop your weapon!" they shout. "Drop your weapon and put your face on the ground!"

I drop the gun and fall to my knees. Shocked. Too shocked to react as reality sinks in.

The men push me to the floor face-first, handcuff me, and flip me over on my back.

That's when they see my badge sitting on my stomach, hanging off that chain that Nick put around my neck. One guy lifts his visor up on his helmet and reaches for it.

"Sasha Aston," I say. "FBI."

CHAPTER THIRTY-EIGHT

They lead me out of the house. It takes two of them to keep me upright because my legs are not working. "Shock," the guy on my left says, as he hands me off to someone else. "She's OK, she's just in shock."

The new guy hugs me tight. "Sasha," Jax says, his whole body trembling. "Sasha, look at me."

I look up at his face. His blue eyes are filled with more fear than I've ever seen. I start to cry and bury my head in his chest.

"Say something," he whispers into my neck. "Say something so I know you're OK."

"I killed him, Jax. He tricked me. He tricked me into shooting him point-blank in the head."

Jax says nothing to that, just holds me tight and walks me

out to the ambulance so they can take a look at me. Make sure I'm OK. But I don't know if I'll ever be OK. I'm not sure if killing Nick will end my life or save it.

I'm only sure of one thing right now.

Nick Tate is a liar. Nick Tate is a liar and I fell for it. I let him goad me into ending his life. I let my love for Kate and my fear of Garrett control me.

I know in my heart there's no way Nick would ever hurt Kate. Never. Not in a million years.

He made me kill him. He made me do my *job*.

And I might never forgive him for that. I might hate him until the end of time for making me do that.

CHAPTER THIRTY-NINE

I pace in front of the ambulance as they check her over, worried out of my mind even though none of the blood belongs to her. I can't help it. I lost a lot today and I can't bear the thought of losing her too. I need to know she's OK. Not physically. Mentally. What can she possibly be thinking right now? After all that talk of saving Nick. What is running through her mind now that the shock is wearing off and she has to come to terms with what she did?

It takes them thirty minutes to declare her fine, and then they hand her back off to me. She looks me up and down and I'm waiting for it. I'm waiting for what I know is surely floating around in her head right now.

You got what you wanted.

But I didn't. I didn't get what I wanted. I never wanted this.

I hold my breath when she opens her mouth to speak.

"Where the hell did you get a Kevlar shirt made by Roberto Moreno Diseñador?"

I laugh, I can't help it. "Who?"

"That shirt." She sniffs. Her crying stopped as soon as she got to the ambulance. Sasha Aston is not a crier. Not in front of anyone but me, anyway. "It's a Roberto shirt. That's his logo on the pocket."

I look down at the white dress shirt parading as a Kevlar vest. It's got a hole in it, right in the center of my chest where Max shot me. But sure enough, Sasha's finger traces a logo embroidered with white thread, so that you can't see it unless you know what to look for.

"That's how James shot me, Jax. When everyone thought I was dead. He gave me a Roberto original. Where did you get this?"

I shrug. "I don't know. It was on the plane when I went to meet Adam this morning. He had one too. And it was a good thing, because Max Barlow shot us both. These designer shirts saved our lives."

"There's something in the pocket." She unbuttons it and withdraws a key. We both stare at it for several seconds, confused.

"Sasha!" her pilot friend calls from across the yellow police-line tape. "Sasha!"

We walk over there together. Her legs are steady now, but we're both silent as we think about these shirts. Putting the pieces together in a new way.

"I'm OK, Harrison," Sasha says when we get close enough.

"I'm fine, but Nick…" She stops talking to stop the tears.

Harrison holds her from across the tape. They embrace like that for a few minutes and then he pulls back and extends his hand. "I'm Sasha's friend, Harrison."

"Jax," I say, unable to call myself by my last name. I just can't be a Barlow anymore. Not after what I found out today.

"I have a message from Nick, Sasha. He sent me a text just before that gunshot."

"What?" Sasha looks at the cell phone Harrison is holding out to her. "What's it say?"

"Read it," Harrison replies. "I have no idea what it means."

Sasha takes the phone and squints down at the message.

"Well?" I say, impatient. "Tell me what he says."

She looks up at me, her face changing from confusion to understanding before my eyes. "It says, *I left you a gift at that hotel room.*"

My own understanding creeps in slowly. "The hotel where he left you ten years ago?"

She nods up at me.

"Let's go," Harrison says. "We can be in Rock Springs, Wyoming in three and a half hours." He doesn't wait for us to answer, just takes off across the field in the direction of the airstrip here in Falls City.

Sasha walks off after him, not even looking back at me.

And I follow. With a new appreciation for what it means to be friends with Sasha Aston.

People love her fiercely. She's right. They will die for her. Even sick and twisted fucks like Nick Tate will give their lives for her. Carting her ass around in a private plane is nothing to this pilot.

WASTED LUST

He'll do whatever it takes to make her happy, no questions asked.

And so will I.

CHAPTER FORTY

The three of us are a nervous wreck as Sasha pushes her key into the door of the hotel room she shared with Nick ten years ago. She takes a sharp inhale, then twists the key and turns the handle.

The cock of shotguns make us all freeze in the blowing snow, but Sasha, confident in her trust of Nick's final message, pushes the door open anyway.

The two men lower their weapons and come forward, only to be pushed out of the way by two women.

There is shouting—the good kind—and crying. Also the good kind. And she is folded into a foursome embrace for several long seconds.

They notice Harrison next, and the greeting starts again,

but this time only from the men, who slap him on the back as they usher us forward into the room. A moment later the door is closed and the room goes dim because the curtains are drawn tight.

I look around, stunned.

Stunned faces look back at me.

There are six girls pressed up against the far wall near the bathroom. Three who look to be sisters under five. One who looks to be a teen, holding a baby. And one who sits alone at the small table, a book clutched to her chest and her feet swinging like she hasn't got a care in the world. She looks up at me with her brown eyes and she smiles. And then she takes an envelope out of her book and places it on the table, pushing it towards me with one pink finger. "He said to give you that."

"What?" I look around and every face is turned to me. I know the men. I've seen them in pictures. James Fenici and Merc, whatever his real name is. "Hey," I say, starting to get nervous since both these men, and the women with them for that matter, are Company assassins. "I have never seen this kid before."

James walks over and plucks the envelope off the table. "Where did you get this?" he asks the little girl. She shrugs and no answer comes forth.

"What's going on here, James?" Sasha is confused, as am I, and she steps back from James and leans into me a little. I appreciate the gesture.

"I'm not sure yet, Smurf. Merc and I got a text this morning that said to come here immediately. Luckily Harp and I were off the coast of Oregon and I still have pilot friends with planes in San Fran. These six don't say much." He gestures to the frightened girls still pressed up to the bathroom vanity. "Of course, only one has any idea," he says again, this time with irritation. "But I'm pretty sure they're Company."

"Fuck you," the teenager spits. "You don't know shit about me."

"You don't know shit about me either, sister. So shut your trap until I figure this all out." James looks at Sasha. "See what I mean?"

Sasha smiles and then turns to the little girl with the book. "What are you reading?"

"*Little House in the Big Woods*. But it's not for me. It's for you." She holds the book out to Sasha, who looks at James and lets out a long breath before accepting it. "He wrote something in the front, but it's in cursive and I don't read cursive."

Sasha takes the book and opens it to the front and starts to read. "'You didn't lose it, Sash. Your childhood is right here in this book. You can take it back anytime you want and all you need is a story. Love, Nick.'" She holds it to her chest for a moment, her eyes closed. And then she looks up at me and smiles. "He set this up. He set all of this up. Read the letter, please. Read it. I need to know why."

"What happened, Sasha?" The blonde woman with James steps out from behind him. "What happened to Nick?"

Harper Tate, I realize. Nick's twin sister.

Sasha hugs her and starts to cry. "I'm sorry, Harper. I swear to God. I'm so fucking sorry."

"Shhh," Harper says, smoothing down Sasha's hair. "It's OK. Just tell me what happened."

I grab the letter out of James' hand and rip it open. I don't want Sasha to have to tell this girl she killed her brother. Ever. I know she'll have to eventually, but I can buy her some time at least.

Dear Jax,

> *You have every right to hate me. Everyone in this room has every right to hate me. But I want you to know I did my best.*
> *The girl with the book is my daughter, Lauren, and I'm giving her to you.*
> *Because she's Company. And if I'm dead right now and you're standing in that hotel room, my plan worked. I killed a lot of people to get to this place. A lot of Zeros and these girls are the last of them. Be patient as they adjust, especially Angelica. She had it the worst and will need some time.*
> *I met a girl a while back. Just some girl in Miami one weekend when I was there doing a job. And she kinda grew on me. I got attached. I got careless. And I never thought about the consequences until it was too late. I was in love with her and she was carrying my child.*
> *I sent her away to keep her safe. But she died during childbirth and it wasn't even a murder. Of all the ironic ways for her to die, that had to be it? God is cruel.*
> *I didn't find out what happened for months. It took me that long to get the courage to try to see the baby. I knew I had to walk away and never look back. I had*

to stay far, far away from that baby. Never claim her as my own. Never see her grow up. And that's when I decided if I had to give her away, I might as well make it count.

I'm not sorry for killing your little brother. I am sorry that he was a pawn in a dangerous game and he paid for it with his life. But Max Barlow had every intention of turning him into me. Or James. Or Sasha, or Sydney, or Harper. Michael never had a chance.

So condemn me. You earned it. I deserve it. But I'm not sorry and I hope you don't take it out on my daughter. Because I already told her you were her real dad and you're a great guy. :)

These other five… well, you get to a place when none of it makes sense anymore. When I came for Angelica, I was at that place. I was already planning on letting the baby live. And the three little ones, they are too young to be considered collateral damage. But Angelica reminded me of Sasha. She put up a good fight when I came for her. Her sarcasm, her confidence, and her strength changed my black killing heart that night. I figured the little ones are easy. The little ones will get over it and never remember. But maybe Angelica deserved a chance too.

It's not our fault we were born into the Company.

So hate me. I'll get over it.

But don't hate these kids.

There's a suitcase under the bed with all their passports and papers that makes it clear who goes home with *whom. Tell James I'm sorry, but he gets Angelica. Tell him he needs a new smurf because Sasha belongs to you. And Harper deserves that baby. She's wanted one for years and was too afraid to try. But these girls are here. They're already Company and that can't be changed. So maybe one day when the girls are older, Harper and Sasha and Sydney will realize it's really over. We won and they can move on and have their own babies without being afraid the Company will take them away.*

Sydney knew the three half-sisters. She killed their father a couple years ago and I know she did that out of love and justice, not revenge. So I figured they were in need of a familiar face.

Tell Sash I love her. I always loved her and I did this for her as much as I did for my own kid. Make sure she understands she can't save everyone, but she did save me. And I thank her, from the bottom of my rotten heart. I thank her.

I'm sorry it ended this way. But I hope you'll be there to help her get through it. And I hope you stay in the FBI and keep her safe.

I put all my trust in you, Jax. Don't let me down.

Your friend,
Nick

I hand the letter to Sasha, who reads it sniffling back tears. She hands it to James and the rest of them read it together.

Harper doesn't ask her question again, but I'm sure, even if they don't know the details, they know the outcome.

Merc grabs the suitcase and plops it on the bed. Just as promised, there are papers in there for each little girl. James walks over to the one named Angelica, who is still clutching the baby tightly to her chest. I'm not sure which of them needs that comfort more. But does it matter?

"You're stuck with me, brat. It's your lucky day. I am known throughout the world for having mad motherfucking parenting skills."

Angelica stares at him, her eyes darting back and forth. And then she bursts into tears.

James pulls her into a hug. "It's OK, Crybaby Smurf. We'll get through it."

Sydney is already pulling coats on her charges, talking softly as she does it. Smiling even. I can feel an air of relief in the room as they are all bundled up. And then when they are all ready to go, they even start to chat with one another. Just another day as a Company girl. Sydney knows better than anyone how serious an undertaking this is. So she lines the little girls up near the door and then waits for Merc to hug Sasha goodbye. They whisper promises to stay in touch, and then the five of them are outta here.

Harper reaches for the baby and there's a moment when I figure that Angelica won't be giving her up, no matter how much sweet talk Harper feeds her. But I'm wrong. She hands her over and starts to gather her things.

Harrison asks if we need a ride, and I'm about to say yes, but really… what's the hurry? We've got nowhere to be. I tell him no thanks and he gives me a knowing nod and says he'll leave the rental car and call a cab back to the airfield.

A few minutes later Harper has the baby buckled into a car seat and she and James turn to give Sasha a hug goodbye with the same promises Merc and Sydney just muttered.

I shake James' hand as he goes through the door, and my best guess is that we might never see these people again.

But I'm wrong a lot. A lot.

About Max, who was not the runner of rats, but the rat himself.

About Nick. He murdered children, but he saved them from a life of torture and killing too. All of them. Whether they knew it or not.

About Merc and James. Two murderers who only fight for their families now.

But about Sasha mostly.

She didn't need me to save her from her past. She needed Nick to do that. But as she takes Lauren's hand and lead her to the bed with the Little House book, I can see her future.

With me.

"Hey," I say, as the cold air from the door recedes as I close it. "You got room for me over there?"

Lauren pats the bed and Sasha smiles as I scoot in next to them.

Hate is hard, I decide. It's hard to hold a grudge for so many years. All the planning and plotting. All the sleepless nights filled with rage and thoughts of revenge. Regrets and remorse. Those are all the hallmarks of hate.

But love is easy. Love is listening to Sasha read a story that takes her back to a simpler time. Love is watching Lauren's eyes grow heavy from the telling. Love is me letting out that breath I feel like I've been holding since I was fifteen.

Love is easy, and not one moment of it is wasted.

EPILOGUE

Sydney

Six months later

The desert. It took me more than a year to get used to the summer heat. But Merc promised an oasis and that's what he gave me. We started the remodeling as soon as we got back to the little house in the middle of the desert scrub two and a half years ago.

First we added two bedrooms. Merc was always talking about kids. But it was a touchy subject for me. I know what it means to have a Company child.

Still, I went along with him. It made him happy. And once he got started on the remodeling he just couldn't stop. The entire backyard is like a five-star hotel in Vegas. A pool that could fit a hundred with a walk-in beach. Waterslides, and waterfalls, and water, water, water everywhere. It's a kid's backyard dream.

WASTED LUST

So here I sit in a hammock, under the shade of those palms that look more like giant umbrellas than trees, with an automatic mister keeping things cool. Two-year old Lily is on my stomach, sleeping away, not a care in the world.

Daphne is splashing her way across the length of the pool, having just learned to do the five-year-old version of the butterfly stroke. I smile at that. Merc whistles encouragement and tells her to keep going. When she makes it to the far edge, she bobs up and takes her goggles off to squeal about her achievement.

I clap softly, not wanting to wake up Lily.

"OK," Merc says, taking his attention back to three-year-old Avery. She is standing at the top of the waterslide biting her nails. "Your turn to shine, Ave."

She shakes her head no, and pouts. "I'm skered."

"Baby girl," Merc says, standing up in the water to his full height of six-foot-four. "I'm big, darling. I've got arms like an octopus. I'm gonna swoop you up the second you hit the water."

Avery was the one who took the most time to adjust. She's just starting to warm up to us. She doesn't really remember me from her other life. All she knows is that she's in a new place with people she doesn't recognize.

But every day we come out here to play. And every day she stands up there and Merc stands at the bottom in the water, promising to catch her. And every day she cries until he comes to rescue her from the slide and carry her down.

I expect that today too. But she sits down this time.

Merc shoots me a smile, but just a quick one. His eyes returning to Avery before she thinks he's not paying attention.

She screams all the way down and plops into the water.

Merc's long arms do in fact, swoop her up to safety. She spits out water and wipes her eyes.

I wait.

And when she giggles and hugs him hard, pressing her face into his neck, I start to believe the promise he made me two years ago. I was Avery once. And Merc saved me too, so I know how she feels. He promised to be good to my daughters.

And he's made good.

Everything is good.

Harper

One year later

"Just put the fucking blindfold on," James growls to Angelica. "Jesus fucking Christ. I'm the motherfucking head of this family. You're supposed to do what I say."

"Harper," Angelica says, her hand on her hip. "He promised not to swear in front of Hannah."

"Harper," James says, his tone softening. "She's eighteen months old. I get another year, at least, before she starts saying fuck."

I have to hide my smile or Angelica will drag this fight on for hours. And I know James is in a hurry. So I act like a mom. "James, she's right. Put a dollar in the jar."

He squints at me. "Are you fucking kidding me?"

"That's two dollars. Actually," Angelica laughs. "That's seven.

Jesus Christ counts too."

"Jesus Christ is not a swear word."

"Is too."

I hitch Hannah up on my hip and grab the mason jar off the galley counter. "Pay up."

He shakes his head at me and takes out his wallet and sneers at Angelica. "I only have Euro, brat. If you don't know the exchange rate—"

"We'll call it an even six. You can owe me the extra twenty cents."

She's so smart. And such a smart ass. I hide another laugh, this time from James. He pulls out six Euros, drops them in the jar, and then holds the blindfold out again.

"Put it on."

She's not going to budge, so I interject. "I'll put mine on first, how's that Angelica?"

James smiles at me and then turns to Angelica. "My lovely wife will demonstrate." He ties the red handkerchief around my eyes and whispers in my ear. "I love you, you know."

I don't hide my smile from anyone this time. "I know." I don't know what he's got planned but he's had us sequestered below deck for days. He even covered the portholes so we can't peek out.

"Now you," he says to Angelica. She lets out a huff, but I can only assume she concedes, because there is no arguing.

"Finally," James says, taking Hannah from my arms and then guiding me forward to the ladder that will take us up to the garage.

We're going somewhere, I know that much. Maybe Bora

Bora for vacation? I can use some shopping time.

"Climb, lionfish. And be careful. Wait for me and don't fuck—" He stops to correct himself. "Don't fall in the water."

Angelica and I climb, and when we get to the deck, she presses her body against mine as we wait for James to tell us what to do next.

"OK, one at a time, ladies. Let me put Hannah in her baby seat and I'll be right back."

He coos softly to her as he buckles her in the tender boat inside the yacht garage. I love hearing him talk to the baby. He can make her smile no matter how hard she's crying. She loves him so much.

"OK, Angelica, you first." Angelica stumbles, complaining, but James is different now. Soft. And protective. "I've got ya, just step down."

I'm next and when I'm settled in the tender boat, Angelica reaches for my hand. This is difficult for her. She's blind, she has to trust James. And even though I think most of their arguing is an act, just like it was with Sasha when she was that age, she's scared to trust people.

I squeeze her hand in encouragement.

After that the engine roars to life and we ease our way out of the back of the yacht. The sunshine hits my face and I count my blessings. I'm so, so lucky.

I enjoy the ride and when he cuts the engine, my heart beats a little faster. I don't hear anyone. We can't be in Bora Bora. That place is busy with tourists all the time.

"Where are we?" Angelica asks.

"Take off your blindfold and see," James replies.

I reach up and drag the soft fabric down my face.

"An island. How original," Angelica quips. "I've seen nothing but islands for the past year."

But I see what she does not. The structure built into the side of the hill of this island is not a hotel.

"It's a house," I say.

James has baby Hannah in his arms as he hugs me tightly. And then he folds Angelica into the hug too. "Not a house, baby. A home."

I have to frown to stop the tears. How many times have I asked him if we could settle over the past eleven years? Hundreds, at least. And his response was always the same. *We can't, Harp. We can't stop running yet. Not yet. It's not safe.*

He kisses me softly and whispers into my mouth. "We're safe now. We're *safe* now."

Sasha

Two years later

Lauren is riding horses with Princess Rory, Princess Ariel, and Kate as Five calls out equestrian tips from the rail of the riding arena in Spencer and Veronica's back-yard stable. He just got back home from his summer college program at Stanford a few days ago and can't take his eyes off his queen for a second. In a couple years he'll be heartbroken, because Rory will graduate from St. Joseph's and he'll have his bachelor's degree in computer engineering. There's no way he can attend high school with a bachelor's degree. I mean, he's pretending now, and Ford and Ash let him get away with staying at St. Joseph's because, well, he's Five. He's persistent. He wears them down.

He wants what his heart wants.

I understand his longing.

I long for something too.

"She is a natural," Jax says, pointing to Lauren as she rides her pony.

"Yeah," I agree. But I'm distracted. The party is fun. Everyone is here at Spencer's house for Labor Day. Rook and Ronin's daughters, Sparrow and Starling, are eating watermelon and playing patty cake. Veronica's two other girls, Princess Belle and Princess Jasmine—Five's nomenclature caught on. Like I said, he's persistent—are swimming with Sydney and Merc's three girls. Angelica is getting her hair braided by Rook, and Harper and James are teaching little Hannah, and Spencer's son Oliver, to kick their feet in the water. All the other guys, but Jax, are sitting at the swim-up bar in the pool, watching sports. And all the other girls, but me, are tanning on lounge chairs at the water's edge.

"What's wrong?" Jax asks, sliding into the hammock under the giant buckeye tree. "You feel OK?"

I nod hesitantly.

"You're lying."

I'm not. I'm really not. And I can't hide the smile that forms on my face as he tries to figure me out. But I don't have any words for this. So I just take his hand and place it on my belly.

He cocks his head at me, questioning. And then we both

burst out laughing.

"We win," I say, gazing up into his eyes. And then I place a hand on his scratchy jaw and kiss him the way he kissed me that very first time. Back when I was having a very bad day and he was there to make it better. When he refused to take no for an answer and challenged me to resist him, and I realized I couldn't. When he promised me safety and he delivered.

I wasted ten years lusting after a dream life I was never meant to live.

I won't give up a single moment doing that again.

Because love should never be wasted.

We win.

END OF
BOOK SHIT

Welcome to the End of Book Shit, fondly called the EOBS around these parts. I write these at the end of every book in place of an Author's Note and it's just a way for me to talk about the story and have my say without getting reamed for having an opinion on Facebook.

So if you're new to me, hi. ;) I write these just before I have to publish. They are 100% last minute and never edited, so you might see some typos.

I think Wasted Lust was the most emotional book I've written to date. For sure, 321 tore me up, that ending was everything I had pictured in my head and more. But this book had characters I knew. Characters I loved. I had just met Ark, JD, and Blue in 321, so I wasn't as invested in them and the story.

But even though I feel you can read Wasted Lust as a standalone, there's a lot of baggage with these characters in this book. A lot of past wounds and heartbreak. A lot of loss that fills them up and changes how they see the world. And every bit of that loss and heartbreak along the way was mine too. Because these characters are real to me. I live in their heads as I write each scene. I not only know them, I AM them.

Sasha is in a lot of books. Slack, Come Back, Coming For You, one sentence about her in 321, (unnamed) and a huge reason why Merc was the way he was in Meet Me In The Dark. He loved her. He was the man who took her in before Ford Aston gave her a forever home. He picked her up when she called, heartbroken after being denied the only thing she ever thought she wanted. He showed up as the ace in the hole when the whole world was crumbling down around her, and he put down that rifle in MMITD to save her life. He was big, and mean, and deadly and he loved her like a daughter.

James was the same way. They fought in the Dirty, Dark, and Deadly series like brother and sister. And it was hard to figure out just where Sasha stood with these killers because she's been playing a game with a dangerous enemy since she first appeared on the pages of Slack with Ford Aston.

I think the best scene to sum up the relationship between these men (including Nick) and the women they love (mostly Sasha, but also Sydney) is that ending of Come Back. If you haven't read the book, I won't spoil it. But it's possible to kill someone and save them at the same time. And this was what Wasted Lust was for me.

I always knew that Nick made his bed back in Coming For You. And once he did that there was no going back. If he believed that what he did was right—and he did, and it was—then he had to see it through to the end.

I take my hat off to Nick Tate. He's the hero and the bad guy all wrapped up into one not-so-neat package. And I cried my eyes out for him. He deserved very tear for being ugly, and ruthless to the point of making me sick. But also good, and brave, and loving for setting everyone free.

The advanced release copies went out to people last weekend

(today is Monday, June 22) and I've already gotten more messages about how this book touched people than any other book I've published before. Thank you, ARC readers. I love that you are so connected with this story and felt the same way that I did when it was over.

After building a world, and weaving a plot, and becoming each and every character through twelve books (Tragic, Manic, Panic, Slack, Taut, Bomb, Guns, Come, Come Back, Coming For You, 321, Meet Me In The Dark, and, finally, Wasted Lust) it's hard to wrap it all up and not feel a profound sense of loss. I don't write traditional romances. I like stories—in movies or books—that live in reality. And for sure, I asked you to believe in this shadow government called The Company. But if there was a Company, and if there was a mother-daughter pact, and if there was a network of people who use innocent children to fight their wars—then this is exactly what that world would look like.

I think that's why people respond so positively about my books. I take a fictional scenario and I make it real. Horrifyingly real, in some cases (Merc anyone?).

But each book, and every single word I ever put down on paper, has meaning. So even though I didn't enjoy writing Sydney and Merc's story, it was *necessary*. How could you ever (*ever*) understand what it meant to be a Company girl if you had not had Sydney's story? You couldn't. You would not feel the same about what these people did, and what it took to break free, if you didn't know what it really meant to belong to the Company. To be their property.

If this is your first book by me, I take my hat off to you, reader. :) It's very complicated, it's filled with hidden meaning and call-backs, and it's not an easy read. I do think it's a standalone—everything you need to know is in here. All you have to do is trust me.

But if this is your first JA Huss book, you're missing out on a great story.

A. Great. Motherfucking. Story.

Because even though you think you know the end and that's all there is to it, you have no idea what it took to get here. So if you liked this book and have not read the others listed above (in order)… go back and read.

Because it's never about the end, my friend.

The only thing that matters is the journey.

If you enjoyed this book please do me a favor and leave a review on Amazon. Even if you didn't purchase your book on Amazon that review means a lot to me over there. Indie authors need your help to get the word out about their books and the best way to show support is to write a review. So please, just take a moment and write a few words about how Wasted Lust made you feel. I would so, so appreciate it.

***

Rook and Ronin are not over. :) I have a HEA book starring Ford and Five Aston coming out in December 2015 just before Christmas. If you want to be notified of that release, FOLLOW my author page on Amazon or join my newsletter.

I have the next book, SEXY, up on pre-order at Amazon and iTunes. SEXY has all brand new characters, all brand new storyline, all brand new everything. It will release on September 9, 2015 and it's gonna be fun.

I have a very special group of friends who support me and I'd just like to say thanks.

Jana Aston, you are the reason I'm where I am in 2015. That's all you need to know. You are the reason.

Michelle New, your graphics are amazing and your help leading up to this release will never be forgotten. I have no words to express my thanks for all that you've done for me, simply because you wanted to do it.

Kristi Carol, #Thumbs, #LongLiveKristyBlazen – thank you for all your help on the New Adult Addiction blog. That site would be dead without you.

And thank you to all my street team members. You make a huge difference in my life.

Veronica LaRoche
Trisha Lukasik Hudson
Tiffany Saylor
Tiffany Rochelle
Tiffany K. Halliday
Tami Estes
Sarah Geiger
Sandra Stroh

Paige Nero Gast
Nicole Tetrev
Nicole Alexander
Misty Crook McElroy
Michelle Tan
Lindsey Miller
Leah Davis
Laura Helseth
Krista Lohss Davis
Katie Terranova
Jennifer Mirabelli
Holly Brama
Heidi Tieman
Christy M Baldwin
Brandee Price
Beverly Gardner Tubb
Ashley Blackwell
Amber Gladson
Amber Asher
Ali Hymer

ABOUT THE AUTHOR

JA Huss is the USA Today bestselling author of more than twenty romances. She likes stories about family, loyalty, and extraordinary characters who struggle with basic human emotions while dealing with bigger than life problems. JA loves writing heroes who make you swoon, heroines who makes you jealous, and the perfect Happily Ever After ending.

CPSIA information can be obtained at www.ICGtesting.com
Printed in the USA
LVOW08s0205160716

496557LV00005B/420/P